Veil of Illusion

Veil of Illusion

Patricia Sheehy

for Barbara —
wishing you lifetimes
of happiness. Best of luck
in all that you do —

Patricia Sheehy

Oak Tree Press
Springfield IL

Oak Tree Press

Oak Tree Books may be purchased for educational, business, or sales promotional use. Contact Publisher for quantity discounts.

First Edition, June 2004

Cover Design by Michelle L. Corby

Cover Art *Lady Illusion* by James E. Sheehy

10 9 8 7 6 5 4 3 2 1

Library of Congress Cataloging-in-Publication Data

Sheehy, Patricia, 1946-
Veil of illusion / by Patricia Sheehy.-- 1st ed.
p. cm.
ISBN 1-892343-35-5 (alk. paper)
1. Women--Fiction. I. Title.
PS3619.H445V45 2004
813'.6--dc22
2004011028

Acknowledgements

No book comes into this world on its own. It takes the faith and hard work of many to transform a story idea into printed reality. To all of my family, friends, and colleagues, thank you for your part in making this happen.

I am indebted to Billie Johnson of Oak Tree Press and her creative team. They make the process of bringing a book to market a wonderful adventure that celebrates the author's vision every step of the way.

My writers group serves as part inspiration, part perspiration, and one hundred percent friendship as we strive to help one another achieve success. I'm forever grateful to my writing pals: Rita Isaacson, Mary Ann Libera, Marge Mehler, and Joy Smith.

An enormous hug of appreciation to my husband, Jim, for his patience and encouragement — for listening, reading, collating, and doing all the hundreds of things that free me up to write. Thanks for all of it, including the fabulous pastel painting that graces the cover.

For their unconditional support, enthusiasm, and good humor, I thank the women of my family, who understand the magic and power of love: Kathleen Frattaroli, Christy Sheehy, Patty Sheehy, Ann Tupper, Janice Antolini, Karen Belanger, Dolores Herchuk, and Lisa Millerick.

To all of my readers, I hope you enjoy this book and the ones yet to come. You are why I do this, so let me hear from you. Now, together, let's pull back the veil between illusion and reality and see what's in store for Caitlin McKenna Saunders.

— PS

Dedication

for my parents, Joseph and Sophie Herchuk,
who gave their children roots and wings
and for my husband, Jim,
whose love makes all things possible.

Chapter One

Summer came early to Connecticut, making it the hottest June on record. Caitlin Saunders lifted the hem of her long black skirt and peeled it away from her legs, fanning her overheated skin with the mass of dark fabric. She then linked arms with her mother, a gesture that Nora McKenna would ordinarily shrug off, and steered her across the cemetery to the waiting limousine.

"You're just like me now," Nora told her daughter. "I was a young widow. And now you. Except you're even younger. Only thirty-one. Still, history repeats...like a genetic flaw...I can't believe David's dead. A car accident of all things." She'd been saying the same thing in various ways for the past three days.

"Mom, it's okay. I'll be okay. So will you."

"Maybe you should come to Florida. Live with me. Don't wait forever, like I did—"

Caitlin patted her mother's hand. "I'll be fine. Honest."

"Hey, wait up." Caitlin's neighbor and good friend, Liz Warner, ran to catch up with them and then slowed down to their pace. "Who's that?"

Caitlin pushed her auburn hair away from her damp forehead. "Who?"

"Him." Liz nodded over her left shoulder. "Back there. Leaning against the tree. He's been there the whole time."

All three women glanced over their shoulders as they continued walking. "No idea," Caitlin shrugged.

Apparently "no idea" wasn't good enough for Nora. She stopped abruptly, forcing Caitlin to a halt. Letting go of her daughter's arm, she turned and stared at the man, her mouth drawn into a thin line of concentration. "Hmmm...he wasn't at the wake...not at the funeral services either."

"How could you possibly know that?" Caitlin asked. "He's too far away to tell—"

"Believe me, I know." Nora wagged a tanned finger at Caitlin. "Your mother pays attention to things." It was the story of their life: Nora stating absolutes, Caitlin challenging them and then being made to feel foolish or inadequate.

"You would do well to be more like me," Nora continued. "Keep your eyes open, Caitlin. You're starting all over again—"

"Yes, Mother," Caitlin said, rolling her eyes and throwing Liz a look of resignation. Nora was always keeping her eyes open. At sixty-one, she was still looking for just the right replacement for her long-dead, dear husband. But so far, no luck.

"I saw that look," Nora said. "I know what you think. You think I'm shallow and old-fashioned but you'll see. You're without a husband now. You'll see how hard it is."

"Don't worry," Liz said, slipping her arms around Caitlin and Nora. "I'm here for Catie. We'll get her life back to normal."

Whatever that means, Caitlin thought. Normal left three days ago when David died. And then again last night, when Maryanne, her fifteen-year-old stepdaughter, packed up nearly everything she owned and left—right after the wake, without any warning and barely a word to anyone—back to live with her mother. Normal. Was there any such thing?

"Let's go," Caitlin said, tugging at her mother's arm. "Everyone's probably back at the house by now."

As they hurried toward the waiting limousine, Caitlin glanced back over her shoulder, but the man leaning against the tree had disappeared.

* * *

Derrick Secor could have attended the wake and funeral, paid his respects like all of David's other friends. "An old pal, from high school," he would have told her. And it would have been the truth. But instead he'd decided to hang back, watch everything from a distance, pay Caitlin a visit—one-on-one—when everything had calmed down, when she was lonely, when she would need him. Meanwhile, he'd make a trip back home, see his dad, visit David's parents. The Saunders would fill him in on things, give him bits of information that would help pay David back for all his good deeds. Yep, that's the way it would go.

There was something sensuous in the way she pulled her skirt away from her legs, fanning herself in the heat. She was a looker. This was good. Seemed nice as well, the way she took care of the older woman. Probably her mother. Not that nice really mattered. Once they'd spotted him—who was that blondie?—it was time to make tracks. He'd contact Caitlin Saunders soon enough.

* * *

Everybody stayed at Caitlin's house far too long after the funeral, eating, drinking, telling old stories. It was as though by leaving—getting back into the rhythm of their daily lives—they were accepting David's death. And nobody was quite ready to do that.

Eventually, as night claimed the day, folks did head out, one by one, hugging Caitlin, promising to see her soon, promising things would get better. Friends gave Nora a ride to the airport. Liz cleaned up, putting away left-over pastries and casseroles. Still, David's parents lingered, hunched over in matching wing chairs, unable to understand how their only child could be dead when they were still alive. It wasn't right. It wasn't the natural order of things. And where was Maryanne? they kept asking. She was David's daughter—their only grandchild—she should have come back with them after the funeral. Why didn't she? Nothing made sense to them. Or to Caitlin.

When they finally did leave, the silence was shattering. Caitlin slipped into an old cotton nightgown, soft from years of washing, and crawled into bed. Her body throbbed with the pain of being alive. All she wanted to do was escape. She closed her eyes tightly, willing herself to relax, concentrating on the breeze from a small oscillating fan as it played with strands of her hair, then washing across her face before moving away to travel the length of her body. Through the open windows, she could hear the buzzing of insects and the occasional thumping of a stray June bug as it threw itself against the screen.

She wriggled beneath the sheet, surrendering to the heaviness around her. She slept fitfully at first, but then fell into an unnatural stillness, as though suspended in time and space. While she slept, she had a sense of slipping away from her body—her mind fully awake as she watched her sleeping self from the outside—both participant and observer in a dream more real than reality.

As though paralyzed, Caitlin was unable to move, unable to unite mind and body, which now seemed distinctly separate to her. Her conscious self moved upward toward the ceiling and then toward the open window. It was then that she noticed the slender silver cord that seemed to keep her safely inside the dream. Looking out toward the midnight sky, she wondered how far she could go without severing its hold on her.

David called to her. He was there, right beyond her reach. She could hear him now, beckoning her to follow. Could she trust the dream? If only she could know for sure—she would go...she would follow the voice...David's voice...the voice that spoke no words. But she hesitated, and in that hesitation, fear seeped in, turning the dream into nightmarish shades of black and purple.

It was then that Caitlin's body fought against its paralysis. Her arms and legs thrashed, kicking away the sheet, pushing hard through the heavy air. Sweat soaked through her nightgown. She gasped for air as she shot into a sitting position.

"No! Stop...stop!" she screamed into the empty room.

With a loud swishing sound, and a sudden rush of air, the silver cord retracted and Caitlin was fully awake. She drew herself up against the headboard, hugging her knees to her chest, trembling and cold, despite the heat. The fan continued to wash warm air across her body. Outside, the air was still and quiet. All night, she sat and listened and watched, afraid to sleep, afraid of what sleep might bring. And all night, she couldn't get the sound out of her mind—the loud swishing sound that penetrated skin and bones with laser-like precision and seemed to settle somewhere deep inside her.

Chapter Two

After five days of reading sympathy cards, piling up unopened bills, and listening to the endless chiming of her grandfather clock, Caitlin returned to work. Now she wondered if she'd done the right thing. Maybe Liz was right. Maybe it was too soon.

The air conditioner blasted waves of cold across her back. She shivered and pulled her linen blazer tightly to her body, as though that one simple action would melt the layer of ice just beneath her skin. "Oh for God's sake," she said, getting up from behind her desk. "It's summer out. It's supposed to be hot. If you all like the cold so much, move to Alaska." She pushed the thermostat up to seventy-four with a determination that challenged anyone to stop her.

She looked around the large one-room office. It was exactly the same as before. Her life, she noted, would forever be divided into before and after. And in this after-world, it seemed that nothing had changed.

Just like every other morning, the sun fell in patches, filtering through the large red maple on the office's front lawn, creating a mosaic of squares and rectangles on the walls and hardwood floor. Mahogany desks gleamed in the bright light. In late evening, brass desk lamps would burn softly, casting a warm glow on the oriental rug, woven in shades of navy, ivory, and burnished copper. It was a room filled with grace and the sense of old money, the perfect setting for a real estate office in an upscale Yankee town. If it really was the same, Caitlin wondered, why did she feel so misplaced?

Making her way through phone messages and unopened mail, Caitlin wished someone had at least made neat stacks of the papers and files she'd left scattered on top of her desk when she thought she'd be back the next morning. That was nine days ago. A lifetime ago. David's lifetime. But a hard rule in the real estate business is never, ever, touch another agent's desk. She regretted now being involved in a business where people didn't trust each other.

"You okay?" Lauren asked as she hung up the phone. She'd done little more than offer a quick, embarrassed hello since Caitlin had arrived. "Maybe we shouldn't have left you alone all morning. We were trying to be normal, give you space and all that crap. Do you wanna talk?"

Before Caitlin could answer, Debbie shot across the room, landing in the chair by Caitlin's desk, her brown hair flying in every direction, strands standing on end long after she had settled down. Ditzy Debbie. That's what they called her. Now that Lauren had broken the ice, it was just like Debbie to want to tell Caitlin, in detail, just how David's death was affecting her.

"I've been crying and crying. Can't seem to stop." Debbie dabbed at her eyes with a worn tissue. "I can't sleep. I can barely eat. I just don't know how you're doing it. Imagine, losing your husband, no warning. Just like that." She tried snapping her fingers but no sound came out.

Lauren rolled her eyes and handed Debbie a fresh Kleenex. "We've missed you," she told Caitlin, her large breasts resting on the desk's surface as she leaned across it. "Nobody's griped about the air conditioning in way too long. Deb here has been weeping at everything, even more than usual for a woman with out-of-whack hormones. And you know it's not just postpartum—your grief is her grief. Anybody's grief is her grief. Even she's been out of sorts." She nodded toward Amelia, formal and controlled Amelia Simpson, owner of Colonial Realty and a descendent of one of the first families to settle Riverside, Connecticut. While Lauren lowered her voice for the last bit of information, she clipped her words in an attempt to emulate Amelia's precise manner of speaking.

But the humor was lost on Caitlin. "I'm going to lunch," she said, ducking under her desk for her purse.

"Honey, it's not even noon," Lauren said tapping the face of her watch, "you can't go yet. Besides I thought we'd go together."

"I'm going now." Caitlin stood up and pushed passed the two of them—these friends who didn't know how to be with her, the new widow, as though her condition was contagious and the only thing to keep it at bay was distance or awkward, insensitive humor. "I'm sorry. I need some air..." She rushed out the front door before they could stop her, before she had a chance to figure out exactly what she would do next.

Closing the heavy door behind her, Caitlin took a few steps forward and then stopped; she stood perfectly still, looking down the long front walk that led to Main Street, wondering what to do with herself. She didn't really feel like eating. Especially alone. But she couldn't go back in either. So now what?

Coming toward her was a small-framed woman with short, jet-black hair and tanned skin. She was wearing a cotton turquoise dress with a full skirt that gently grazed her bare legs. A silver chain rested on her neck and hung low on her dress, a nugget of clear crystal dangling from the chain, bobbing up and down against her chest as she walked.

There was something familiar about the woman and Caitlin found herself staring, almost to the point of rudeness. They were about to pass, the woman's full skirt nearly touching Caitlin's straight one, when she stopped and looked hard at Caitlin.

"Catie. Catie McKenna!" The stranger practically shouted as she grabbed hold of Caitlin's hand.

The noon rays were hot on Caitlin's face as she struggled to maintain her composure. She hated being caught off guard. Even more, she hated people knowing more about her than she knew about them. And this woman knew her name. "Actually, it's Saunders," Caitlin said.

"Well you were McKenna, right?"

"Well...yes, that' right...And you're...?"

"Josephine. Ford? Bennett High? Class of eighty-nine."

"Josie! I didn't recognize you. You look terrific! Not that you didn't back then, but, wow, look at you!" Caitlin openly stared at her old high school acquaintance, admiring the style she'd been able to achieve without actual beauty. Her nose was still too large, her fiery eyes too wide apart, but there was something about her, an odd combination of openness and mystery. "What are you doing here?"

"Looking for a rent...I'd love a house, but at this rate, I'll settle for a condo, even an apartment—I'd really like Riverside, though, especially Old Riverside, but everything's so expensive. What about you?"

"I work here. I'm afraid we don't have any rentals. But I'll ask around, see what I can do."

"Thanks. I'm getting desperate...I'm also starving. Let's have lunch and you can tell me all about the last 13 years. Has it really been that long? Don't you still feel 18? By the way, you look pretty terrific yourself. You haven't gained an ounce, lucky you. I'm always battling ten pounds. On again, off again." She laughed, patting her behind. "Mostly right here—"

Once she remembered who Josie was, Caitlin realized that she hadn't really changed at all. She still talked like a runaway train, fast and all over the place. And she still had that look of something wild running loose inside her. Next to her, Caitlin felt like a geranium, the nice, no-risk variety—the house plant everyone could depend on. Nobody else since high school had made her feel quite like that; at least nobody that she had chosen to befriend all these years. Yet, there was something so compelling about Josie that Caitlin couldn't help but be drawn in. Besides, here was a possible client.

"Let's go to Sweet Sensations," Caitlin said. "It's just down the street. They have soup, salad, light sandwiches. And they have the best pistachio ice cream in the world."

"Just what I need," Josie laughed.

Sweet Sensations had been renovated to look like an old-fashioned ice cream parlor, right down to the soda fountain and swivel stools covered in red vinyl. Toward the end of the counter was a manual cash register that made a dinging sound when a sale was made and, at the very end, was a small glass case filled with penny candy—fireballs, bubble gum, licorice whips. Caitlin and Josephine settled into a back booth, both ordering tuna on rye and iced tea.

"And leave the check open for dessert," Josephine told the waitress before turning her attention to Caitlin. "What a kick. You must come here all the time."

"Sometimes. Not often."

Caitlin was sorry now that she'd agreed to lunch. The last time she'd been here was with David, a few weeks ago. They met for lunch and then walked down to the river, holding hands, peering into people's backyards, trying to see into living room windows as they strolled by. They'd laughed a lot that day, especially when a woman caught them peeking around the corner of her house trying to get a better look at her landscaping. She shooed them away as though they were a couple of kids.

Caitlin put her fingers to her temples and tried to rub away the pain. A massive headache was settling in. "David just died," she said, barely audible.

"I'm sorry, what?" Josie asked. "Who just what?"

"David. My husband. He died. Nine days ago. I'm a widow."

"Oh my God. I'm so sorry. How? Do you want to talk about it?" She reached across the table and stroked Caitlin's hand.

"Car accident. This is my first day back to work."

"I don't know what to say...I'm so sorry...do you have children?"

"No," Caitlin answered quickly. "Well, not really. A stepdaughter. Fifteen. She was living with us, but she moved out the night of the wake. Before the funeral, can you believe it? She blames me for David's death. Says it's all my fault. But I can't imagine why and she won't tell me. Anyway..."

They fell quiet, Josie unsure of what to say and Caitlin simply not wanting to talk. A hearty laugh from a table in the middle of the room broke their silence and Caitlin chuckled, wiping away tears that were ready to spill across her cheeks. "I'm a lot of fun. Sorry. I was just thinking about how empty the house will be when I get home tonight." She pushed away her half-eaten sandwich.

Josie finished her lunch while Caitlin twisted her paper napkin into a long spiral and occasionally sipped her iced tea. As much as Josephine had a well-deserved reputation for talking, she'd apparently learned the art of listening along the way. Caitlin relaxed a little, feeling oddly safe with her, like she might with a stranger at a coffee counter. "I had the strangest dream the night of David's funeral," she blurted out. "It still haunts me..."

"Wait. Before you start, let me order a dish of Dutch chocolate ice cream—one of my many weaknesses—and a dish of pistachio for you. Just pick at it if you don't want the whole thing."

Josie let a spoonful of the rich chocolate ice cream melt on her tongue, obviously enjoying its rich, dark flavor. "This is fabulous...so, tell me about the dream. Don't leave anything out."

Caitlin fidgeted with her spoon, taking small bites of ice cream. "Well..." She hesitated. "Okay...it's like this. I was lying in bed, totally exhausted, and I fell into this kind of paralyzing sleep. All of a sudden, it seemed like I was outside of myself, like my mind and body were separate things. I could look down and actually watch by body sleep. I mean, how weird is that? The part of me that was outside—if this makes any sense at all—wanted to join David—whatever that means. I was by the window, looking out at the sky..."

"And then?"

"I panicked. I woke up shouting and punching the air. There was this loud swishing sound...I don't think I'll ever forget it...and then there was this silver cord...it disappeared and it was like I was one person again."

"Wow. Sounds like a classic out-of-body experience to me," Josie said.

"You mean like something out of a Shirley MacLaine movie? Caitlin laughed. "I don't think so."

"Exactly like that." Josephine glanced at her watch quickly.

"Ohmygod, I'm late again. I really want to talk with you about this, but I have to pick up my daughter at Parks and Rec in, like, five minutes and it's a twenty minute drive from here. By the way, I have somebody I want you to meet. His name is Marc Gallagher—"

"My God, Josie, David just died—"

"What? Oh geeze, Catie, I didn't mean...I'm not that insensitive... Marc's a developer. Last time we talked, he mentioned looking for a piece of land up this way. I'm in public relations," she offered by way of explanation, "always putting pieces together, looking for opportunities."

"Sorry."

"Don't be." Josie handed Caitlin money for her share of the bill and tip. "I really have to run. Listen, I don't think it was an accident that we met today after all these years. As a matter of fact, I'm convinced there are no accidents; everything happens for a reason. Here's my number, home and work." She handed Caitlin her business card and then started for the door. "Let's get together on Saturday for breakfast or shopping or whatever," she called back over her shoulder. "Meanwhile, try to find me a rent."

The door to Sweet Sensations shut with a bang. Through the window, Caitlin caught the sway of Josephine's turquoise dress as she ran down the street toward her car. It was as though Josie was a hologram—three-dimensional and real one moment, a vaporizing swirl of color and energy the next. Her sudden departure left Caitlin with a disquieting emptiness and the uncanny feeling that something important had just begun.

Chapter Three

When she arrived home early that evening, there was a note taped to her front door: Come over for a swim and burgers. Kids would love to see you.—Liz.

As tempting as a swim sounded, Caitlin wasn't in the mood for chatter. And one thing Liz always had was chatter. It was her way of filling dead space, as though she was afraid of what would happen if everyone was quiet at once. Her conversations were full of everyday events and town news; in a way, she was soothing to be with because she demanded very little in return. All you had to do was nod your head now and then and come up with the appropriate amount of exclamation or indignation. But sometimes the chatter became white noise, like the engine of an airplane. It could either put you to sleep or give you a headache.

Caitlin felt disloyal even thinking negative thoughts about Liz. Over the years, they'd become much more than neighbors. They'd become friends, as well. But by some unspoken agreement, they stayed at the surface of their lives, never exploring one another's flaws or feelings, and rarely, if ever, revealing deeply-held beliefs. It was a polite friendship; still, it was a good one. They were there for one another when it counted.

Caitlin picked up the phone and called across the street. "I'm not sure what I feel like doing. I can't seem to make any decisions..."

"You have to eat." Liz interrupted.

"I know. Start without me. If I'm there, I'm there. I'm just not sure."

"Okay. But try."

Caitlin kept the phone in her hand long after they'd said goodbye. Putting it back on the receiver meant doing something else with herself, and she couldn't for the life of her figure out what that should be. The only sound in the house was the ticking of the grandfather clock, the one she and David bought with their wedding money. Every fifteen minutes its Westminster chimes reminded her of passing time. Of the passing of life. She stood in the kitchen and listened closely for any other sounds. They were there, lifeless and mechanical: the dripping of the faucet, the motor of the refrigerator working overtime in the unseasonable heat. But that was it—three sounds in a house that used to be filled with the noises of being alive. Maybe Liz's house was a good idea after all. She changed into shorts and a T-shirt, grabbed her bathing suit, and left.

"I'm running away from the silence," Caitlin announced as she entered the Warner's back yard. "Got any noise here?"

"Have we got noise," Steve laughed. "That's all we have."

Steve was a handsome man, with high cheekbones and skin that always looked tanned. In the summer, it bronzed deeper, highlighting the green specks in his cool gray eyes. Caitlin stopped and looked at Steve, almost as though she was seeing him for the first time. His laugh—it hadn't reached his eyes. The corners of his lips had turned up, his mouth had opened, showing perfectly straight white teeth, and a soft chuckle had hit the air. But his eyes had remained untouched. Has it always been that way? she wondered. Caitlin made a mental note to take closer notice. It was interesting, she thought, the things she was suddenly paying more attention to. I wonder—

"She's in the kitchen," Steve told Caitlin, interrupting her private assessment. He called out to his wife through the open windows. "Lizie, Catie's here. And she looks thirsty. Pour her a glass of that new Chardonnay."

"Just seltzer water. And lemon, if you have it," Caitlin shouted. Then she turned to the two blonde-haired children now standing beside her. "Hey Jessie. Hi Jason. Got any hugs for an old, tired lady?"

"We're wet," six-year-old Jason warned.

"That's okay. Wet dries. Come here, you guys."

Caitlin opened her arms to Jason and his eight-year-old sister, Jessica. Over the years, they had filled the empty spot in Caitlin's life where her own children should have been. Not having any had been one of David's decisions, and loving him had made it worth it. Until now.

They hugged her hard, leaving pools of water on her shorts and legs, and then dove back into the pool. "Come on in, Catie!" Jason begged. "We can play basketball. You and me against Jessica."

"Hey! We talked about that!" Liz hollered as she carried a tray of hamburger patties and two drinks from the kitchen to the patio. "It's Mrs. Saunders to you. Don't make me tell you again. Children don't call adults by their first name. She'll play with you later."

"You know I don't mind," Caitlin protested. "I actually kind of like it."

"Oh, I know you don't mind. But I do. These kids have to learn about respect. As it is, they're too mouthy." Liz settled into the chair next to Caitlin while Steve lit the grill.

"My juice," Liz whispered, sneaking a look at Steve and then the children.

Immediately, Caitlin knew that the cranberry liquid had more than ice in it. Steve didn't approve of Liz drinking hard liquor in front of the kids. Wine was okay; it was civilized, somehow. And, of course, he had no objection to the imported beers he enjoyed. Liz got around Steve's mandate by pouring herself a healthy glass of juice and lacing it with vodka whenever she was in the mood for a real drink. Caitlin often wondered what would happen when one day Jason or Jessica took a drink out of Mommy's glass. She couldn't decide what would be worse for Liz—a slightly tipsy child or Steve's discovery of her duplicity. Oh well. Who was she to question, she with no husband, a long-gone stepdaughter, and no children of her own. It was their way of managing things and, apparently, it worked for them.

"How are you doing?" Liz asked, patting Caitlin's hand. "I've cried every night since David died. I would want to die myself if it was me."

"Okay, I guess. But watching your kids...I wish now, more than ever, I'd had children. At least one. Then there'd be someone left for me to love, some part of David to hold on to."

"You guys figured Maryanne—"

"Would fill my need? Yeah, right...talk about life turning on a dime."

"Have you heard from her?"

"Not a word."

"Anytime you need a kid-fix..."

"I know."

Patricia Sheehy

Caitlin sipped her seltzer while Liz took a long gulp of her juice and then put the cool glass to her forehead.

Caitlin nodded toward Jessica and Jason. "I'm still planning on taking them to Ogunquit for our annual September get-away, if it's okay with you. I made the reservations last month, before—"

"Of course it's okay," Liz interrupted. "But are you sure? I mean, you know..."

"I'm positive."

"But, Catie, all alone?"

"I really want to. It'll help, I think. It's something to look forward to. So, what will you and Steve do while I whisk your kids away for a weekend?"

"Who knows? Right now my heart's not in anything. It's all been too much." Her brown eyes turned glassy. "You know, I complain a lot, but I'd be lost without Steve and the kids. I mean, who would I be without them?"

"Thanks. So you mean I'm nobody now?"

"Oh God, Catie, of course not. I didn't mean...it's just that...well, first David and then Maryanne...you're stronger than I am, that's all."

Liz swallowed hard and took a long sip of her drink. Pulling her blonde hair back into a pony tail, she held it in position for a minute to cool her neck, and then let the thick mass drop back against her shoulders. "Enough of this sad talk," she declared. "How was your first day back at work? Oh, guess what? Sylvia's upgraded her diamond earrings, can you believe it? And I hear Andrea Fishman is having an affair."

Caitlin sat back and listened to Liz drone on, glad for the chance to feel invisible for a while, not compelled to talk or even respond. She watched the clear water bounce along the sides of the pool as the kids jumped off the diving board and swam to the shallow end, only to get out, run around the pool, and jump in again.

"Hey, Catie, you okay?" Liz asked. "I was telling you about Andrea, did you hear a word I said?"

"Sorry. I went off into this fugue state."

The time for silence had passed. "I ran into an old high school friend today," Caitlin told Liz. "Well, not a friend, exactly, just somebody I kind of knew. We used to make fun of her, call her Josie the Gypsy. Her clothes were kind of cheap and she wore too much jewelry. Now to see her, you might call her the same thing, but it's really a compliment."

"Where?"

"Where, what?"

"Where'd you run into her?" Liz asked.

Caitlin noticed an edge in Liz's voice. Curiosity? Jealously? One thing about Liz—she hated coming in the side door, finding things out after the fact.

"We bumped into each other outside the office. I was going to lunch. She was on her way in, looking for a rent here in town."

"Why? Where's she living now?"

"I didn't ask. I hate to admit it, but I was pretty self-absorbed."

"Maybe she's getting a divorce."

"She has a daughter, that's all I know." And then for no particular reason, at that very moment, Caitlin broke into tears. "I miss David so much! Why did he have to die? Why?" Her voice turned hard, angry.

"Oh, Catie, don't cry. You're making me cry. Who knows why these things happen. It was just God's will, I guess. That's what Steve says. You just have to have faith."

"Yeah, right. Like faith is going to keep me warm at night or make me laugh. Or remember my birthday. I don't think God's will has anything to do with it. Why would God want David to die? I mean, why now, in the prime of his life, when he had me and Maryanne and everything to look forward to? I think it's just a cruel joke and I want to know why."

Across the yard, Steve took the last hamburger off the grill and slammed the cover shut. "Burger time," he announced, "and they look great, as usual."

Nobody moved to join him. Jason and Jessica took another dive off the board; Liz and Caitlin halted their conversation mid-stream, and by silent consensus, laid back in their chairs, putting their faces up to the last warm rays of the day.

Steve sat down at the picnic table alone. "Come on guys. It's dinner time—J & J...Elizabeth...Caitlin. Get over here. Now."

Reluctantly, they each obeyed.

Chapter Four

The phone by her bed kept ringing, commanding Caitlin to shake off sleep and answer it. Why didn't her machine pick up the damn thing? Just shut up. Shut up. Leave me alone. She pulled David's pillow over her head, breathing in his scent, praying for the world to go away. The ringing stopped. Oh, thank God. She released her hold on the pillow. But the reprieve was short lived, less than thirty seconds, and the incessant ringing started over again.

"Pick it up!" she hollered to the answering machine downstairs in David's study. "Pick it up. Leave me alone." But that wasn't about to happen, she realized, remembering she'd turned it off after the funeral. She was tired of getting messages. Tired of listening to well-meaning folks, including her mother, "just checking in." Mostly, she was just plain tired.

So now the phone by her bed kept ringing. She should move the answering machine into the kitchen, out of David's study. That was the real problem; she didn't want to go in there, listening to the day's messages, pretending things were normal, pretending that David and Maryanne would be home any minute, that they would all return their calls as soon as possible.

"Okay, okay!" she hollered at the intrusive noise. "Hello," she mumbled into the receiver, trying hard to sound alive.

"Did I wake you?"

"No," Caitlin lied. She always lied when she was caught sleeping, as though sleeping later than the caller somehow suggested that she was inferior. "Who is this?"

"It's Josephine. Ford? Really it's Ford-Newman. We said we'd trying and get together today. Are you sure I didn't wake you?"

"No, no, you didn't wake me...I was just getting into the shower... the water was running." Caitlin's eyes searched for the digital clock on the bureau. Nine o'clock on a Saturday. This woman was unnatural!

"Well, what do you think? Lunch and a little shopping, or shopping and a little lunch?"

Nothing. That's what Caitlin thought. Just let me crawl back under the sheets and go to sleep. Aloud she said, "Sure, great. Whatever."

"Okay. I'm leaving now. I have lots of errands. Let's meet at the mall around eleven—in front of the bookstore—we'll take it from there."

"Fine," Caitlin said to the dial tone. Josie had hung up and was probably halfway down the street. Caitlin threw herself back on the bed, already dreading the day.

* * *

The air-conditioned mall was filled with young families and senior citizens trying to keep cool as the heat outside once again sizzled to a record high. Young parents were buying up bubble water and ice cream cones, trying to keep tots off the escalators and under some semblance of control, while white-haired, thick-waisted folks sat on benches, cooing at the babies and clucking at insolent two-year-olds. It seemed to Caitlin that she and Josie were the only two people between the ages of 35 and 60. Apparently everyone else their age was home in their air conditioning, or sitting by some cool body of water sipping cocktails and catching rays.

"Hi," Josie said softly, coming up behind Caitlin. "They're adorable, aren't they?"

"They sure are," Caitlin agreed, unable to take her eyes off twin sisters stretched out on the tile floor playing Go Fish. About seven years old, they had ringlets of blue-black hair, snow-white skin, and black eyes. Their long lashes cast shadows on their cheeks as they concentrated on their game. "Can you imagine how filthy they're going to be?"

"But can you imagine how much fun they're having?" Josie said.

It felt like a reprimand to Caitlin. She'd sounded just like her mother with that comment about getting filthy, worried more about appearances than experiences, and Josie had caught her in the act.

"I mean, who cares," Josie continued, "about a little dirt compared to the memory of having no air conditioning in the house and enough money for only a small treat—one ice cream cone to share—and so their parents bring them to the mall for the afternoon. They walk around for awhile, savoring the thought of a strawberry cone, the ice cream filled with deep red chunks of real fruit. Or maybe it'll be chocolate—rich, dark, delicious chocolate. They sit down on the cool tile floor for awhile, take out the cards they brought from home, and begin to concentrate on their game. The ice cream cone will be the very last treat of the day and the winner gets to pick the flavor."

Caitlin took a long look at the girls and then at Josie. "How do you know all this?"

"I don't," Josie smiled. "I only imagined it. Who knows why they're here. Or how much money they have. But it certainly makes a little dirt seem insignificant!"

How strange she is, Caitlin thought. So different from anyone else I've ever known. Liz would be absolutely neurotic about kids sitting on a dirty floor and she wouldn't find Josie the least bit amusing. As a matter of fact, I'm not sure they'd like each other much at all, she thought. Well, who knows how much I'll really end up seeing Josie anyway. I'll help find her a rent, if I can, and that will probably the that.

"Well, here we are," Josie said as they walked away from the bookstore and the scene of the two girls. "What shall we do first?"

"Are you always so cheerful?" Caitlin asked. "I need coffee before I do anything. I haven't had one cup yet today."

"Coffee it is. And we might as well eat at the same time. Nice cameo," Josie said as they settled into a booth at Friendly's. "It suits you."

"Thanks," Caitlin said, touching the antique broach David had given her two years ago. It had been so unlike him, buying an expensive gift spontaneously—especially jewelry—without thinking it through or comparison shopping. But he'd been so insistent, as though the cameo had taken hold of him in some strange way. They'd gone to the beach for the weekend, but it turned out to be overcast and cool; rather than return home, they decided to go treasure hunting in all the little antique shops they'd seen along the way.

It was only the second shop they'd gone to, a small dank place where merchandise was piled, rather than arranged. Very little light came in through the porthole-type windows, so lamps of various sizes had been turned on, casting pockets of yellow glow throughout the store. Caitlin was rummaging through an old trunk when David called her over to the jewelry case. His voice had a rush to it, an excitement that made her immediately put down her books to see what he had found.

"Look at this." He held the cameo up to the light of a small brass lamp. "I want you to have it."

"It's beautiful," Caitlin admitted, running her index finger across the bisque-colored carving of a woman placed in a setting of gold filigree. "But don't you want to look at others? I mean, we've never really explored cameos. We don't know anything about them."

"No. This has your name all over it. I knew it the instant I saw it." David turned to the small man behind the counter, who was pretending to be busy arranging and re-arranging other pieces of jewelry. "How much?"

A broad smile filled the man's round face. "Three-fifty. A special price, just for you. Pay me cash and that includes the tax."

"David, $350!" Caitlin whispered. "We can't blow that kind of money just like that! You like to think about things...don't you want to think about it? We can come back tomorrow."

"Do you like it?" was all David asked, all he wanted to know.

"Well, of course..." Caitlin said, touching the cameo once more. "How could I not like it."

"Then it's yours."

"You've made a good choice," the little man said. "A good choice. This here cameo dates back to the late 1800's. See here, you can tell by the type of setting, and the lock. Earlier, and there would be no safety catch; but this has a small one. Nothing like what we're used to today, but it's something. Yup, you made a good choice. Look at the color on this one compared to all the others." He pointed to the array of cameos in his case. "They're all shell cameos, every single one of 'em, but see how your background has a brownish tint, not pink like the others. Much more valuable. Not nearly as common.

"And look at this." The man was excited. He'd made a sale and now he wanted to educate them about it. "See how all the angular lines and the strands of hair flow smoothly from one to the other? This was carved by a true artist. Excellent polishing. Not like those cheaper cameos, ragged edges, few details. Yup. This is a beauty all right."

Running her fingers across the cameo, Caitlin heard a voice calling to her: "Earth to Catie, Earth to Catie, do you read me?"

"Josie, I'm sorry. I drifted away. You mentioned the cameo and I began remembering the day David bought it for me. He was so insistent. Anyway...let's order."

"I'll have to be careful about what I say from now on or I may lose you for good," Josie laughed. "Any luck finding me a rent?"

"There's not much out there. How large a place do you need?"

"Two bedrooms would be perfect. Living room, large kitchen or dining area. I'm not fussy. But I do need two bedrooms so my daughter can stay over and feel like she has her own space. If I absolutely have to, I'll settle for one large bedroom—but I mean large—and I'll create a private space for her. Courtney will be living with her father, but I want her to be able to come stay with me on weekends."

"Divorced?"

"Just about. We're still in the same house, though, which is totally weird."

"You're living together? In the middle of a divorce? That is weird."

"The laws are screwy. There's no-fault divorce, which makes it all easier, I suppose. But you both get to stay in the same house until it's final. So nobody leaves any sooner than they have to."

"And you're the one leaving?"

"Yeah. It's the right thing. I want Courtney to stay in her home, and I'm the one who needs out. So—"

"Hence the rent. Are you okay?"

"Mostly. I'm scared and excited all at once. Sometimes I'll sit quietly in the rocker in our living room, late in the afternoon when the sun filters in, and wonder if I'm crazy. You know, is it really so bad? Am I just chasing the proverbial elusive dream? Will I wake up in a couple of years, suddenly sane, wanting exactly the life I've just thrown away with no way of getting it back? Then other times, I walk around the house, touching things, hearing Greg's voice nagging at me, telling me to stop wanting so much..."

"What do you mean? What do you want?"

Josie waited until the waitress had delivered their food and checked to see if they needed anything else before she answered. "Life. Aliveness," she said, taking a bite of her grilled cheese and tomato sandwich. "Don't get me wrong, Greg's a terrific guy. If you met him, you'd love him. Everybody does. But we've gone dry." She leaned in across the booth needing to have Caitlin understand. "Here's the thing. We've reached this horrible place. We don't smile or laugh or share anything. I need to learn more, do more, and he resents it because that's not where he's at. So I'm always either accounting to him or apologizing. And he's always shaking his head in disapproval. We have a terrific colonial on a country road, a great daughter, and a filled-up life. But it's just not full..."

"It's ironic, isn't it?" Caitlin observed. "Here, I've just lost a husband I'd give anything to have back, and you're—" she stopped, knowing her thoughts would come out awful.

"Throwing mine away? Don't worry about hurting my feelings. Life is messy," Josie said. "Hey. We're getting too heavy here. This is supposed to be a forget-your-problems-let's-have-fun day. Let's finish up and go shopping."

As they scanned store windows, Josie asked, "What season are you?"

"I don't know. I just wear what I like."

"Oh, you should be analyzed. It's fun and it really makes a difference." She stopped walking and made Caitlin stop as well so she could study her. "Greeny-gold eyes...creamy skin, golden undertones... and that auburn hair...are those streaks natural or do you have it done?" Josie didn't wait for an answer. "Whatever...they're great. You're a classic autumn. I think I heard only seven percent of the population has autumn coloring. That makes you a rare bird. It also means that this gorgeous white blazer would look much better on you if it was ivory."

Caitlin recoiled as Josie touched the arm of her jacket. Who was this woman to tell her how she should look? David had surprised her with this blazer last July, for no reason at all except that he loved her. A blend of linen and cotton with brass buttons, it went with everything, and Caitlin found she wore it almost like a uniform in hot weather. And this self-styled gypsy had the nerve to tell her it didn't look good?

Josie was oblivious to Caitlin's reaction as they continued walking through the mall, passing by window after window. "These clothes are too ordinary, too stuffy, especially for summer. There, look at those outfits." She pointed to a window just ahead. "They're terrific. Cool, easy to wear, and they're loose enough so you don't even need underwear."

Caitlin looked at Josephine. Was she here in the mall without underwear? The two of them certainly were a pair! Caitlin in her Talbot blazer and sleeveless coral dress with matching belt and straight skirt. Her auburn hair was lightly streaked to add dimension rather than color, and cut chin-length with fringe bangs skimming her forehead. She wore gold love-knot earrings, one long gold chain and, of course, the cameo.

And then there was Josephine: bare legged, wearing black and white sandals, a wide skirt and sleeveless, tunic-style blouse, unbuttoned to reveal just the slightest amount of tanned cleavage. The blouse was belted with a length of round silver disks that looked as though several Indians had spent years hammering out the intricate designs. Long silver earrings dangled and swayed every time she moved her head.

Suddenly Caitlin envied Josie's style. Cool. Free. Fun. It's how she wanted to feel. "Let's go inside and try some of those on," she told Josie. "I'm in the mood for something new after all."

Chapter Five

There's a psychic fair next Sunday, wanna go?" Josie asked the next day as she and Caitlin lounged in Caitlin's back yard with the thermos of margaritas Josie brought and a bag of tortilla chips unearthed from the bottom of Caitlin's "goodie" drawer. She was running out of food. She'd have to go shopping soon. It was something she'd been dreading—and avoiding—grocery shopping for one when there used to be three.

"What's a psychic fair?" Caitlin asked, sipping her margarita, wrinkling her nose. "Too sour."

"Are you kidding? There's no such thing as too sour." Josie took a deep sip and smiled. "Perfect. But if you don't agree, next time you can make them."

"Psychic fair?" Caitlin asked again.

"What world have you been living in? You really don't know about them? It's where intuitives—kind of like fortune tellers, but the real thing—read your life. Past, present, future. They tell you whatever your spirit guides want you to know..."

"Spirit guides?" Caitlin laughed, waving her hands in the air and imitating music from The Twilight Zone. "Do-do-do-do..."

Josie chuckled, rolling over onto her stomach so she could look at Caitlin as they talked. "Seriously. It's a great way to explore the ideas of psychic energy, karma, reincarnation—things beyond this physical world." Josie banged the wooden arm of her chair.

"You mean things that go bump in the night?"

"No. No. We're not talking about ghosts or things like that." Josie sat up, excited by the topic and her apparent desire to educate Caitlin. "There are a lot of psychic readers at these fairs. All kinds. They tap into the energy of the universe, so to speak, and can tell you amazing things. Come with me. Please. It'll be fun."

"I don't know. Maybe. You're way over my head with this stuff. Tell me more."

"Well, I'm not an expert on this or anything," Josie said. "The way I see it, it's a lifetime journey, discovering the truth about ourselves and the challenges we carry over from past lifetimes. A good psychic reader can see what's going on with you, maybe even point out some stuff you need to know to make good decisions. Things like that."

"I'm not sure I buy it. Past lifetimes? That's what you call reincarnation, right?"

"Exactly. The way I see it is this: our spiritual goal is to return to God, and we do that by going through many lifetimes of learning and growing, both on the earth plane as well as other levels of existence. I can't accept that we only get one chance, one lifetime, to do it all. Or that this one lifetime is the only criteria to judge whether or not we get to heaven, or whatever you want to call it. The Buddhists call it Nirvana, which means perfection."

"Hmmm..."

"Call me crazy if you want. And you don't have to believe any of it. But come to the fair anyway. Just as a hoot. It's so much more fun going with someone. And your reader may never even get into past lifetimes. She may have her hands full reading this one!"

"I'll let you know. Meanwhile, tell me more about—"

The phone rang interrupting her next question. "Hi, Liz," Caitlin said as soon as she picked up the receiver.

"How'd you know it was me?"

"I'm psychic!" Caitlin laughed, looking over at Josie.

"So, what are you doing?" Liz asked. "I kind of figured you'd be over for a swim, it's so hot out."

"Liz, I can't keep barging in on you and Steve. You guys have your own life, you don't need a fifth wheel."

"But you and Dave always come over for a swim on Sundays. What's so different now?"

"You know..."

"No. I don't..."

"Oh, Liz. David's gone...that makes everything's different."

"Not really. You're still you. And it's so hot out. Come on over."

"Josie's here." Caitlin made her voice extra cheerful, as though Josie being there was an ordinary occurrence even though she sensed her new friend's presence was somehow a betrayal of Liz. "She showed up on my doorstep with her bathing suit in one hand and a thermos of margaritas in the other, and we've been running through the lawn sprinkler."

Liz's silence hung heavy, and for a minute, Caitlin actually thought the line had gone dead. "Liz? Are you there?"

"Oh, Catie, I'm sorry. I was just thinking, mentally counting hamburgers. Bring Josephine over. I'd love to meet her. Why should you two be running through lawn sprinklers like a couple of project kids when we have a pool right here?"

"Are you sure?"

"I insist. Come over in about a half-hour; that'll give me time to straighten up around here. We'll have a swim and then the usual, hamburgers and salad."

"Okay. If you're sure. Josie brought over some strawberries. We'll bring them for dessert."

Liz was dying to meet Josie. Of that, Caitlin had no doubt. And she was equally certain that Liz had looked out her front window and seen the unfamiliar yellow car in Caitlin's driveway. So why the wounded silence when she heard Josie was here? Knowing and knowing are two different things, Caitlin decided, running her fingers through her hair. Poor Liz. She had such a need for absolute order in her life, right down to her friendships. She couldn't tolerate anything rearranged or out of place. How like her to want to straighten up the house, and they probably wouldn't even go inside. Caitlin remembered back to when she first met Liz. It was a year before Caitlin ever saw the inside of Liz's house—because it wasn't fully decorated yet—even though Liz had been inside hers almost from the day they'd moved in.

* * *

In exactly one half-hour, Caitlin and Josie strolled over to the Warner's.

"Hi, I'm Elizabeth," Liz said in her best suburban voice, extending her hand to Josie. "This is my husband, Steve, and the two fish are Jason and Jessica. I understand you brought a suit?"

"Hello, I'm Josephine Ford-Newman," Josie said, rising to Liz's formality, as though she immediately understood what was going on. "But call me Josie. All my friends do, and since you and Catie are so close, I hope we can become friends too. My suit's right under here." Josie lifted one corner of her hot pink T-shirt. "We were sunbathing at Catie's, although I must admit the pool looks a lot more inviting than her sprinkler." Josie smiled her most engaging smile and waved to the kids in the pool. "Think I'll join them if you don't mind." She peeled off her shorts and shirt and jumped in before Liz could say another word.

"Look at her," Liz whispered to Caitlin as they sat down. "It's unnatural for anyone over thirty to look that good. Where are her lumpy thighs? Where's the tummy bulge?"

"Come on, Liz, lighten up. She's really nice. Give her a chance. She thinks her hips are too big, if that helps any."

Liz took a long drink of her cranberry juice and vodka, studying Josie as she did a few laps. "So, what have you two been talking about all afternoon?"

"Just stuff. Nothing much," Caitlin answered, feeling worn down and suddenly tired of what other people thought, tired of feeling guilty about her every move. She closed her eyes and listened to Liz drone on, telling her about a fight Jessica had with Kristen, a girl down the street, how she thought the Allens might be moving, and how she was certain that John Chapman was having an affair because he came home late almost every night and Lois constantly looked as though her eyes were swollen from crying, although she was quick to talk about all the pollen in the air and how it affects her allergies.

As the day began to cool, the only things left in the pool were a stray raft, bobbing up and down as the water moved with the evening breeze, and two pairs of dangling feet, impatiently waiting for the go-ahead signal that would let them swim again, now that the mandatory half-hour waiting after dinner had almost come to an end. The adults sat around the redwood table, finishing the last of the coffee, too lazy to begin clean-up.

"You'd think they'd get tired of it," Liz halfheartedly complained, waving her two children back into the pool. "They're in that water from sun up to sun down, day after day."

"They're beautiful children," Josie said. "Very well behaved and fun to be with. I always wanted blonde hair like them, but I got stuck with this." Josie tugged at the short, dark hairs framing her face.

"Caitlin mentioned that you have a daughter. How old is she?" Liz asked.

"Actually, I had two, born a year apart. But one died. Her name was

Allison. Courtney's twelve."

"Josie!" Caitlin's voice registered her shock. "I didn't know. Why didn't you tell me?"

Josie shrugged. "You're going through so much of your own stuff right now. It was five years ago. Leukemia. I've found a place for the hurt so it doesn't ache quite so much, and I've learned to accept it."

Liz's face revealed genuine pain as Josie talked about the unthinkable—about what it was like to lose her daughter and the difficult years that followed. Steve listened just as intently, nodding at the right times, twisting his mouth just so to register the appropriate amount of concern. But, just like his laughter, Caitlin noticed that the pain never reached his eyes. Would anything ever reach that high, touch that deep? Caitlin turned her thoughts inward. Why she was spending so much energy these days examining motives and emotions? It was as though David's death had given her the ability to view life through a highly polished lens.

Caitlin's introspection had taken her away from the conversation. She was jolted back at hearing Josie talk about her psychic explorations.

"My traditional religion just wasn't giving me enough answers," Josie was saying. "I mean, why was my daughter taken before she had a chance to really live? There had to be an answer. When my minister couldn't help me, I began talking with priests and nuns. I even went to a rabbi. They all told me basically the same thing: that it was God's will and I shouldn't question His infinite wisdom. That just didn't cut it."

"But that's just what it was, God's will!" Liz protested. "Just like David's death. Ask Catie, she understands. You didn't like the answer so you threw out your religion? You have to have faith."

"I do have faith," Josie replied calmly, slowly. "A lot of faith. And I didn't throw out my religion. I broadened it, expanded it. Like I was telling Caitlin—"

"Catie? You've been filling our Catie's head with this garbage?" Steve said, his jaw tightening.

A knot was forming in Caitlin's stomach. She pressed her hands against the pain, willing herself to take long steadying breaths. Watching Josephine meet Steve's intense gaze, not backing down from the harshness of his voice, Caitlin knew she was witnessing the undercurrents of a real disagreement. It was exactly the kind of situation her father had warned her about all her childhood, drilling into her the maxim about never mixing politics or religion with food and drink, molding her into a socially acceptable, never-make-waves type of woman. The kind of woman David loved, the perfect wife who never publicly voiced opinions on any controversial topic. Now, here she was, no David, and in the middle of a tidal wave of controversy.

"Caitlin's a grown woman. My ideas aren't going to bite her," Josie responded. "Like I said, I began exploring different religions in my desire to look for answers. Is this really our only chance to get it right or do we have lots of lifetimes, lots of opportunities? I looked for answers that would work for me. And I found them. I'm probably more spiritual now than I've ever been in my life."

"But..." Steve said.

"But, what?" Josie interrupted, jutting out her chin, ready to deflect the next punch.

"You go to psychics instead of church, and you court the devil with this junk about coming back over and over again in different bodies."

"Shh, keep your voice down. The kids will hear you." Liz touched her husband's arm.

"Excuse me? 'Court the devil?' Me? I don't think so." Josie said.

"What would you call it? Mark my words, if you don't change your ways, you're going to end up in hell." Steve hissed his message through clenched teeth.

Josie's eyes continued to meet Steve's. "I don't believe in hell," she said softly.

It seemed to Caitlin that Steve and Liz sucked in their breath at exactly the same time, and she knew for certain that she hadn't exhaled for close to a minute now. The only one functioning close to normal was Josie.

"I think this conversation is a bad idea." Caitlin pushed back her chair and stood up. "Why don't we call it a night?"

"Let me just say one thing," Josie said. "You invited me into your home and I feel bad if I've made you uncomfortable or angry. But my beliefs are my beliefs and there's nothing wrong with them. They're not evil, and neither am I. Yes, I go to psychics. They help me to connect with undiscovered parts of me. But I also go to church. Not often, but I do go. I even believe in the Bible—don't look so shocked, Steve—I really do believe in it—but I also believe it's been tampered with along the way by men of the cloth more concerned with politics than the truth, so I accept it symbolically rather than literally. And, yes, I believe in reincarnation." Josie stood up, knowing it was definitely time to end the evening. "We probably knew each other in a past lifetime and fought like cats and dogs then, too," she said with a smile.

"Never know." Steve returned her smile, attempting to reclaim his role as the gracious host. He extended his hand to Josie. "At least it wasn't a dull evening!"

"Steve's right. It definitely wasn't dull," Liz said, as she walked with Josie and Caitlin to the front of the house. "It was very interesting meeting you, Josephine. I'm sure we'll see each other again sometime."

"I'm sure," Josie answered, a slight smile tugging at the corners of her lips. "Thanks for dinner."

Liz hugged Caitlin goodbye, then whispered, "I'll say an extra prayer for you tonight. I don't know how you're managing." She looked over at Josephine, who was already halfway across the street. "But maybe you're not."

Chapter Six

They'd already driven around the block twice looking for a parking space. Caitlin strained her neck to get a look at Old Towne Nursery down at the corner of the street. "They must be having some kind of huge plant sale."

Josie didn't answer. She just smiled that closed-lipped smile of hers, as though she had a secret she wasn't yet ready to share. On the third time around, she saw some people leaving and quickly swung into the vacated space. They were parked right across the street from their destination, and right in front of the Riverside Congregational Chapel.

Tacked to trees just outside the brick VFW Hall were large-poster board signs with the words "PSYCHIC FAIR 11–5" written in colored markers—pink, blue, purple, and yellow. They might as well have drawn balloons and clowns on the signs, Caitlin thought, as she and Josie climbed the cement stairs to the entrance of the old brick building. They pulled open the heavy door and stepped inside to a cacophony of sound and color.

"My God, all these people! No wonder we couldn't find a parking spot." Caitlin stood in the doorway taking in the unexpected numbers of men, women, and children—all sizes and ages, looking at books and music, and talking with one another. "Are they all here for readings?"

"And you thought Old Towne was having a two-for-one sale," Josephine joked.

Caitlin stood and watched for a minute before nudging Josie. "I have to go to the bathroom."

"Again? You went before we left the house."

"I know. I'm like a faucet when I'm nervous."

"Catie, you're at a psychic fair, not a public hanging!"

"I know. But what if I'm told something that I don't want to know? What if it's something bad?"

"Relax. Readers can only tell you what's revealed to them, and that's whatever your guides want you to know. Listen, you don't have to do this. Not if you're not ready. We can leave, or you can look around at the books and things while I have a reading."

"Let me go to the bathroom," Caitlin said. "I'll let you know when I get back."

"It's through that doorway," Josie said, pointing to the back of the room, "and down the hall on the left, just past the stairs leading down to where the readings are held." She chuckled at the look of distress on Caitlin's face. "Do you want me to go with you?"

"No. I'll find it," Caitlin said, waving Josie away with a sweep of her hand. "I'm fine. I'll be right back."

Caitlin walked across the hardwood floor, purposely stepping on squares of sunshine for good luck. During all of her growing-up years, whenever her parents dragged to one of those myriad events held in halls, from weddings to trade shows, and even her Uncle Jackie's after-funeral luncheon, Caitlin had entertained herself by chasing the sun around the room as it moved in patches throughout the day. Taking giant steps, she would tell herself that it was extra good luck if the only spots her feet touched were those polished by the sun. Here she was now, all grown up and still looking for bits of sun-polished floor. Still looking for luck.

The bathroom was small, but spotless, and that made Caitlin feel better. You could always judge a place by its bathroom. She'd grown up with that bit of wisdom and eventually found it to be true. The cement walls, bumpy and uneven, were painted a sky blue, and even though the paint was chipping, there wasn't a soiled spot to be found. The sink and toilet were pristine in their whiteness and there was a neat pile of paper towels on a glass shelf. Caitlin took a long look at herself in the mirror. She felt like she'd aged tremendously in the last few weeks, although a casual observer would never have seen the difference. The aging had occurred on the inside. She talked out loud to her reflection, "You want new, Caitlin McKenna Saunders? You say you want answers. Well, this is your chance, so don't be a baby." She couldn't quite smile at her reflection, but she did nod, giving herself permission to follow this new path.

Back in the single large room, Caitlin took stock of the space as she look for Josie. High on both sides were rectangular windows, un-curtained to let in the maximum amount of air and light, the same light that created those wonderful patches of sunshine across the oak floor. In one corner, women were selling coffee, iced-tea, apples, brownies, and huge chocolate-chip cookies. The center of the room was left empty so people could move about freely, but nearly all of the wall space was taken up by tables covered with books, rocks, jewelry, and even clothes. Trappings for the spiritually challenged, Caitlin thought, feeling that she had crawled under the carnival fence and was about to be discovered by a band of Gypsies.

"What is all this stuff?" Caitlin asked Josie, finding her at one of the far tables.

"Books. Rocks. Clothes."

"Very funny."

"Listen. Can you hear that CD he just put on?" Josie asked, nodding toward a man at another table. Flutes and a piano seemed to be playing to a background of chirping birds, cascading water, and soft breezes.

"That's really nice," Caitlin said. "Sort of like being on a Caribbean island."

"Exactly. It's a meditation tape. I have the same one at home. I'll lend it to you. Listen, the registration line was long so I took the liberty of signing you up for a reading. I'm having two. If you don't want it," Josie hastened, "I'm sure I can sell your spot to someone else."

"No. I'll do it." Caitlin said, taking the ticket from Josie's hand and digging into her wallet for ten dollars. "Why are you having two?"

"For fun. Each reader tunes into something different. I generally have a couple when I come, sometimes even three."

"Now what?" Caitlin asked.

"We have to wait about ten more minutes, and then we go downstairs. Each reading takes twenty minutes, so come back up here when you're done and wait for me while I have my second one. You can look at the books, or whatever."

Josie browsed for the next few minutes while Caitlin stood with her back against the far wall, watching the people. They were all so ordinary; that's what surprised her the most. They were the same people you would see at the grocery store or the movies. Two young women walked in, dressed in tank tops and jeans, one carrying a baby not more than six months old. They headed right for the registration table, apparently familiar with the routine of these fairs. Liz would just die, Caitlin thought, exposing a baby to all of this. It seemed to Caitlin that even she could feel the energy in the room; but it felt good, positive, if that was possible. She began to relax a little.

Two other women, apparently strangers, stood close enough for Caitlin to hear their conversation.

"Man, it's hot in here," said the heavier woman. She seemed to be in her early twenties. She had long dark hair, a deep tan, and lavender eye shadow. "I've never done this before, but I understand it's fun."

"More than fun. Helpful," said the other, much older, woman She looked as though she'd just come from church, wearing a sun dress covered by an appropriate short white jacket and sandals with a small heel.

"Are they really accurate?" asked the first woman.

"You'll be amazed at how accurate they are. Just relax. I do this a lot. I also have a psychic in Massachusetts that I consult once a year. What the readings really do," she continued, "is tell you what you already know, deep down, and help you deal with things. I've made some major decisions based on my readings. Sometimes a reader can see the future, not just the past or present, so ask anything you want."

Caitlin would have liked blending into the wall a while longer, listening to the two women, but Josie was tugging at her elbow. "Come on. Let's go downstairs. It's almost time."

As they walked through the narrow hallway and down the stairs, Caitlin finally thought to ask. "Who's reading me? Have you ever had him?"

"It's a her. That's all I know. They recommended her at the registration desk. Said she's different, and very on target."

"Different, how?"

"I don't know," Josie smiled, this time a wide, full-cheeked smile. "Honest, I don't know." She laughed at the skeptical look on Caitlin's face. "Just go with it."

They separated at that point, each directed by a young woman to their assigned reader. "Janet Lee is in the middle row at the back table," the girl told Caitlin as she pointed to the back of the room, "all the way down."

Caitlin couldn't see who she was headed toward. She simply walked to the back of the basement room, which had been set up cafeteria-style with rows of tables, one after another. She looked at each reader as she passed. For the most part, they were normal men and women, a little poor-looking perhaps, dressed primarily in polyester and worn cotton. But normal. Maybe designer clothes just weren't a priority with psychics.

The readers sat at their tables waiting for their clients. Some had candles lit; others had crystals or amethysts in front of them. Some had crosses, and one women even had a crystal ball.

Caitlin reached the back of the room and spotted the sign JANET LEE on a table before she actually connected with the person. She sat down on the aluminum folding chair and looked up at her psychic reader.

She had only an instant for everything to register, and in that instant, she had to bite her tongue, first to keep herself from crying, and then to keep herself from laughing out loud, hoping that Janet Lee could not, at that very moment, read her thoughts. There, across from her was the person who was going to help her begin her search for inner truth. There was Janet Lee, the one person in the room who seriously looked as though she'd belonged on the Atlantic City Boardwalk telling fortunes for fifty cents.

Even in the windowless room, light bounced off Janet Lee's translucent skin, giving it the luster of fine pearls. A line of thick, brown pencil circled each eye, and then extended outward toward her temple. Her full lips were stained red. Janet Lee's long yellow hair was turned under, pageboy-style, with bangs rolled so tightly that Caitlin wanted to poke the straw-like hair to see if the roller was still underneath. A black sequin hat, secured by a large brass hatpin, was centered firmly on the yellow mass. An amethyst-colored sun dress hugged her large breasts and slender waist, and a print black shawl covered her shoulders. Around her neck, resting on bare skin, was a silver cross.

"Hold out your left hand," Janet Lee demanded, breaking the almost eerie silence that had begun to bond them. Caitlin did as she was told.

Without ever invading Caitlin's personal space or touching her outstretched palm, Janet Lee began to talk. "Oh, honey," she said softly. "I feel your sadness. Such pain. You've just lost someone. Someone very close. Your husband, perhaps?"

How could she know? Caitlin looked down at her hand, suspended in air. It felt as though she had plunged it into the center of an electrical mass. From her wrist, across the palm to the fingertips, and then around the back of her hand, there was tangible energy. She could feel it vibrating, pulsating; it was the energy that helped her keep her hand still and the muscles of her arm strong and unflinching. "That's right,"

Caitlin finally answered.

"I see a second loss. Very close to the first," Janet Lee continued. "This one is still here, on the earth plane. But gone from you. You want things to be right between you. The guides want you to try. But things may not work out. You may have to go separate ways. You will be working out a lot of karma in the coming year. I see a lot of relationships changing, moving in and out of your life. Try to keep the ones you want. Work at them. The others, let them go. You understand what I'm saying?"

"Yes...I think so."

"Oh. I see so much. It's all coming at me at once." Janet Lee rubbed her forehead, as though trying to sort out the various messages. "More people. I see new people coming into your life. Be careful. I'm being told to warn you. Someone will seem like a friend, but don't be fooled. Remove the mask. That's what I'm being told to tell you. We all wear masks, honey, you know that. Remove the mask. That's all I can tell you."

It sounded like a bunch of carnival hype to Caitlin. Strangers coming into her life. Right. Would they be tall, dark, handsome strangers? But the part about David was true. But two losses? David and Maryanne? It had to be Maryanne. But those could just be lucky guesses. Maybe she looked sad. But what about the energy around her hand? Where was that coming from?

"Good things will start to happen for you," Janet Lee continued. "Keep your eyes open. Always open. Ahh, I see change. No, I see the opportunity for change, for you to change. This would be a good thing."

"What kind of change?" Caitlin asked.

Janet Lee looked into Caitlin's eyes. "You'll become more you, the real you. Not the face you show the world. You don't always show what you believe, what you feel. You try too hard to be liked. You're going to be given challenges, opportunities to decide what's more important—how you feel about yourself or how others feel about you."

Janet Lee continued to study Caitlin's palm, never once actually touching her. Caitlin's right hand was sweating, her heart pounding, as she sat waiting for whatever else this funny-looking woman would tell her about herself--for other truths she could read from the lines in her hand.

"You're in a period of learning, of receiving new information. That's good. You work with houses. You draw them. No, you used to draw them. Something beginning with the letter A...artist, architect...You wanted to design houses. But now you do something else. You sell houses now, don't you?"

"Yes, that's right," Caitlin said, "but how could you know?"

"Lately you've been thinking about that lost dream. I see an old road being uncovered, brushed clean. You could travel down it now, if you wanted to. You could go back to school and study. You've been thinking about it, haven't you?"

"Kind of...a little bit," Caitlin said. "But I haven't told anybody." Afraid to move her left hand and break the current that still surrounded it, Caitlin slid her right hand across the table and touched Janet Lee's arm. "How do you know all this?"

"I'm psychic, honey," Janet Lee laughed. "That's how I know. One more thing, before our time is over. David, that's your husband's name, isn't it?"

"Yes." Caitlin's reply was soft, choked.

"He's been with you the whole time here. He's gone now, but he left you roses. Psychic roses. For healing. He said to tell you they're white."

A bell rang and their time was over. Caitlin pulled her hand back, close to her body, shaking it free of remaining bits of energy.

How could she know? How could Janet Lee possibly know? David always brought her white roses. Never pink, or red, or yellow. But white. Always white.

Chapter Seven

When the mail arrived on Saturday, Caitlin examined the return address a full minute before opening the envelope. After reading the card and note through once, she immediately ran over to see Liz.

"Look at this," Caitlin demanded.

"It's a sympathy card," Liz said, taking it from Caitlin. "An expensive sympathy card," she corrected, turning it over. "Who pays five dollars for a card?"

"That's what I'd like to know. Read the note. Tell me what you think."

"Who's Derrick Secor?" Liz asked after reading the note. "Actually it's M. Derrick Secor," she said, re-reading the signature. "I'm definitely impressed," she added, fanning the card in mock appreciation. "Nobody writes with a fountain pen anymore, except maybe the idle rich. Do you think he's rich?"

"Beats me. He could be anything. I've never met him, and as far as I can remember, David never even mentioned him."

"Well, you're going to see him, aren't you?" Liz asked, re-reading the note. "Holy you-know-what, it's tonight! He says he'll pick you up at seven unless he hears from you by noon. After that he'll be unreachable until he actually gets here."

"It's almost noon now. What's the number?"

"No way." Liz tucked the card under one thigh, refusing to hand it over to Caitlin. "I think you should go. It'll be good for you. Besides, aren't you curious?"

"Curious? About what?" Caitlin tried to grab the card from Liz. "Let me have it. In a few minutes he'll be unreachable, whatever that means, and I don't want him coming all the way from Massachusetts for nothing."

"He's on the border, Catie. That's not exactly East Jebrew. He just wants to take you to dinner." She pulled the card out from beneath her leg and read "to meet David's wife and express his condolences." She handed the card over to Caitlin. "Aren't you curious about him, about how he found out about David dying? I think you should go. At the very least, it'll give us something new to talk about."

"It's too soon. I'm not into dating."

"It's not a date. It's an old friend of David's who feels bad about his death and wants to meet you. I think it's nice. And it'll give you a chance to find out all those little things about David's past that husbands never get around to telling you."

Caitlin was starting to waver. "That's true. That part could be fun." She looked at her watch. While they talked, it had ticked its way past noon. "Thanks a lot. It's too late to call now anyway. He could have given me a cell phone number if he really wanted me to reach him, don't you think? Now I'll have to go, unless, of course, I just don't answer the door."

"And you're way too honest for that. You'd die from a thousand guilt trips standing behind a door while he keeps ringing the bell waiting for you to answer. So, what are you going to wear? You have to look gorgeous."

"Stop it. You just got done convincing me it's not a date—"

"It's not. But you don't want him to think David married a frump. Wear that new purple outfit. The one you bought with whatshername. It really does look nice on you."

"Her name is Josie. And it's periwinkle not purple. I'll see. I don't even want to think about it right now. Like Scarlet would say, I'll think about it tomorrow."

"Tomorrow's too late," Liz laughed. "For Scarlet, and for you. As a matter of fact, Derrick Secor will be here in exactly six hours and forty-seven minutes!"

Chapter Eight

Derrick placed the flowers on the passenger side of his silver Mercedes and patted them gently. "Nice touch, Secor. Definitely a nice touch."

Everything was going smoothly. She didn't call. That was a good sign. He'd stayed by the phone until nearly three, with the answering machine on, wondering if she'd try to cancel. He wouldn't have picked up, though. He would have made her believe he was already on his way down to see her. But no call. Perfect.

Derrick settled back in the leather seat and pulled a small black notebook from his inside breast pocket. Flipping through pages of dated entries, he found the one he wanted. Callahan's Flower Shop, long-stemmed white roses. Next to that entry, he wrote the name Tess. That was the name of the girl who'd waited on him. She'd know exactly which roses to give him. They were long and lush, and they were Caitlin's favorite.

Finally, it was time to go. He checked his reflection in the mirror and then put the car in gear. Next stop, Corey Lane.

* * *

Caitlin stood behind the closed front door, hiding from view of the side windows, twisting her diamond-studded wedding band until her finger actually began to burn. Liz was right. She couldn't do this, hide like a thief in her own home. When she could no longer bear the insistent ringing of the doorbell, she took a deep, steadying breath and readied herself to meet a piece of David's past.

"I was about ready to get in my Mercedes and drive back to Massachusetts," a seductive voice greeted her. "I'm Derrick Secor. You must be Caitlin. And these are for you."

For one long moment, Caitlin was unable to move. Standing before her was a man about six feet tall, with hair so dark it was almost black, and smooth tanned skin with cheekbones tinted just slightly pink from the summer sun. He was holding out a dozen roses to her.

"Are you all right?" Derrick asked.

Caitlin shook her head slowly. "I'm sorry. You startled me." She backed away so he could come in.

"You look like you've seen a ghost."

"Really, I'm fine. It's just that for a moment..." her voice trailed off. "For a moment I thought I was seeing a ghost. David's ghost. You have the same coloring and build." Caitlin took a deep breath. "But I can see now that you don't look anything like him. Not really."

Derrick's hair was longer and darker than David's, worn away from his face in what Caitlin considered a GQ style. He was elegant where David was more casual. "David would never wear double-breasted jacket. You just took me by surprise, that's all. I'm sorry." What a dumb thing to say—David would never wear double-breasted jacket—you're losing it, Caitlin.

"No, no, don't be sorry. I'm flattered if I reminded you of Dave, even for a minute. He was one terrific guy. Here, these are for you."

"White roses. From Callahan's." Caitlin looked directly into Derrick's dark eyes, which, like his hair, were more black than brown. She took the roses without speaking, almost as though she was on automatic pilot, the way she'd been at David's funeral, nodding her head, accepting condolences, not really hearing or seeing. Or feeling.

Derrick stood perfectly composed. "Is there something wrong with them?"

"No. No. they're fine. I just don't understand—"

"The flowers? I wanted to bring you something in the way of condolences." Derrick's voice was quiet and sympathetic. "I rode around town until I found a florist that looked good. It turned out that they knew you. The girl said you loved white roses." He reached out and placed his hand on both of hers as she clenched the cone of white and lavender paper that was the hallmark of Callahan's Florists. "You're trembling."

"David always gave me white roses. From Callahan's," she explained haltingly. "Seeing you, seeing the roses..." She touched his arm. "I'm okay now. And they really are lovely. Thank you. Come in. I'll put these in water." She waved Derrick toward the family room and went into the kitchen for a vase. She lingered there, inhaling the fragrance of the roses, inhaling the memory of David, and fighting back her tears. This was a horrible mistake. Going out. Having this man in her house. Let's just get it over with, she told herself, already looking forward to the evening's end.

When Caitlin joined Derrick in the family room, she found him engrossed in a photo album. She could have sworn she had put it back in the desk drawer this afternoon. But obviously not.

"He sure didn't change much all these years. Except for the glasses. I wear them too. Hate to admit it, but I do. Contacts." Derrick said, pointing to his eyes. "Wore them tonight to impress you. I hate putting those suckers in."

"They look nice," Caitlin told him, not knowing what else to say.

"Thanks," Derrick smiled, a grin so appealing it was hard not to respond.

Caitlin sat down next to him, pointing to special pictures in the album, reliving moments of personal history, pulling Derrick into the life she and David had built. When they reached the end, Derrick flipped back several pages as though looking for something specific.

"Mind if I keep this one?" He asked, pointing to a picture taken on the beach in Maine last summer. "To remember Dave by." It was one of the few pictures of David alone. He was sitting on a cliff along the Marginal Way, the water below splashing hard against the rocks, his short dark hair tousled by the wind. Dressed in a rugby shirt and khaki shorts, deck shoes on the ground next to his bare feet, it was the way Caitlin would always remember him—natural, blending into nature. How could she give away that memory to some stranger in a navy blazer with brass buttons and wing-tip shoes? Nobody had ever left a hole in her album before. Not even David's mother, who was forever collecting photos of her only son.

"It's my only copy," she told Derrick.

"But look at all the pictures you have," he said. "I only want one. I'll make myself a copy and get it back to you. I promise." He had already started to remove it from the album, slowly, gently, as though Caitlin might not notice. His eyes were so compelling, his voice so convincing, it seemed unreasonable not to give in.

"I guess," Caitlin told him, getting up and walking away as he removed the picture, leaving an empty place in the middle of the page. "But make sure you send it back."

"Will do. Shall we go eat? I'm famished." Derrick stood up and smoothed out the lap of his trousers. "I was so afraid I'd be late that I got here extra early and had a chance to scout out your little town. Found the perfect place for dinner. It's right on the river. Lucky for us, they had a cancellation and could take us at eight. We'd better head out."

He has to be talking about The Whiting House. "Where are we going?" she asked anyway.

"You know, I can't remember the name. But I know just where it is. Big red colonial, set up high, overlooking the Connecticut River."

"The Whiting House?" First Callahan's and now The Whiting House...

"That's it. You and Davie ever go there?"

"Dave," she corrected. "His name is Dave. We go there all the time." Caitlin grabbed her shawl, eager to get the evening over with.

* * *

Midway through dinner Caitlin realized she was actually enjoying herself. Derrick might be a little too impressed with himself, but he definitely had charm. He knew the right wine to order, he spent money comfortably, and he was never short of conversation.

For a few moments, she sunk deeply into the sense of being cared for again; she could almost feel Derrick's strong arms cradling her, protecting her from life's storms. She flashed ahead in her mind, imagining him bringing her tea on a drizzly autumn day and tucking an afghan under her cold feet. For awhile, she almost forgot about David. But then, that wasn't exactly true, because all they did was talk about him. It was as though David was alive, in the next room waiting for her, and Derrick was in charge of watching over her until he got back. Caitlin smiled at the image.

"What are you smiling about?" Derrick teased. "Here I am telling you the heartbreaking story of my first prom, and I see the corners of your lips turn up. This was not meant to be an amusing story."

"Oh, nothing. It's silly...it's just that being with you, talking about David, I don't know...I felt safe for a minute...like everything was okay."

"It's not silly at all. I'm glad I make you feel safe, and I think Dave would want me to keep an eye on you. You're too fragile to be thrown out into the world alone." Derrick reached across the table and put his hand on Caitlin's.

"I'm not that fragile!" She pulled her hand from under his. "I can take care of myself perfectly well, thank you."

"I know you can. But you shouldn't have to."

She rubbed her hand as though trying to restore blood and feeling. "Not to change the subject or anything, but with all these stories, you still haven't answered my earlier question. If you two were such great friends, how come I never heard of you?"

"Okay. True confession time. Maybe you heard about me as Milton. I shouldn't even be telling you—nobody calls me Milton and lives to tell about it. What a loser name to hang on a kid. As soon as I moved away, I changed my name. I'll never be Milton again. Ever."

As Derrick talked, Caitlin's mind flashed to his signature. M. Derrick Secor. One mystery solved, she thought and couldn't wait to tell Liz.

"Anyway," she heard Derrick continue, "it's not that Dave and I were such great friends, as much as we were always thrown together and then became friends. All through school there we were—Saunders, Secor—alphabetically arranged with nobody between us. Except for seventh grade. A bully by the name of Seaman moved into town. He was there just the one year and then his dad got transferred. So there we were again, Saunders and Secor." He signaled for the bill while finishing off his scotch. Handing the waiter his American Express card, Derrick waited another long moment before continuing.

"In high school we had the same home room for four years. It made us buddies. But Dave was always the one the girls wanted. They were crazy over him. And why not? He came from the right side of town, he was good in sports, he always had cash in his pocket and gas in his car. I got the cast-offs. Except once..." Derrick stopped talking and Caitlin could see by the set of his jaw that nothing could convince him to finish that last thought.

"But, look at you. You're very handsome, you must know that. And you're obviously making good money. It couldn't have been as bad as all that in high school."

"Style, Catie. I've developed style. Make enough money and you can buy good looks. The computer business, and a few good investments. Microsoft set me up for life. I have no complaints. But I'm still lousy in sports and I've been through two wives." His voice hardened. "It didn't have to be that way, though."

"What do you mean?"

"Nothing. Enough said. More than enough."

The silence was filled with tension, and Caitlin wasn't sure why. If they hadn't just started their coffee, she would have suggested leaving. Instead, she stretched her mind, looking for something to discuss. "Any children?" she asked.

"One. A boy. He's in South Carolina with his mother." He studied Caitlin as though looking at a prized possession under a magnifying glass. "You really are lovely. But then Davie always did know how to pick them. Is Brenda still a looker?"

"Dave," she corrected again, an automatic response to the nickname Dave had always hated. "She's put on a few pounds," Caitlin said. "Actually—this is horrid, but it feels great to say it—she's gotten fat. But I didn't know you knew her. How?"

Derrick shook his head in mock disapproval. "The voluptuous ones are always the first to go. Their bodies seem to grow down and out. What a shame. I'll bet you were a late bloomer, Catie. That's why you kept your figure."

Caitlin found herself blushing. "How did you know Brenda?"

"I was around that summer when Dave got back from Europe. With his new bride Brenda. That's when I met her. Just once. But that was enough to assess the situation. She was a looker, and she fawned all over him. Imagine going to Europe to celebrate your independence, finally out of college and on your own—free from all those ties that bind--and coming back with a wife! He had people back home to consider, but Dave being Dave, he saw something he wanted at the moment and, without giving it another thought, he went for it. And now look. He got tired of Brenda, and he got you. Lovely Caitlin."

"I don't think I like this." Caitlin picked up her purse. "You make David sound so..." She searched for the word..."so pragmatic. Just for the record, he didn't leave Brenda for me. They were already separated. You make it sound like he was in habit of trashing one relationship for another. He wasn't like that. Not at all. He was a wonderful man, and we really loved each other—"

"Whoa...Whoa, settle down. I didn't mean to hurt you, and I didn't necessarily mean you when I said Dave went after whatever he wanted. It was just an observation. That's how he used to be. It was one of the qualities that you had to admire about him. He always got what he wanted." Derrick had put his hand over Caitlin's again, as though the simple gesture could actually stop her from getting up. And something about it did.

"You sound so bitter. Almost as though you didn't like him. Why are you here? Why did you want to see me?" she asked.

"You've got it all wrong. I admired Dave. I really did. Anyway, to answer your question, I was home, visiting my dad—he hasn't been well since my mother died a couple of years ago—and I ran into Dave's father. He told me about the accident. I went over the next day and spent the whole afternoon with the Saunders, looking at old high school pictures. You must know how his mother is about pictures! Anyway, it brought back a lot of memories. When they told me about you, it was like something inside clicked. I knew I had to meet you. I never liked Brenda, disliked her, in fact. But if Dave hadn't married Brenda—if he'd done what he was supposed to do instead—well, then, he'd have never met you. I guess I just wanted to see if the end was worth it all. And, looking at you, I'd say it was."

Caitlin's stomach churned. Was there something about David that he knew and she didn't? "I don't understand. What are you saying? What was he supposed to have done?"

The set of Derrick's face told her she wouldn't find out. Not now anyway. "Just ignore me," he said. "Sometimes I speak out of line. We all distort the past. We give things more importance than they deserve. Dave was a great guy, and a good friend. And meeting you is the best thing I've done in a long, long time." He turned his attention to the bill, quickly calculating a tip for the waiter and signing the charge slip. "We're all set here. Ready to go?"

The ride home was quiet, but by the time they reached Corey Lane, Derrick seemed to have relaxed once again. "It's a nice street, Caitlin. Traditional. Quiet. It's just right, isn't it?" Walking her to the front door, he reached for her hand. "I'd like to see you again."

"That's not a good idea. Thanks for tonight, but..."

"Why not?"

"I'm not ready to date. I wouldn't feel right."

"I'm not asking you for a date," he laughed. "I just thought we could get together and talk some more. I have hundreds of stories to tell you about Dave and Edmond High. Little things, fun things. It's a way to keep him alive, Catie. You'd like that, wouldn't you?" His voice was seductive, cool water cascading across smooth marble.

"I don't know...it's such a confusing time for me."

"Come on." He teased her with this eyes.

"As long as we're clear that it's not really a date."

"Clear as crystal. How about I come by around noon next Saturday and we'll go on a picnic. I'll pack the lunch."

"I can't. I have lunch plans." That wasn't exactly true. She was hoping to have plans, as soon as she got up the courage to call Maryanne and invite her to lunch.

"Dinner then. We'll make it a picnic dinner."

"I don't know. Maybe it's not a good idea—"

"Caitlin, Caitlin." Derrick touched her head and smiled. "What's the harm? You just said yes. Don't go back on your word. Dave would want you to be with an old friend now. Maybe I can help. Like I said, together, we can keep David alive. You'd like that, wouldn't you?" he repeated.

"I guess," Caitlin said. "All right. Why not?"

"Great. I'll be here around three." Derrick started to walk away, but he ran back just as Caitlin was closing the door and quickly kissed her on the cheek. "Until next week."

Caitlin's face burned from the kiss. This whole thing was a mistake and now she was locked into next Saturday. Maybe she would call him and cancel. For now, all she wanted was a shower, a warm, cleansing shower. She locked and double locked the front door and then checked the back one. Ever since the movie Psycho, she'd felt uneasy about taking a shower late at night, alone in a house so empty. But, tonight the need was greater than the fear.

She let the warm water cascade over her body, rinsing away the contradictions of the evening. Caitlin knew she couldn't wish for David to be alive again, but she wished desperately he could somehow help her move ahead with her life, make decisions, figure out what to do next.

The evening kept replaying in her mind. She'd see the sweet Derrick, the one who made her laugh and didn't shy away from talking about David, as so many people had done after his death. And then there was the angry, sullen Derrick who turned to granite when she broached an apparently forbidden topic. There was the smooth, sophisticated Derrick who drove a Mercedes and enjoyed flaunting the rewards of financial success. There was the little-boy Derrick, still afraid of coming up short, of being second best. Most compelling—and frightening—of all, there was the Derrick with secrets. All this in one man, in just one evening!

Caitlin laughed out loud. "Oh, David, wherever you are, I wish you could help me with this one. Should I see him again? I want to. I think. But there's a part of me that's afraid. Is it only myself I'm afraid of, or is really him?"

Caitlin rinsed the shampoo from her hair and then stepped out of the shower into the steamy bathroom. Still naked, she put her ear to the closed door, thinking she had heard a sound coming from somewhere downstairs. Her heart pounded as she opened the door just wide enough to peek into the hallway and listen for footsteps, or the opening and closing of drawers as a thief rummaged through her things. But the house remained silent--almost too silent, as though the intruder knew she was listening and he, too, was holding his breath. Caitlin shivered as beads of water began to evaporate from her skin.

"Nobody's there," she whispered to herself. "Calm down. Don't get carried away."

She could call the police, but the closest phone was in the bedroom and she was now convinced that the intruder had made his way upstairs and was just around the corner, knife in hand, waiting for her to emerge. She listened again. Nothing. The clock chimed midnight, twelve long, loud chimes, giving him an opportunity to make his move unheard. Caitlin closed the bathroom door and locked it. She grabbed her terry cloth robe, wanting to be covered in case she had to make a run for it, but telling herself all the while that she was silly, that it really was only the wind, or the settling of the house.

Steam had escaped through the open door and the fogged mirror over the sink was beginning to clear. To keep herself focused, Caitlin began combing the tangles from her wet hair, tugging at little knots, not caring if she was splitting carefully trimmed ends. Keep calm, keep busy, she was telling herself, nobody's out there, nobody at all. Then she saw her eyes go wide and watched the color drain from her face. Her mouth opened to let out a scream that wouldn't come. Beyond her own image in the mirror, Caitlin saw the reflection of a man's face, his brown eyes piercing her as they stared with an intensity of purpose. Her heart pounding wildly, she turned to confront the man who'd been watching her from a corner of the small room. Only he wasn't there. Trembling, she turned quickly to see if the face was still in the mirror. All she saw was her own tear-stained reflection. David had disappeared.

Chapter Nine

Caitlin found herself obsessed by the image in the steam-filled bathroom. Had David really come to her at the very moment when she was begging him for help? If so, what was he trying to tell her? All the next day, while she stayed busy with chores, she kept sending up a silent prayer: "Please come again, David. I promise you, I won't be afraid this time." At the same time, she was filled with a panic that clenched her stomach and burned like acid. He was dead and she didn't understand visits from the other side.

Meanwhile, she had real-life relationships to work on. She called Liz first thing Monday morning. "Hey, stranger, how about if I stop by before heading to the office? We can catch up on things." She tried to keep her voice light, tried not to give any hint of her nervousness, of her fear that their friendship was somehow in jeopardy.

"I don't have any coffee on. Steve's trying to cut down, so I've stopped making it in the morning." Caitlin could hear the reservation in Liz's voice. Except for showing her Derrick's card, they hadn't really talked since the fiasco with Josie.

"I'll bring my own. Have coffee, will travel. See you in a minute." She hung up before Liz could make up some lame excuse about having to start on her household chores.

Caitlin knew that Janet Lee was probably talking about Maryanne when she told her to mend broken relationships, but it made her face the problem with Liz—if there even was a problem—and she decided to try and straighten things out before they got out of hand.

"Hello?" Caitlin called out to Liz, letting herself into the house.

"Out here. On the deck."

"Feels like rain. Again. Kind of an ugly summer so far," Caitlin said as she joined Liz.

"Guess so. I can't stand the humidity."

"Maybe the rain will help."

"Maybe."

Caitlin took a long swallow of coffee, hoping her next words wouldn't ruin things. "Liz, look, I need to do a reality check here. Are we okay? I feel like we've had a fight, even though I know we didn't."

"Everything's fine."

Caitlin could tell she was lying by the way she fingered her hair and tried to maintain eye contact. It was an unnatural stance, wide-eyed and unblinking, head cocked just slightly to the right. Liz made a huge distinction between lying, which was purposefully deceitful, and "social fibbing," which was simply the civilized way of dealing with awkward situations.

"Liz, talk to me. Please."

"Oh, Catie," Liz's voice was high-pitched and sad. "I can't bear the thought of David being gone. What are we going to do without him? I wake up in the middle of the night trembling. I look over at Steve and wonder if I'm next. Am I the next widow?"

Caitlin's skin prickled. "But you still have him, don't you?" She noticed the sharpness of her own voice and immediately felt bad. "The middle of the night," Caitlin confided, "that's when I miss David the most. I roll over and there's nothing on his side of the bed except empty pillows. Sometimes I panic...I get all knotted up inside thinking I've forgotten him, afraid I will forget him." Caitlin took a deep breath, gulping down the lump that had begun to choke her voice. She wanted to tell Liz about David coming to her, his face in the mirror, but she didn't dare.

She wished it would rain. The thick, gray air was too much to bear. She pulled the front of her blouse away from her wet midriff and blew warm air down her chest. If it wasn't all so sad, Caitlin might have actually laughed at the panicked look on Liz's face as she swirled her tea with her index finger, concentrating on the little waves she was making in the china mug. Liz was so bad at facing feelings.

But, for once, Caitlin didn't care. She wanted Liz to understand how uncomfortable her own life was right now. "You know," she continued softly, trying to make eye contact with Liz who continued to avoid her gaze, "I'm always looking at pictures, imprinting David's face on my brain. I wear his after-shave to bed. I actually hug his suits—can you imagine that?—so I can feel their texture and breathe in the smell of his skin. But you know what I can't get back? Do you know what I've already lost and it's driving me crazy? His voice. I can't get his voice back. I want to hear him laugh one more time. I want to hear him say, 'Catiedid, I love you.' I even want to hear him snore!" Caitlin laughed, but it came out more like a half-cry. "If I could just understand why he died. Knowing would make everything so much easier."

"We'll never know," Liz said, looking past Caitlin at the clouds rolling toward them with ominous speed. "Death is one of the mysteries of life. It's going to rain any minute now."

Caitlin ignored the weather update. "Liz. Liz, look at me, please." She walked over and bent down by Liz's chair, taking her hand. "Where's David right now? This minute. Not his body, I know where that is. It's lying in a cold coffin six feet beneath the ground. Or is it eight? I can never remember. But where's David?"

"With God," Liz answered softly.

"Do you really believe that?"

"Of course I do. He has to be...he was a good man..."

"But...I don't know...so you belief in an afterlife?"

"I guess. I don't know, Catie. Ask Steve. He's better at this stuff than me."

"I don't want to ask Steve. I want to know what you think, what you believe. Maybe it's all a big joke. We die, we're dead."

"Don't say that. Of course there's an afterlife." Liz's voice was small and frightened.

They were both quiet for awhile. Caitlin stood and leaned against the railing of the deck. "Josie says all the answers are deep inside of me, that I can find them if I just search for my own quiet truth. She says we all know the truth, we carry it with us from lifetime to lifetime, but that we cover it up with all kinds of false reality."

"Josie!" Liz practically snorted, her nose wrinkling in distaste. "Now, there's trouble looking for a place to land."

"Just 'cause she's different?"

"Different? Different is streaking your hair green or wearing a short dress to a formal party." Liz laughed, too high and too long. "Just listen to yourself. Lifetime to lifetime? She's a gypsy, a pagan—"

"She's not a pagan," Caitlin said. " She's just more...open. I don't know...it's hard to explain. But I like her."

"Congratulations."

"Liz, don't be like that. I don't want her to make a difference between us."

"Yeah, well tell that to Steve. He's having a real problem with it. He actually wanted to go over this week and, as he says, talk some sense into you."

"Oh, for God's sake." Caitlin's stomach churned with impatience. "Why is he having such a problem? Josie's my friend, not his. Or yours."

"You heard her, going on about spirits and reincarnation and life hereafter! If Steve hadn't gotten so upset, I'm sure she would have entertained us for hours with her talk of other worlds. It's totally... well...I don't know...it's just not right. It's wrong."

"Different doesn't mean bad."

"Don't fool around looking for some 'truth' that will just lead you astray." Liz was practically begging. "Just have faith and everything will work out."

"I don't know," Caitlin sighed. "And I have such a need to know. When I'm with Josie, I feel hopeful, opened up to the possibility of discovering new ideas. Then I talk to you, and I get confused all over again because I know you wouldn't do anything to hurt me. Don't you want to know more, explore more?"

"No. I'm very happy just the way things are. Like Steve says, why go looking for trouble?"

Caitlin looked up at the darkening sky. "It's all so complicated. I promise I'll be careful."

"Good. Now, enough about that. Tell me all about Derrick. Every single detail..."

* * *

By the time Caitlin left Liz, her head was spinning. How she was going to balance Josie and Liz? What if she was forced to make a decision between the two? What if she chose Josie over Liz and then Josie just upped and disappeared one day? Josie was definitely the type. Where would Caitlin be then? No, she couldn't do that. Besides, Liz was too important to her. But if she chose Liz, she'd have to be content, or at least pretend to be content, with looking at life the same way as Liz. The only answer was in not choosing. She could manage that. Nodding her head in determination, Caitlin resolved to keep both friends. She smiled thinking of the old Girl Scout song: Make new friends, but keep the old. One is silver and the other gold.

"And Liz is definitely gold," she said out loud. I'll just be careful when I'm with her, she thought. We'll talk about things other than Josie. I won't even mention her name anymore and things will get back to the way they used to be.

Settled in at the office, Caitlin had two more calls to make before she could actually get down to the business of selling houses. First, the painless call. She dialed the public relations firm Josie worked for.

"You must be pretty important there," Caitlin joked when she finally got her on the phone. "I had to go through a receptionist and a secretary before they'd let me through to you."

"I wish. They just try to keep me well hidden—inaccessible to impossible clients," Josie said. "What's up?"

"Good news and bad, as they say. I found a rent for you, an adorable little house right here in Riverside, practically on top of the Connecticut River. The man who owns it has to go to a nursing home, but his kids don't want to sell the house out from under him. They want to keep it and rent it out as long as he's still alive."

"That's great! Not for the old man, but for me. What's the bad news? One year's salary in advance and my next born child?"

"Not that bad," Caitlin laughed. "It's not available until September."

"Not to worry. I'll take the house without even looking at it. I trust you. And, believe it or not, the timing works out fine. I have a lot of vacation time coming, so I'm taking Courtney and we're going to spend the month of August at my folk's place on the Cape. They'll be out of town. Actually, they'll be out of the country."

"You're going to the Cape? For a whole month?"

"August is usually a slow time for me. It'll be good for us. We need some mother-daughter time."

"But, Josie, a whole month?" Fear slipped into Caitlin's voice as she suddenly realized just how much she'd come to depend upon Josie's non-judgmental, unconditional friendship.

Josie laughed. "You'll be fine. I'll call you a couple times a week. And I want you to promise me that you'll come for Labor Day weekend. Marc Gallagher will be there—I told you about him—and a special friend of mine I want you to meet. Listen, I'll talk to you later. I have a client meeting in fifteen minutes and it's a half-hour drive."

Caitlin kept the receiver in her hand, took a deep breath, and prepared to make the call she was dreading. But it had to be done.

Time to try and mend broken relationships. If nothing else, she needed to understand why Maryanne was so angry with her, why she moved out the night of David's wake and hadn't talked to her since. She tapped her pencil on the desk, listening to the phone ring. Once. Twice. The third ring was cut short by a clipped, high pitched voice. Damn, Caitlin thought. Why couldn't Maryanne have answered the phone? This woman had the most unnerving effect on her, even after all these years.

"Hello, Brenda, this is Caitlin. May I please speak with Maryanne?" Keep it sweet; keep it short, she kept repeating to herself. She ran her fingers through her hair waiting for a reply.

"I'm sure she doesn't want to speak with you, Caitlin. I'm really surprised you have the courage to call, after all that's happened."

"Please, Brenda. I just want to speak with Maryanne. Won't you call her to the phone?"

Caitlin could hear her stepdaughter in the background asking her mother who was on the phone. Let's see if she lies, Caitlin thought. Let's just see what kind of a mother she really is.

"Hold on," the clipped voice said and then everything was quiet. Caitlin obediently waited, clenching the receiver so tightly a pool of sweat formed under her hand. The silence went on for so long she began to wonder if Brenda had simply put the phone down and walked away. Then she heard Maryanne's voice, soft and tense, as though she was talking through clenched teeth.

"Hello."

"Maryanne, hi. How are you?"

"I'm okay. What do you want?"

"I've missed you. I thought maybe we could talk."

"So talk."

"Not like this. Not over the phone. Let's have lunch on Saturday. I'll pick you up; we'll go anywhere you want. We could spend the whole day together, if you like."

Silence again.

"Yeah. All right. Just lunch," Maryanne said.

"Where shall we go? How about someplace nice, maybe down by the beach?"

"I said just lunch. Friendly's, at the mall, at one-thirty. I'll get a ride. And don't be late. You're always late for things."

Chapter Ten

The week passed in a blur of anxiety and sleep deprivation. Too many worries and conflicting emotions were assaulting Caitlin all at once; she felt off balance and much too vulnerable. Seeing Maryanne would be trying at best. The last thing she needed was Derrick. By Saturday morning, she'd made the decision to call and cancel their dinner plans for that night, but he wasn't home. She left a message on his machine, praying he would get it and not make the trip down.

She then went into Maryanne's room and collected a few of the things she'd left behind in her hasty exit, things that had been important to her stepdaughter before tragedy stepped in. There was her tennis trophy. And the photo Caitlin had taken of David trying to teach Maryanne to golf for the first time—a terry cloth hat sat precariously atop her new perm and her face, freckled from the sun, was one huge smile as she sent the ball flying toward the first tee. The camera had caught David just behind Maryanne, high in the air, jumping with enthusiasm. Under the bed, Caitlin discovered the Irish knit sweater she had given Maryanne last Christmas. All of that, and more, Caitlin stuffed into a brown grocery bag. Methodically, she rolled down the top of the bag to keep it closed, taking one last look around the room before leaving.

"You're early," Maryanne observed as Caitlin slid into the booth.

"Ten minutes to be exact."

"But you still beat me. Have you been here long?"

"Long enough to drink a whole Coke. You look like hell."

Caitlin was determined not to let Maryanne goad her into the kind of edgy banter they'd had when they first lived together. It was hard to know sometimes what was teenage stuff and what was out and out hostility. "Well, you look great," Caitlin told her. "I love your hair short like that; it really brings out your eyes."

"Thanks. It was my mother's idea. Let's order. I'm, like, starving to death and I don't have much time. I told Brett to be back in an hour."

"You're still seeing him? That's nice. But an hour's so short. I'd hoped we could shop after lunch. I'd like to buy you a new outfit. I missed your birthday, and turning fifteen is pretty special, so I though I'd make up for it."

"Yeah, well, it's already passed so why make a big deal. Besides, I told you, lunch only. My mother buys me everything I need."

"Okay, no problem," Caitlin said quickly. "I just though it would be fun." Don't try so hard, she told herself, even as she tried again. "Vanessa called the other day. For your phone number. Did she reach you?"

"Yeah. We talked. Can we order now?"

"Sure," Caitlin said, signaling to the waitress. "The usual?" She asked Maryanne.

"I guess."

"One tuna salad sandwich, one patty melt, extra onions, medium well, one coffee, and she'll have another coke. We'll share an order of fries." Caitlin told the waitress.

Once the waitress left, Caitlin put her elbows on the table and leaned in across the booth, talking softly. "I miss you. It's so quiet in the house now, without you and all of your friends. Remember the time Vanessa slept over and the three of us overdosed on popcorn and all those old movies I rented? Your father thought I was crazy—" Caitlin stopped and smiled. "We had some good times. Don't you think?"

"Yeah, well, that's ancient history. Besides, you didn't exactly like my moving in. Do you remember that?"

"That's not true. Well, maybe; but only in the beginning. It was hard, a teenager living with us. It was so different from our weekend visits. All those years, you lived with your mother, and then boom, you were on our doorstep. Literally. But that was over two years ago. I think we all adjusted. Didn't we? I even think we had a lot of love going on. Don't you?"

No answer.

"Maryanne...don't you?" Caitlin asked again.

Maryanne's eyes filled with tears. She looked up and met Caitlin's gaze. But just for a moment. And then the waitress delivered their food. Nothing worked after that. It was as though all systems had shut down and Maryanne was not about to give her stepmother a break. Not even one. Caitlin tried a half-dozen different topics, from fashions to friends, and, in desperation, real estate. But Maryanne wouldn't give Caitlin the courtesy of a real conversation. Halfway through their meal, Caitlin could no longer take Maryanne's monosyllabic answers. Time for a hammer and chisel, she thought. Time for some truth.

"Maryanne, you obviously don't want to be here, so why are you?"

"Because my mother told me to. She was in the background when you called, ordering me to accept. She wanted to know just what you had to say for yourself."

"Well, at least that's honest. I was hoping maybe you missed me," Caitlin teased. "Just a little?" she added when Maryanne didn't respond. "By the way, I brought you some of your things." Caitlin patted the bag she had placed next to her on the seat. In the silence that followed, Maryanne's last words suddenly registered with Caitlin. She sipped her coffee, trying to make sense of them. Finally she asked, "What did you mean by that comment, what I have to say for myself?"

"You know," Maryanne said, looking at Caitlin through squinted brown eyes. "Like, what you have to say about Dad's...you know, Dad's dying and all."

"No. I don't know. What more can I possibly have to say about it? He was my life. I loved him beyond measure. He died and I miss him desperately. What else is there? Except that I miss you, too."

Maryanne shifted her small frame, crossing her legs and then uncrossing them, all the while playing with the straw in her Coke. Still she said nothing.

"Just tell me," Caitlin said. "Whatever it is, I'll understand. I promise. Why did you pack up and run off like that, right after the wake, the night before his funeral, for God's sake? I was a mess. I couldn't deal with whatever it was. But I can now." Caitlin reached out across the booth to touch Maryanne's hand, but she kept it just out of reach. "I really thought we were a family, the three of us. All of a sudden, your dad dies, and then you're gone two days later. Would staying, at least for a little while, have been that awful?"

"I can't believe you. You kill my father and you want me to stay? Mom said you were nervy." Maryanne crumpled up her napkin and threw it on top of her half-eaten burger. "Thanks for lunch. I have to go. Brett hates to wait."

Caitlin half stood as she stretched across the table and grabbed Maryanne's arm, forcing her to stay seated. "Oh no, you don't. You don't drop a bomb like that and just leave. You owe me an explanation."

"I don't owe you anything. Let go of me!"

Caitlin softened her grip as Maryanne reluctantly sat back down. "Maryanne, this isn't how I wanted today to go. Please, can't we just talk—"

"About what? About how you killed my father?"

"How can you say such a thing?" Caitlin whispered, afraid everyone in the restaurant was listening. "It was an accident, you know that. The police explained it all. The pavement was still so hot when it started to rain that his car hydroplaned when he tried making that curve on Edison Street. He hit a tree before he could regain control. How can you possibly blame me?"

"If you have to ask—" Maryanne was shaking her head in disgust.

"Of course I have to ask!" Caitlin's hands were wet with perspiration and she could feel pools of sweat staining her blouse.

"Okay. You want to know? I'll tell you. I wasn't going to say anything, but you're, like, pushing me into it. Besides, my mother says it's sickening how you're going around acting so innocent and all, instead of guilty like you should be. She hears how you are from other people. They tell her how hard it is for you, how sad you are. They feel sorry for you. Mom says they should feel sorry for her. She's the real widow. Dad was hers until you took him away, and if you hadn't done that he'd still be with us, and if he was still with us, he'd be alive today because he'd never have been on that road in the first place. My mother is always home on time to cook dinner, and besides, we hate Chinese food. So, it's all your fault!" Maryanne swallowed a gulp of air and swiped tears away from her flushed cheeks.

"Oh my God. Where is this coming from? Maryanne?"

"Mom said you wouldn't own up to the truth. If you had never met Daddy, he'd still be with us, because I know he and Mom would have worked things out and gotten back together. It's all your fault that they didn't! And if they had gotten back together, he'd still be alive. He was getting take-out—AGAIN—because you were late. You're always late. You're always too busy selling houses to cook dinner. If he hadn't been on that road getting you Chinese food, he'd still be alive."

So there it was. The truth. Or, at least Maryanne's version of the truth. "But, it was still just an accident, no matter how tragic, or how much we miss him now. Don't turn your anger on me. I loved him. You know that. Blaming me won't bring him back and it'll just drive a wedge between us. Your father wouldn't want that. He'd want us to be close, more now than ever. Besides, when you come right down to it, he could have been on that road for a hundred other reasons. We'll never know. But to accuse me—"

"He called and left a message. He was on that road because of you. You killed him."

"Oh, Maryanne—"

"I have to go." Maryanne got up to leave and this time Caitlin didn't stop her.

"Maryanne," Caitlin called after her, holding up the brown paper bag stuffed with miscellaneous memories. Hearing her name from across the room, Maryanne stopped and looked back briefly. Then she turned around and kept walking until she was out of the restaurant and part of the anonymous crowd pushing its way through the mall.

* * *

Caitlin rushed home, her mind focused on a single thought—get inside as quickly as possible and turn on the answering machine. David's voice. She would hear David's voice. It wasn't lost to her after all.

Running to his study, she pressed the on button and rewound the tape. She cursed herself for not having used it since the funeral, but keeping pace with all those small, yet demanding, odds and ends of her life had required too much energy. She didn't want to hear the voices of well-meaning friends whose lives were still cruising on normal. She didn't want the obligation of returning calls and making them feel good about her life and how she was coping. Clearly, she wasn't coping well at all.

She pushed play and listened, fast-forwarding past her own voice telling callers to leave a message for "Caitlin, David, or Maryanne."

There. There it was. David's voice. Talking to her. "Catie, obviously you're not home, or else you just don't want to talk to me." He chuckled into the phone. "It's already five-thirty. I'm leaving now. I'll pick up Chinese. Tell Maryanne I'll stop and get her a meatball grinder. Hope you closed the deal."

A high-pitched beep signaled the end of David's message and the beginning of the next, this one from her mother. Caitlin stopped her mother's voice mid-message and rewound the tape, listening to David once again. And then again. And again. There it was. David's voice. She closed her eyes, breathing in its timbre and cadence, smiling at his humor, laughing and then crying at the warmth of her husband, lost to her forever, except for this one bit of magnetic tape, that could be ruined in an instant. She had to stop playing it. What if it broke or got worn? She turned off the machine, removed the cassette and put it carefully into her blazer pocket. She would go out right now and find a place to have it copied. Surely one of the electronic stores could help her with reproducing it. She'd get several copies, in fact, just in case. That way she'd always have his voice, even when she was old and gray and the pain of all this had dulled to a quiet throb. If that ever happened. A quiet throb seemed so welcoming right now.

She knew the tape was in her pocket, but still she slipped her hand in for reassurance and then patted her pocket as if for safekeeping. She would go right now, head back to the mall and have copies made. But she was so hot. Overheated, actually. She needed to splash water on her face and get something cold to drink. The kitchen. First she would go to the kitchen, and then to the mall. Nothing made perfect sense right now, except for those two actions: the kitchen and then the mall.

Caitlin ran cold water across her wrists, splashing her cheeks and forehead and gulping greedily from a bottle of spring water. Reaching for a towel, she glanced out the small window above her sink, nearly choking as she caught sight of the dark-haired man standing by the stream that ran through her backyard He was skipping stones across the water. "David!" Caitlin gasped.

Tears streamed across her face and strands of hair stuck to her wet cheeks as she ran outside, open-armed toward her husband. David!" she cried out. "David!"

"That's quite a greeting. I'll have to come around more often," an amused voice told her.

Caitlin nearly tripped over her own feet as she skidded to a stop. She froze as the man came closer. When he was only inches away, adrenaline reached her limbs and she lunged at him, slapping his face, punching his stomach and arms. "How could you do this to me?" she screamed. "How?"

He grabbed hold of her arms, and, pinning them behind her back, held Caitlin tightly to his chest until her body stopped twitching and her sobs had begun to fade. After a while, she pulled back and blew her nose into the dish towel she still clutched in one hand.

"Catie, honey, I don't understand. What's gotten you so worked up? Was it your lunch?" He stroked her hair, gently taking single strands from her cheeks and pushing them back behind her ears.

"Yes. No! I mean, yes, but—"

"But, what?"

"Derrick." Her voice was as limp as her body and little more than a whisper. "From up there," she pointed to the kitchen, "you looked just like David. I don't understand." She stepped back and examined him. "You're wearing glasses, they're identical to his...and your clothes...one week you show up in a designer jacket and wing-tipped shoes, and now you're bare-legged, in cotton shorts and a madras shirt. And Docksiders. Your hair...it's...I don't know...I can't put my finger on it... the color, it's the color! It's just like David's."

"Caitlin," Derrick laughed, holding her shoulders securely, "last week we were going to dinner. This week we're having a picnic. I do have more than one style of clothes. The haircut is just a haircut, something short and cool for the summer. The color's the same. It just seems different because of the cut."

Her icy stare let him know she wasn't convinced, although she would have been hard-pressed to explain why. At that very moment Caitlin's mind flashed to the blank spot in her photo album. Her skin prickled as a cloud passed over, casting a cool, dark shadow across the two of them.

"Come here," Derrick said tenderly, pulling her stiff body to him. "I'm sorry if I startled you, truly I am. I got here early. You weren't home yet, so I came around back. It's beautiful here, Catie."

"Your car—?"

"It's out front," He chuckled. "You must have been very preoccupied."

"I guess I was. I called you. To cancel tonight."

"You did? Well, I'm here, so let's make the most of it."

He held Caitlin protectively against his chest, rubbing her back, stroking her hair, rocking back and forth with the summer breeze, as though soothing a wounded child. It was that child in Caitlin that surrendered to his warmth and allowed herself to be held. It felt good to be cared for again.

Chapter Eleven

Without knowing quite how it happened, one day in late August, Caitlin realized that she and Derrick had been seeing each other regularly—nearly every weekend, in fact, since mid-July. Liz was delighted. Josie, on the other hand, left for the Cape and then called her almost every day, expressing her doubts about this man who had wormed his way into Caitlin's life, inch by inch, by turning himself into the image of her dead husband. Caitlin brushed away Josie's concerns, citing all the wonderful things he'd done for her in the past weeks—movies and concerts and Saturday afternoons with Jessica and Jason. It was almost as though they were a family. It was almost as though...

Caitlin was never able to say the words out loud—especially to Josie who seemed to have a habit of making too much of things—but the truth was, with Derrick around making her laugh, becoming part of her already established life, looking so much like David, it was almost as though David had never died. As horrible as it sounded, if she closed her eyes hard enough and didn't think about it too much, Caitlin could actually convince herself that Derrick was David, that her husband was there and nothing, absolutely nothing, in her life had changed. But the illusion only lasted for a little while. At some point, Derrick would do something—some unrehearsed look, some spontaneous action—that made him more like himself than David, and reality reared its head. It was always a hard moment. And when it happened, Caitlin was always glad that she hadn't given in to Derrick's continual, but quiet, insistence for a more involved relationship. It was during those moments of harsh reality that Caitlin missed David the most and wondered what exactly she was doing with her life.

The person most pleased with the turn of events was Liz. She'd become Derrick's biggest supporter, constantly praising his good looks and generosity. She was overwhelmed at Caitlin's extreme fortune, finding such a perfect man so soon after losing David. It had to be the luck of the Irish. What else could it be? "It's just like old times," she confided to Caitlin, as the four of them ate at the Whiting House the weekend before Labor Day. Liz wriggled comfortably in her chair, absolutely delighted with the way things were working out. Everything was normal again.

"Well, they're not quite the same," Caitlin reminded her, not so quick to let Derrick replace David in everybody's mind.

"Oh, honey, I know. But just look at him. He's almost the spitting image of David. It's hard to believe he looked any different when you first met him." Steve and Derrick were so engrossed in their own conversation about stocks that they were virtually ignoring the ladies. "And the way those two get along, you'd think they'd known each other forever. It's a nice feeling, isn't it?"

"I guess," Caitlin answered, glancing over at Derrick once more to make sure he wasn't listening. "It's just strange," she whispered, "the more I see him, the more he becomes like David. I don't know if it's deliberate or coincidental, or just my head playing games with me, but sometimes I have a hard time separating the two in my mind. First it was the hair and the clothes. And the roses! Every time I see him now he brings me one white rose. And then last week, he was looking for some aspirin in the medicine chest and he ended up putting on some of David's after-shave. When he came back downstairs, I had a hard time remembering that he was Derrick. It's not an easy brand to find, but he must have bought some because he's wearing it again tonight!"

"When you think about it," Liz offered, "is it really so bad? I mean, it must make you feel comfortable—"

"But it's eerie, don't you think? It makes me uncomfortable. Visibly he's so much like David that I have a hard time keeping them separate. But in other ways he's not like David at all. He has an edge to him, not violent or anything, but something. It scares me sometimes. When he's being Derrick, with a capital D, I have no trouble keeping him and David separate in my mind. But when he's being the softer Derrick, the

David-Derrick, then I get all confused. I feel like I'm sinking into this dark hole and when I wake up I won't know who I am or who I'm with. I must sound crazy. I know I'm not making any sense, but, Liz, I don't want to forget Dave, not yet, really not ever, and I don't want to replace him with someone who just seems like him. I mean, who is Derrick Secor?"

"Replace, huh?" Liz smiled. "He's gorgeous. And rich. I can't believe all the things he's bought for the kids. Every Saturday it's something new. They think he's great, and so do we. Steve and I both agree he's the best thing that could have happened to you."

Caitlin's face grew hot. "I know he's generous. Almost to a fault. He's always buying me things, too. Expensive things. But I'm trying really hard to keep my head straight about this. And you're not helping. Don't you think the similarities are just a little bit spooky?"

"Personally, I'd just sit back and enjoy being treated like a queen," Liz said. "I think you're making way too much of a few coincidences. After all, he and David grew up together; they probably developed at lot of the same tastes and mannerisms."

"I didn't think of that," Caitlin said. "Maybe you're right. Josie thinks he's up to something. She doesn't trust him at all."

"Catie, every time you mention that woman's name, it's connected to chaos if you ask me. She's just jealous and stirring up trouble for no good reason. You deserve to be happy, whether she thinks so or not. Just sit back and be pleased that you have Derrick in your life to help you forget." Liz took a satisfied sip of Chablis.

Caitlin looked across the table and studied Derrick for a minute, admiring his high cheekbones and the fullness of his lips. While Steve continued on about the bull market, Derrick returned her look with a wink that made her blush.

"You're right," Caitlin whispered to Liz, "I do like him. Except, I still can't get him to talk about his two marriages. And he has this little black notebook. I know I've told you about it. He never actually takes it out in front of me, but sometimes I come into the room unexpectedly, or too quietly or whatever, and I see him reading it or make notes."

"So?"

"So? What do you mean, so? He tries to act nonchalant, but he always has this I've-been-caught look on his face."

"Catie, for heaven's sake, it's probably his appointment book. Will you stop looking for trouble where there is none?"

"That's the whole point. It's not his appointment book. He leaves that lying all over the place. No, it's something else. When I asked him about it, he just looked at me with this icy stare, and said it was nothing, just notes. But I'm dying to know."

"You know what they say about curiosity...leave it be, Catie. Maybe it's a list of all his conquests. You know, instead of notches on a belt! Or a journal and he just doesn't want you to know how sensitive he really is. Shh...they're listening." Liz poked Caitlin's thigh before turning her attention to the men. "I hope you two finally figured out how to make a killing in the market so you can drape us in mink coats and diamonds and whisk us away to exotic islands!"

"Okay, Gimme, now you're showing Derrick your true colors. She spends more money than any woman I know." Steve turned to Derrick. "That's why I call her Gimme—it's always gimme this, gimme that!"

Derrick laughed. "So, while we were deciding how to get rich, you girls were deciding how to spend all our money? Is that what you were so deep in conversation about?"

"Something like that," Caitlin smiled.

It wasn't until dessert that Derrick broke Caitlin's confidence and told her friends what she had made him promise not to reveal.

"Aren't you guys curious about why we're doing this on a Friday night instead of our usual Saturday?" he asked innocently enough.

"Didn't really think about," Steve answered. "But now that you've brought it up, I'll bite. Why?"

Liz leaned in closer, while Caitlin sat back in her chair, her face drained of color. "You're doing something special tomorrow? Just the two of you, something romantic, right?"

"Maybe it'll turn out romantic for our Catie here, but it certainly isn't for me." Derrick responded, a tinge of hardness to his voice.

"Derrick, why don't we just finish up and get going," Caitlin interrupted. "I'm tired."

"She's tired, poor thing. She didn't seem tired just a minute ago, did she?" Derrick looked at Liz and then at Steve for affirmation. "Maybe she just wants to get home so she can get up early for her long drive. To the Cape."

"Derrick! Stop playing games," Liz demanded. "You look like the cat who swallowed the canary, or better yet, like the cat who's tormenting the mouse."

"And I'm the mouse. Let's go." Caitlin stood up.

"Not yet, dear—"

"I'm not your dear," Caitlin hissed, "and I don't want to fight. Please." She sat back down, fearful of making a scene.

"Driving to the Cape tomorrow is more important to Catie than spending the day with me," Derrick announced. "And do you know why? To be with Josephine Ford-Newman. And do you know what our Ms. Josephine Ford-Newman has planned for Caitlin?" Derrick paused, giving each of them time to focus on his next words. "A Tarot card reading. She has a psychic reader coming in to help Catie discover her true self—that's what she says—and possibly even why David died! Now does that beat all, or what?"

"Caitlin, how could you?" Liz gasped. "You promised to give up all that stuff."

"I didn't promise to give it up. I promised to be careful, and I am. I really don't see what business this is of anybody's. I've been grown up a long time now. You are not my keepers. Josie's my friend, and if I want to see her, I'll see her."

Steve stared at Caitlin through cool, clear eyes, compelling her to meet his look. For a moment it was though nobody else in the room existed; all noise was blocked out except for the iciness of his voice. "It is our business, Caitlin. At least once a week, you take off with our children, all by yourself, without us to act as a filtering system, and you expose them to your thoughts and your ideas. That's over, right here and now. You can see who you want, and do whatever you want, but as long as your values are so screwed up, you won't be seeing much of us any more. It's not the kind of influence I want on my wife and kids. When you change back to the old Caitlin, we can be friends again."

Everyone at the table was silent. Then all the noises in the room hit Caitlin's head at once—the clanging of dinner trays, the clinking of silverware against china plates, laughter and conversation from surrounding tables, piped-in music, the ringing of the telephone at the reservation desk—and she became more and more dizzy with each passing moment.

She looked at Steve, her eyes wide with disbelief.

"Steve, you can't. Liz..." She reached over and grabbed Liz's hand, squeezing it tightly. "Liz is my best friend. You can't just issue an ultimatum like that."

"I can do whatever I want. This is not negotiable. When you give up Josie and her ways, then we can go back to how we've always been. But not until."

"Liz." Caitlin's voice was high and tiny. "You're not going to go along with this, are you?"

"He's my husband, Catie..." She looked across the table at Steve, her eyes begging him to change his mind, to put everything back the way it was just a few minutes ago. But he sat perfectly still, like carved granite and, Liz being Liz, she had no choice but to stand with her husband on this issue. "Why don't you forget about the Cape and everything will be okay. I told you Josie was trouble."

"Josie's not the problem here. I need air," Caitlin said, standing up so quickly that her chair fell backward and crashed to the ground. As she bent to pick it up, she could feel hot tears against her eyelids. "I'll be outside," she told the three of them, and then specifically to Derrick, "Thanks a lot."

Outside, in the heat and mugginess of the August night, Caitlin leaned against a tall white birch, listening to the sounds of the river below. Standing near the edge of the bank, she watched beams of yellow moonlight bounce off the black liquid. At that very moment, she wanted nothing more than to construct a raft and ride the water to freedom. But just like Huck and Jim discovered on their journey, she, too, was learning that real freedom comes from the heart, from unlocking all those private doors that keep you prisoner. And it comes at a price.

Chapter Twelve

Huge awnings were cranked open to filter out the afternoon sun, while a ceiling fan moved air throughout the open space that served as living area, dining room, and kitchen. No pictures were needed; instead, floor to ceiling windows created the frames through which Nantucket Sound was seen from every corner of the L-shaped room. Caitlin took a long, deep breath, filling her lungs with the salt air.

"Josie, this is incredible," she said. "It's hardly a cottage!"

"I know. Could you just die?" Josie laughed, hugging Caitlin. "I still can't get used to this place. You remember how poor we were growing up? Well, Mom married this terrific guy about ten years ago who happens to be pretty well off. Understatement. It's the best thing that's ever happened to her, and not just because of the money. This was his. Anyway, they decided to spend August in Europe this year, don't you know." Josie patted her head and tried clipping her words in feigned sophistication. "So for a month anyway, I got the deed to Arcadia—that's what they call this humble abode." Josie giggled. "I feel like I died and went to heaven."

"I guess so." Caitlin followed Josie out onto the deck. "A place like this could make a new woman out of you." She shaded her eyes with her hand and stared out at the endless body of water dotted with people walking toward the horizon as though trying to reach the other side of the Atlantic. Already, she was beginning to feel better, as though Corey Lane with all of its problems was a thousand miles away.

"It's low tide," Josie said. "Here on the Sound it means you can walk forever. The key is knowing when to come back! There they are!" Josie shouted, waving to two men walking toward them. "Don't come up," she told them, "we'll come down with something cool and refreshing. Just set up the chairs. Where's Courtney?"

"She went off with her gang ten minutes after we started on our walk," the shorter of the two said. "Looks like two old men, even ones who adore her, just don't cut it." He laughed a deep, hearty laugh, the little roll of flab around his waist moving up and down with the vibrations

"Is the beach okay?" Josie asked Caitlin, "or would you prefer sitting up here on the deck?"

"Are you kidding? The beach is perfect. Why do you think I came, for your good company?" It felt good to joke, to toss words around in a carefree fashion, not worrying about being judged or misunderstood. "Just let me wash the makeup off my face and change into my suit."

"And I'll be in the kitchen mixing up a pitcher of rum coolers."

A few minutes later, Caitlin was dressed in a black bathing suit, a towel slung over one shoulder. "Ready."

"Great, so am I." Josie handed Caitlin a plate of fresh fruit and cheese while she carried the tray of drinks. "Let's go."

The men were sprawled lifeless on the lounge chairs. "Adam Dressler," Josie said, bending down to kiss the thick head of chestnut-colored hair of the man who had spoken to them from the beach, "meet Catie Saunders."

He opened one eye and then the other, before sitting up as though hit with a sudden burst of energy. A broad grin filled his round face. "A pleasure to meet you, Catie. A real pleasure. Josie's told me so much about you." He took her hand, giving it something between a shake and a squeeze.

Caitlin threw Josephine a quick look, wondering just what — and how much—she had told Adam about her. But, instead of returning her glance, Josie was mussing the hair of the other man. "Wine, women, and food, Marc—it's all here, all you have to do is wake up."

He opened his eyes, squinting in the bright sun, the beginnings of a scowl crossing his face.

"Here," Josie said, handing him a tall glass. "But I lied. It's rum, not wine."

Marc sat up and took a long sip. Josie waited until he was finished. "He's the gentle bear type, grumpy when disturbed, but he won't really harm you," she whispered loud enough for him to hear. "Marc, I'd like you to meet Caitlin. Caitlin, Marc Gallagher."

It was his smile, slow and slightly crooked, that Caitlin noticed first; but it was his eyes that threw her off balance—cobalt eyes—sharp, keen, penetrating cobalt eyes that made Caitlin want to pull down the shades and bolt the doors. She blinked furiously under their scrutiny.

"Hi," Marc said in a soft voice, smiling just slightly as he looked up at her. "Nice to meet you."

"You too," Caitlin responded. Out of the corner of her eye, she noticed that Josie had taken up residence in the chair between Adam and Marc. Her only choice was the one right in front of her, next to Marc. "Well, I guess I'll get comfortable," she said, spreading her towel over the lounge chair and lying down, her face tilted toward the hot sun.

"Pass this down to Catie," Josie said, handing Marc the remaining drink.

As Caitlin took the cool glass from Marc, their fingers touched and a shock seemed to run through her body. Feeling herself blush, she brushed her bangs back from her face, blowing air through her lips and over her face, making a production of just how hot a day it was. "Boy, I need this," she announced, sitting up and taking a long sip. "It sure is hot."

"Must be," Marc said, a tinge of humor in his voice. "Your face is all flushed." He grabbed her hand. "Come on, let's go down to the water."

Caitlin pulled her hand away and pressed the cool glass to her face. "No thanks, that's okay. I really want to get some sun. Maybe later." She lay back down, but was unable to relax. Her body felt restless, charged up. She rolled over on her stomach, pressing herself hard against the chair. She buried her face in her arms, trying to blot out the world, listening only to the distant conversations and laughter of the people around her. But all she could focus on was the presence of the man next to her.

"This sun is just too hot." Caitlin stood up. "I think I'll try out the water after all, while the tide is still low."

"Wait up. We'll go with you." Josie patted Adam's behind. "Before this one turns into a couch potato."

Adam groaned. "I just got comfortable. Why do you want to torture me?"

"Because I love you."

"Well, at least it's a reason," Adam said, struggling to get up. "Maybe not a good one, but a reason." He popped a piece of cheese into his mouth and grabbed a few grapes. He took Josie's hand and the two of them ran toward the water.

Caitlin started after them, walking quickly, hurrying to get away before Marc opened his eyes and noticed the three of them were gone.

"Hey," he hollered after her, his long legs gobbling up the distance of sand between them. "I invite you down to the water, you say no and then you go in without me?" He clenched his heart. "How's a guy to feel?"

Caitlin looked up at Marc, noticing the slight cleft in his chin and the deep red stain on his cheekbones from too much sun. A slight wind had kicked up, blowing his straight sandy hair toward his face. As he pushed it back off his forehead, she noticed that it was layered with varying shades of blonde and brown, as though he'd spent his entire life walking the beach. Altogether, there was something very Bohemian about this man—something in the way he carried his tall, lean body; something in the way his eyes seemed to study and probe that made Caitlin feel he looked at life from a different angle. In that way, he seemed a lot like Josie, except that Josie didn't make Caitlin feel uncomfortable as though she was measuring Caitlin's every move.

As Marc and Caitlin reached Josie and Adam, they got caught in the cross-fire of their water fight. Caitlin had started walking past them, heading toward the sandbar, when she felt an enormous splash of water on her bare back. She stopped in her tracks and clenched her teeth, angry without knowing why. She counted to five before turning to confront her assailant, putting a smile on her face, trying hard to be a good sport. But Josie and Adam were off to one side, splashing one another; directly in front of her, though, was Marc, a wide smile filling his face.

"You! I might have known. You could have had the decency to let me get wet first." She knew she was whining, but she couldn't help it.

He just kept coming closer, grinning down at her. For a minute, it looked like he was going to try and kiss her! Caitlin bent down, and, with cupped hands, shot salt water up at Marc, hoping to wipe the smile off his face. But he was too close and the water hit his chest.

"That felt good," he laughed.

"Oh, did it?" Here's some more then. And some more!"

Marc stood laughing while Caitlin furiously splashed water at him. "Now it's your turn," he said, soaking Caitlin with a few swift splashes.

"Thanks a lot!" She felt herself near tears at the assault. She turned with as much dignity as she could muster and began walking out farther into the ocean. When she reached the sandbar, she sat down in the water, letting the sun melt the last bit of anger from her body. She turned to see Marc coming toward her. Josie and Adam were still working their way out, walking slowly hand in hand.

"Hi," Marc said softly, sitting down in the water next to Caitlin. "I'm Marc Gallagher. Nice to meet you."

Tears immediately sprung into Caitlin's eyes.

"I'm sorry if I upset you," he said. "I was just goofing around, trying to get a smile out of you."

This time Caitlin did smile. She wiped the tears away from the corners of her eyes. "No, I'm sorry," she said. "I was acting like a baby. I hate bad sports and that's just what I was."

"Don't worry about it. I know you've had a bad time of it lately. Josie told me."

Caitlin stiffened. "What does she do, go around broadcasting my life story? Am I the token widow or something?"

Marc gave her a long, silent look and then stood up. "We'd better start back. The tide looks like it's starting to come in. Here, put this on. You're starting to get pink." He stripped off his wet T-shirt and handed it to her. "Come on, let's head in."

"I'll wait for Josie and Adam, they're right over there. I'm sure they'll be ready to go soon."

"Suit yourself." Marc strolled off in the water and headed toward shore.

Wearing his shirt, Caitlin walked over to Josie and Adam. "Marc decided to head in," she explained. "I thought I'd wait for you guys."

* * *

"Well, what do you think of him?" Josie asked as they cleaned up the last of the dinner dishes.

"He's nice...so sweet and full of life. I like him, although, I have to admit, he's not exactly what I expected."

Josie knit her eyebrows together. "What do you mean?"

"Don't get me wrong. I think he's great. Just different than I expected—"

"Who are we talking about?"

"Adam."

"Oh," Josie laughed. "I was talking about Marc. You're right. Adam isn't what anybody expects: a short, chunky, Jewish English professor.

He isn't what I would have expected either! It blows everybody's mind. Especially those who know my gorgeous soon-to-be-ex-husband. But I'll tell you something, gorgeous wears thin. Once you hit mid-life, you want someone you can walk into old age with, someone with a little substance. Adam has substance."

"He really is nice, don't get me wrong. But how do you know he's going to make you any happier than your husband did?"

"He's not," Josie said, leaning against the counter.

"Okay..."

"I'm going to make myself happy," Josie answered. "I'm working on that right now, every day. At least I'll have that bit of karma accomplished. It took me a long time, but I've finally realized, here—in my gut, and in my heart — that we can't count on anyone else to make us happy. We have to do that for ourselves and then, hopefully, find someone to walk side-by-side with in life. Your friend , Liz, has a long way to go in that department. She depends totally upon that husband of hers. Every thought she has seems to be filtered through Steve... Steve says this...Steve says that...according to Steve..."

"Liz! Boy, that's a whole other story. I have to admit, you're right," Caitlin said. "She can't express an independent opinion."

"Can she even form one? That's the million dollar question."

"Not nice. She really is a good person. Just under his thumb. Sometimes I was that way with David, but not always. Even now, with Derrick, I find myself slipping into that pleaser routine. The Stepford Women of Corey Lane. Maybe there's something in the water."

"Hey, at least you recognize it."

"I do. And I'm trying really hard to be separate, independent. Maybe that psychic at the fair was right, time to find the real me. Anyway, back to Adam. I really do like him."

"That's a relief," Josie laughed. "So do I. But you still haven't answered my question."

"Which is?"

"Marc?"

"Oh. Right. He's okay. A little intense, though. And not real good about observing personal boundaries. Come to think of it, I'm not sure I like him much at all."

Josie chuckled. "That's Marc, intense with no boundaries. But he is cute, don't you think? And the nicest person you'll ever meet. He'd do anything for you. He really helped us when my brother, Billy, died. Cancer. Marc and Billy were best friends all through college, and then after, they worked in the same firm. He became like part of our family.

I figured you two would hit it off since you've both been through similar experiences. Except he's still having a hard time getting rid of the guilt."

"You mean about Billy?"

"That, and other things. He'll tell you when he's ready. Give him a chance, Catie. He's one terrific guy."

"I hope you're not trying to play matchmaker, and by the way, I have a bone to pick with you." Caitlin put down the dish towel and hoisted herself onto the kitchen counter. She looked out at the Sound, the waves now pounding against the sand. "It's really beautiful, isn't it?"

"I love this time of day. Everyone has left the beach; the sun is setting, but the air is still warm." Josie agreed. "But don't change the subject. What's bugging you?"

Caitlin suddenly felt foolish. "Nothing. It's just that..."

"Out with it!" Josie threw a towel at her. "It's okay to confront."

"Well, I just got the feeling that maybe you told Adam and Marc all about me and it made me feel uncomfortable, kind of exposed."

"Oh, Catie." Josie reached up and squeezed her friend's shoulders. "I would never break any kind of confidence, or do anything to make you feel that way. All I told either of them, including Adam, is that we're old acquaintances-turned-friends, that you're fun and sweet and nice, and that you've just lost your husband. That's it. Honest. What did you think I could have told them anyway? You're not exactly a person with a dark side or jaded past—as far as I know!"

"I don't know," Caitlin admitted. "Maybe more about David. Or Derrick. Or all this metaphysical stuff. I don't know."

"Well, don't worry, you haven't been the topic of our conversations. But I did think you and Marc would hit it off."

"You already said that!" Caitlin laughed, throwing the towel back at Josie and hitting her in the head. "For your information, he's not my type. I go for dark handsome men with an air of mystery."

"Like Derrick?"

"Maybe. Actually, like nobody. Except David..."

"Doesn't it worry you, or at least bother you or something, that Derrick seems to be turning into David, little by little? Obviously, I never met your husband, and I've only been with you and Derrick a couple of times, but from what you tell me, that's exactly what's happening."

"I know. I mentioned that to Liz last night. She said to stop thinking so much, just relax and enjoy. But that's another whole story. I'm so pissed at her and Steve right now I can't see straight."

"Oh?"

"I don't want to go there—"

"Okay, so back to Derrick. Are you sure he's not playing mind games with you?"

"Why would he? He has no reason to. But I have to tell you, one thing is weird. I keep thinking back to David's funeral. There was a man, standing off in the distance, just watching us. Liz spotted him. I swear now that it was Derrick. But he says it wasn't. Why would he lie about such a little thing?"

"Why would he do such a little thing—skulking around at your husband's funeral—isn't that the real question?"

"I don't know. Forget about it. Let's talk about something else." Caitlin jumped down from the counter. "I came here to relax and laugh and forget all my woes. The only one who comes close to letting me do that is Adam. And Courtney. But she's barely around. You and Marc just keep picking at the sores, looking for some source of infection."

"Whoa. Heavy! Sorry, we don't mean to do that. I just care, that's all." Josie's turquoise eyes twinkled. "Maybe Marc does too."

"That's it!" Caitlin laughed. "I'm just going to ignore you from now on." She walked out on the deck and watched as Marc and Adam finished building a fire on the beach.

"Come on down," Adam called. "No wait. I'm coming up first. We need a little something to help keep the throat clear." Adam rushed up the deck stairs and went directly to a large oak cabinet. "Name your poison," he told Caitlin and Josephine.

"Amaretto for me." Josie said immediately.

Caitlin scanned the bottles. "Chambord. I haven't had that in ages."

"And Irish Mist for the men," Adam said, pulling out the three bottles. He then removed four Waterford crystal cordials.

"Waterford? On the beach?" Caitlin asked.

"Adam likes to juxtapose contrasting elements. Fire and ice. That's probably why we're so good together."

It was nearly dark when the four of them huddled around the fire, sipping liqueurs from crystal glasses, talking softly as though they were sharing lifetime secrets, every now and then their laughter piercing the night sea air.

"Quick, make a wish," Marc ordered, pointing to a brilliant flash of light.

"A falling star," Josie whispered, taking Adam's hand. "Boy does that remind me..." her voice trailed off for a minute. "Caitlin, I promised to tell you about meeting my soul mate. I imagine you've guessed it's Adam. And right now seems like the perfect time. Unless, Marc, I'd be boring you. You've already heard the story at least twice."

"Don't stop on my account. I love good science fiction."

They each poured another drink and settled back in the sand. Josie lowered her voice dramatically, talking in smooth, seductive tones, as she brought them back to a time and place a little over two years ago.

"Wesleyan University was holding its annual writers' conference for published and would-be authors. I'm one of those closet wannabes, the kind who wants to pen the Great American Novel, but doesn't have the guts to really try. Anyway, I'd been wanting to attend the writers' conference for years—to give myself the kick in the behind I needed to get started—but I always found an excuse. I'm not good enough; summer's a time for relaxing not studying; I'll make an ass of myself. Whatever. There were always more than enough reasons. So, two years ago, I get their brochure, as usual; I read it, as usual; but this time my excuses just didn't hold water, not even with me. I held onto the registration form for weeks, feeling more and more compelled to sign up until, finally, just before the deadline, I wrote out the check and blanked out the entire week on my calendar. Just like that. I barely discussed it with Greg, except to inform him that he'd be on duty as far as Courtney was concerned. Suddenly, this conference became the mainstay of my existence. Nothing else seemed important..."

"Meanwhile," Adam interrupted, "there I was facing another summer of teaching crash courses in English Composition at UCONN—a full semester crammed into six weeks with apathetic, sun-worshiping students who would spend the entire time gazing out the window. The whole experience loomed larger than life and I felt bored and resentful at the prospect. And then the invitation came. Wesleyan University was requesting that I serve as Poet in Residence for the upcoming writers' conference. I would help aspiring poets learn their art, and I would have the opportunity to talk with and learn from writers accomplished in other genres. It was an irresistible opportunity."

"So, there we were," Josie continued, "two stars destined to collide, arriving on campus at the same time. Even though I lived close by, I decided to sleep there, stay in the dorms, in order to get the full benefit of the conference. Anyway, we actually did collide. We banged right into each other at the first night's cocktail reception. Wine—thank God it was white—all over the place, but it was like it didn't matter at all—our eyes locked and couldn't let go. That night, I kept thinking about

Adam and how familiar he seemed even though I knew we'd never met. I felt intensely drawn to him; yet, physically, he was exactly what I normally didn't find attractive. No offense, dear," she leaned over and kissed him on the cheek.

"No offense taken," Adam smiled, "I felt the same way about you." He ruffled her short, dark hair. "Blondes...curvy, even buxom, thick-haired blondes is what I normally go for..."

"Pieces of fluff, you mean."

"Ouch! Not true. You don't have to be brunette to have brains. Right, Caitlin?"

"Absolutely." Caitlin found herself blushing for no good reason as she played with her auburn hair, tucking and untucking it behind her ears.

Marc moved closer and ran his fingers through Caitlin's hair, picking up strands and examining them in the light of the fire. "I see some blonde streaks in here...hmmm." He lightly knocked his knuckles on her head. "And it doesn't sound too hollow...must be a few brains lurking in there."

Although she remained perfectly still, Caitlin's insides were jumping irrationally at Marc's slight touch. She closed her eyes for a moment, enjoying the sensation of his long fingers moving through her hair. Remembering suddenly that she didn't particularly like this man, she shook off his hand with a smile and quick shiver, edging away from him. "Don't keep us in suspense," she said, "on with the Adventures of the Mated Souls!"

"Good title," Josie said. "Maybe that's what I'll call my book, if and when I ever write it. Okay, where was I?" She took a sip of her Amaretto. As she lifted the glass, light from the fire bounced off the crystal, adding one more layer of illusion to the night. "There we were," she continued, "eyes locked every time we met. I sat in on all of Adam's poetry sessions, just so I could sit back and observe him, watch his movements, watch how his eyes crinkled every time he smiled, see how he appreciated the talent in all of these would-be poets. I'd always be the last one to leave the room and we'd walk out together, standing so close that our arms would brush up against each other. Now, remember, I was a happily married woman. I use the term 'happily' loosely—I was content, sort of—but I definitely was not looking for an affair. And if I was, like I said, Adam is not who I would have chosen, at least not on the conscious level."

"And I was just learning to live alone—and be on my own—coming off a twenty-year marriage in which I was, to use the vernacular, dumped, because I'd apparently grown old and unappealing."

"So, there we were," Josie said, "on some very basic level deeply attracted to one another, contriving ways to spend a few minutes a day with each other, but not willing to admit to anything, fighting it all the way. Whenever we were together, there was an electrical field around us; I felt charged up, on edge, like I would burst at any moment. It was like foreplay, without the touching. But it was larger, more important than just a physical reaction.

"It all came together that second to the last evening. Well, sort of, anyway. About twenty of us signed up for what was described as 'a personal growth experience to help unleash creativity.' We all went to The Morgan Estate, part of Wesleyan's off-campus holdings. It has acres of land and a wonderful stone castle filled with oil paintings of the Morgan family and assorted relatives, dating back quite a while.

"Anyway, the exercise was a take-off on an old Indian ritual called a 'vision quest.' But a rather loose interpretation. We didn't fast and we didn't sweat to death for two hours in order to purify our bodies. But we did sit around a fire and chant and sing, and we did sleep outdoors.

"I had no idea Adam had signed up and he had no idea that I had, but there we were. This place is situated way off the beaten path, set up high, overlooking the Connecticut River. We had a light picnic supper and were free to explore our surroundings until dusk, when we would convene around a large camp fire. I wandered into the house and was studying the portraits, looking into the eyes of these people, feeling strangely connected to them. I went from room to room, almost dazed, as though I was being pulled back into time; my heart pounded, but I wasn't frightened. Not really.

"I walked into the last room, an upstairs sitting room, and there was Adam, standing by a long window looking outside at the rose garden. He turned and looked at me and just smiled. It was though he'd been waiting for me, as though he'd known I would come. Neither of us said a word. I walked over to him, he put his arms around me, and we kissed. It was the strangest damn thing I'd ever felt. I knew him. And I knew that room. We'd been there before. I wanted to crawl inside him, to cling to him and stay in his arms forever but, instead, I ran from him and joined the group starting to form around the fire.

"Adam joined us, but he kept his distance. He didn't know what to make of the whole thing either. The sky was black, dotted with brilliant silver stars, and I was looking up asking God for guidance, for some kind of sign. Just at that moment, a star shot across the heavens. Adam and I both gasped out loud. Everyone else just looked at us, like we were crazy or something. I didn't know it at the time, but Adam had been asking for answers at just that same moment."

As Josie and Adam took turns talking, Caitlin found herself surrendering to the sensations and sounds around her—to fire and water, crystal and starlight, to the rhythmic pounding of waves as they struck the shore, to the sweet scent of their liquors and the intoxicating heat of the fire. And to the storytelling. It was as though she was participating in some ancient ritual. Even as her heartbeat quickened, she relaxed into the feeling of something familiar and safe, of some cosmic memory now being called to the surface. All the tensions of the past months seemed to leave her body, evaporating one by one into the evening sky. Without thinking, she tucked in closer to Marc, almost, but not quite, leaning against his knee. She looked up at him and smiled. He stroked her hair and let his hand settle softly on her shoulder.

"My turn, dear," Adam interrupted. "She'd tell the whole story if I let her. Anyway, to continue on...we sat around chanting while someone in another corner of the property began drumming. Between the heat of the fire and the chanting and the incessant beating of the drum, you lose control of your consciousness, which is the whole idea. To purge yourself. You begin to feel like our mind and body are floating in space. As the drumming continued, we each took our sleeping bag and went off alone with only our journals and a flashlight. The idea was to use this time of inner connectedness to write from a point of pure discovery and creativity."

"I went off toward the river," Josie said, "where I could rest high on its bank and listen to the water rush across the rocks. I had no idea where Adam had gone. All night I half-slept, waking up at odd moments, turning on my flashlight and jotting down thoughts, sometimes one word, sometimes whole paragraphs, all things I had seen, or dreamt, as I laid there under the stars.

"The first image I saw in my dream-like state was a house, high on a hill, much like Morgan House, but I couldn't be sure. I saw myself as a young woman serving dinner to the family and when I got to the son, our eyes met and we were sad. We were sad because we loved each other but knew it never could be. That boy was Adam! I woke up and wrote everything down and then tried to get back to sleep. It was more like a half-sleep, because images kept going off in my mind, like a fireworks display.

"I was in the same house again, but it was years and years later, like another lifetime; and this time I was in the parlor, as a guest. I looked very tired and scared. Adam was trembling. His father was angry, hollering at us. I looked down and saw my swollen stomach. I had no parents. I was an orphan. They had brought me in as a young woman and I had repaid their kindness by sleeping with their son. They sent me away to have my baby. Adam stood by and watched. I never saw him again. Or so I thought. I had one more dream that night. In this one, Adam and I were married. We were so happy. We were so much in love. But he died; he died at sea a year later. We had no time together, no time at all—"

Josie's voice cracked with emotion. She stopped for a moment, listening to the pounding of the waves, breathing in the pungent night air. She took hold of Adam's hand and squeezed hard before speaking again.

"As morning arrived," she said, "I was deeply moved by the night's events, but I attributed the strong images to the ritual and the aloneness, and even to my unexplained attraction to Adam. But, I have to admit, I was haunted by the whole thing. I couldn't seem to shake loose from it.

"The drumming had stopped some time during the night, but it started up and we all regrouped by the fire for breakfast. As soon as he saw me, Adam grabbed hold of my arm and insisted that I read his journal. At first I didn't want to. I actually pushed him aside. But he was so insistent. It turns out that his writings...his images from that night...all of his dreams, if that's what they were, were identical to mine.

"We knew right then and there something bigger than the both of us was at work, some universal force playing itself out—that we'd spent lifetimes together, loving and having that love thwarted. And that now, maybe, this was the lifetime to see it realized. The connection we felt at that moment...it's impossible to verbalize. It was as though we were two huge magnets being drawn toward each other—"

"And, so, here we are," Adam said, weaving his fingers between Josephine's. "Together again."

Chapter Thirteen

Caitlin loved the beach early in the morning, before it was assaulted with artificial sounds. She rolled up her white slacks and walked barefoot along the edge of the water, watching the sun cast its light on the rolling waves.

"Yo, Caitlin, wait up."

She continued walking at an even pace, pretending not to hear the voice now making headway in her direction.

"Cate, hi. Terrific morning," Marc said, breathless from catching up to her. "Just look at that sky."

"Oh, hi." She tried to act surprised.

"Mind if I walk along?"

"Sure. Why not?" What could she say? No? Get Lost? That's what she wanted to say. Almost. This man had the most unnerving effect on her and she couldn't figure out why. And the truth was, she was confused and embarrassed by the way she'd leaned into him last night, by how comfortable she'd felt. Even now, in the light of day, part of her wanted to reach out and hold onto him. She had to stop herself from linking her arm through his and walking comfortably along the beach, as though they'd done it hundreds of times before. He felt that familiar. The other part of her saw him as the enemy. All of her defenses were on guard, as though letting him get too close was the surest way to get hurt. How could she feel so strongly about someone she'd just met?

"How'd you sleep last night?" Marc asked.

"Okay, I guess. I always have a hard time in a new place."

"Are you sure it's the place?"

Caitlin squinted and gave him a long look. Marc met her gaze and she quickly turned her head, kicking the water as she walked.

"What do you mean?" she finally asked.

"Well, as often as I've heard the Adam and Josephine story, last night it left me unsettled. I tossed and turned all night. And I thought about you a lot. It was the damndest thing. I was wondering if you had the same reaction."

"What do you mean?"

"Is that your favorite question? You know exactly what I mean. Did you think about me last night while you were supposed to be sleeping?" He smiled down at her teasingly. "Or maybe you dreamt about me?"

"Only in your dreams would I have dreamt about you. In my dreams, it'd be more like a nightmare."

"Ouch," Marc laughed. "We're touchy this morning. I was just making innocent conversation."

"I don't think you have an innocent bone in your body. You were goading me. And you know it. You can wipe that stupid smile off your face. It doesn't work on me."

"Stupid? And I thought it was charming."

"Guess you thought wrong."

"Hmmm." Marc stopped to examine a conch shell that had washed in during the night. He threw it back into the water and continued walking, his pace faster now so that Caitlin had to take a skip every so often to keep up with him.

"If you want to walk with me, then walk," she commanded. "If you want to run, then run alone."

Marc slowed down, falling into rhythm with her step.

"Well?" he asked after several minutes of silence.

"Well, what?"

"Well, did you think about me last night?"

"Not at all."

"Not even the tiniest bit?"

"Not even. Can we change the subject now?" Caitlin felt her face flush with the lie. But she wasn't about to let him know that she spent a long, restless night caught in the web of Josie's story, and somehow he'd been woven into the tapestry of her dreams. He was the kind of person who'd never let you forget such an admission. Besides, it was none of his business.

"I don't believe you. But we'll let it go for now." Marc pulled Caitlin to a stop, holding onto her arm lightly, their feet sinking into the wet sand. "But here's a question I really do need the answer to: Have I done something remarkably wrong? What have I done to offend you? You've been ornery towards me from the get-go. Except for a few minutes last night, by the fire, when you let your guard down."

Caitlin looked down at her feet, wriggling her toes deeper into the sand. She shrugged. "I know. I'm sorry. I can't explain it. Something about you makes me want to punch you. It's that stupid smile. See, there it is again."

"Go ahead, punch." Marc grinned and extended his upper arm toward her.

"See what I mean. You're infuriating." She shook off his grip and began walking back toward the beach house.

Marc let her walk alone for a few minutes and then caught up with her.

"Here, a peace offering." He handed her a perfectly shaped scallop shell.

Caitlin jammed the shell into her pocket without looking at him. "Do you think we knew each other before? Maybe that's why you're so mad. Maybe I was a real bastard." Marc squinted his eyes and pursed his lips, trying hard to look evil.

"And maybe it has nothing to do with past lives. Maybe it's simply because you're a pain in the ass in this lifetime."

His deep laugh was carried away by the wind. "No, that couldn't possibly be it!"

They walked quietly for a while. Almost back at Arcadia, Caitlin began to feel badly. Why was she so harsh with him?

"Josie says you're a developer." she said. Talking about work was always safe territory.

"That's true."

"I'm in real estate. Mostly residential."

"I know. Josie told me. I'm looking for a tract of land out your way. She thought maybe you could help me."

"Maybe. Sure. Why not?"

"Don't be so enthusiastic. Lady Ice, that's what I'm going to call you."

It was true, she did freeze people out when she was mad or hurt. Or afraid. It was her way of dealing with things until she thought them through; and then, afterwards, she usually wanted to talk the problem to death to try and figure it all out. David had called her an iceberg more than once. Funny that Derrick never assessed her personality, the way people you're close with tend to do. It was almost as though he was more concerned about holding onto her than knowing who and what she really was.

That realization startled Caitlin. She'd never really thought about Derrick in those terms. Her eyes opened wide and she stopped walking so suddenly that a look of fear shadowed across Marc's face.

"You okay?" he asked. "Did you hurt yourself?" He looked down at her feet, expecting that maybe she'd cut herself on a shard of glass or stubbed her toes on a piece of driftwood.

"No. It's nothing. I'm fine. Really."

"You're not fine."

"Really, I am. Thanks."

"Cate?" Marc touched her arm softly, just enough to encourage her confidence.

"It's silly. Something just dawned on me—you ever have that happen where you get struck by a thought and you need to figure it out on the spot? It's not about you, don't get excited. Anyway. I'm fine. I'll figure it out later."

"Okay. If you say so." He reached out and tousled her windblown hair, and she didn't stop him. They walked the rest of the way in comfortable silence.

Back at Arcadia, they steadied each other as they washed the sand off their feet under the outside faucet and then walked up the deck stairs together.

"So, do you think you can find me about thirty acres?" Marc asked.

Chapter Fourteen

C atie, meet Sara Livingston," Josie said, more in the form of an announcement than an introduction, nudging Caitlin awake. She had fallen asleep on the deck, listening to the surf, feeling the hot sun beating down on her back. Caitlin lifted her head and smiled hello. As she struggled to regain her senses, she wished Josie had warned her that someone was coming. What time was it anyway?

"Don't tell me you forgot about the Tarot card reading," Josie said. "We talked about it last week. On the phone? Remember? When we were making plans for this weekend."

Caitlin struggled to a sitting position. She took a long drink of warm iced-tea and lifted her face to the sea breeze. Nearly awake now, she turned to the two women standing above her. "Oh, right. Listen, I'm not sure about this. I think maybe I've changed my mind. No offense, Sara. Nice to meet you." Everything was so peaceful; why tempt fate? She could go back and tell Liz that nothing had happened and everything could go back to the way it was.

"No offense taken," Sara said in a no-nonsense, raspy voice. "You do what's right. When it's right." Her black hair, apparently rinsed too often with too much henna, looked almost purple in the harsh sunlight. It was pulled back loosely with a rubber band. Sara reached back now to tuck errant strands behind her ears and readjust the silver earrings that weighed heavily on her ear lobes. She stood, eyeing Caitlin, as though trying to determine her worth. Feeling like an insect trapped under the microscope of a probing scientist, Caitlin squirmed and finally stood, needing to know she could expand her boundaries and even escape.

"But you have to," Josie begged. "To help find out what's going on in your life, including..." She lowered her voice conspiratorially, "that strange appearance of David in the mirror." Turning to Sara, who was studying the ocean, giving them space to talk, Josie said, "She really wants this. She's just afraid. You know how it is the first time."

Sara continued looking straight ahead, wisps of hair blowing about her tanned face. She took a deep, cleansing breath. "It's so lovely here. I hate living inland." Her brown eyes met Josie's as she nodded toward Caitlin. "She does what she wants. When she wants. You know that. I'm thirsty."

Josie grabbed Caitlin's arm and dragged her inside as she went to the kitchen to get Sara a glass of seltzer. "Don't forget the lemon," Sara called out to her.

"Catie, please," Josie said, pouring three glasses of seltzer and squeezing lemon into each one.

Caitlin sighed, but didn't respond.

"I know I shouldn't beg," Josie said, "and I don't want to force you or anything, but I think you'll really be happy you did it."

"I don't know. I'm already in enough trouble over this weekend. I feel like my life is out of control. Maybe it's just not worth it, trying to find answers this way. Besides, she's kind of strange. Be honest, don't you think so?"

"A little," Josie smiled. You get used to it. Go take a shower. You'll feel better." She pushed Caitlin in the direction of the bathroom, handing her a tall glass of seltzer and lemon. "Don't worry, be happy!" she said. "Just go cool off. Then come back ready for the reading of your life!"

* * *

Sara Livingston was a sturdy, big-boned woman with large, capable hands. Wordlessly, she nodded toward the dining area once Caitlin had decided to go ahead with the reading. They sat around the oval, glass-topped table, Sara on one side, Josie and Caitlin on the other. Sara moved about, settling herself into the upholstered chair, until she found just the perfect position for the length of the reading.

Caitlin and Josie watched silently as Sara willed herself into a trance-like state. Her hands lay open, palms up in her lap, as though serving as a receptor for the energy she was attempting to channel. Her breathing became increasingly more deliberate, hypnotic in its depth and rhythm; her shoulders relaxed and her face flushed a gentle pink. When she was ready, she opened her eyes and smiled a gentle, reassuring smile. "Shall we begin?"

From the few minutes she had spent with Sara when Josie introduced them, Caitlin noticed how Sara spoke quickly, almost harshly, in staccato-like sentences. But in this altered state, she seemed more articulate and her voice was soft and smooth, almost melodic.

Sara picked up the oversized deck of cards and began shuffling, the turquoise and silver ring on her marriage finger bobbing up and down with the rhythmic movement. "Tarot cards must be approached with respect," she explained to Caitlin, "but they are nothing to be afraid of. To fear them, is to fear yourself. They are just a tool, a mirror, if you will, of the truth—all the truths within you, past and present, and even the future—truths you're aware of and truths you haven't yet revealed to yourself."

Caitlin reached for Josie's hand, glad that she was sitting right beside her. "When you say that you—I mean the cards—reveal truths, what do you mean? What kind of truths?"

Sara put the cards on the table, tapping each side of the deck until she had a perfectly square stack. Then she looked directly into Caitlin's eyes. "Truth is hard. Harsh, even. So we hide, setting up walls and mazes and creating new truths for ourselves. We live illusions, shadows of truth. But," Sara pointed a short, chubby finger at Caitlin, "at some point during each of our lifetimes, we're given the opportunity to pull aside the curtain, to take a look at the other side and see what lies beyond that veil of illusion. This is your time."

Caitlin took a deep, steadying breath, uncertain whether this was, indeed, her time. If life was an illusion, then illusion was harsh enough for her. Truth could only be harder. Harder to witness, harder to bear. Did she really need any more? Josie must have sensed her dissonance because she held Caitlin's right hand tightly and pushed downward, keeping Caitlin in her chair. They each exchanged glances, knowing, but not lending words to what was happening. Then Caitlin let out a sigh and smiled weakly toward Sara. "I'm okay. Let's do it."

Sara pushed the deck toward Caitlin. "Shuffle the cards, and then cut them into thirds. I have cleared the deck from all past energy. Now you will shuffle. Your energy and truth will be absorbed by the cards.

That is what I will reveal."

Caitlin did as she was told, her fingers feeling clumsy with the oversized cards. After a few seconds, Sara closed her eyes and filled the room with her voice, speaking in a commanding, resonant tone. "For the purposes of this reading, we will set our egos aside. We call upon the higher spirits to guard and protect us and to lead us to the path of information that will be most helpful. We ask that the white light of God surround and protect us. Only good may come to us; only good may go from us. Nothing of evil is welcome or allowed. Amen."

Sara opened her eyes and smiled broadly at Caitlin. "Ready?"

Without waiting for an answer, Sara took the cards from Caitlin and dealt out three cards. "First, a quick look at the present. These three cards represent body, mind, and spirit. Remember, Tarot cards are simply a mirror of the way things are—they can't fabricate; they can only reflect."

The pictures on the cards were intricately drawn symbols and designs rendered in beautiful, muted colors. According to Sara, Caitlin's present state of affairs was reflected in the cards now before her: King of Rods—The Lovers—The World.

"Let's deal with this King of Rods," Sara said. "There's a strong, manipulating man in your life. Domineering, extremely self-confident. He will ask you to make a choice. When it happens, trust your instincts--your deep, inner instincts. Your gut. Right here." She made a fist and tapped her stomach. "Follow your gut. Your choice in this matter will affect some old karma that needs resolving."

"What man? What kind of choice?"

"That is all I know. That is all the cards are revealing. But you will know when the time comes."

"The right choice? What does that mean?"

"It's something you must discover for yourself. But be sure to listen to the inner you."

Sara picked up the three cards, put them to one side, and began dealing out twelve more, this time in circular fashion. Not certain if she and Josie were allowed to talk, Caitlin squinted and shrugged her shoulders, trying to let Josie know she was puzzled. This was all too cryptic for her. Too much like that whole Janet Lee reading. Men and secrets and life choices that couldn't be revealed. What was the point of it all?

Josie laughed out loud. "We can talk. But we should keep it down so Sara can concentrate. What's with the look? You gotta' know she's talking about Derrick."

"I was thinking maybe Steve, especially after what happened Friday night—"

"Talk about altering reality," Josie chided. "When will you see the truth about that jerk? And I don't mean Steve. He's a jerk, too, but in a different way."

"I might be mad at Derrick for the other night, but he's been nothing but kind to me. He's actually taken a lot of the pain away from David's death."

"Another thing you haven't exactly dealt with—"

"Okay." Sara interrupted. "Here, the cards are laid out in the twelve astrological houses, each one representing a different side of a person's life. For instance, this first one, in the house of Aries, represents personality—your window on the world, so to speak—how people see you and how you present yourself to the outside world. Right now you're undergoing a period of heightened activity. You're always busy, always doing, but without accomplishing much."

Caitlin's heart pumped faster. That's exactly how she'd been managing her life lately. If she wasn't out with Josie or Derrick or Liz and the kids, she was working, even when there was no work to do. Anything to keep from thinking. Anything to keep from going to bed, from hearing noises and seeing ghosts in the middle of the night. "What's that card in the middle?" she asked.

"It's you. The card in the center always represents the person asking the questions. She may not look like you physically, but her spirit mirrors yours. See the red roses surrounding her? They're symbolic of passion, desire, beauty, and cultivation. But notice the crown, how it's sharp and spiked. You're a determined woman, who's generally a little bit on guard. Because you've been hurt—I'm not sure if it's this lifetime or a previous one—you tend to be cautions. But you may be cautious with the wrong people, and not cautious enough with the ones you should be. You need to reassess some of your judgments. However, once you commit yourself, right or wrong, you're fiercely loyal, almost to a fault."

Sara studied the next card and then looked up at Caitlin. "The Nine of Rods. See how he holds one rod on his shoulder, in readiness to defend his position. Again, like before, we see that you're facing a radical evaluation of your life here on the physical level. All the cards keep pointing to the same thing," Sara continued. "You're going to have to make changes, choices, if you want to grow. That's what this lifetime seems to be about, dealing with past karma, letting go of old baggage. Oh, fun." She smiled, pointing to another card. "This shows that you will experience a lot of activity very rapidly in terms of love affairs and creativity. Some things are already on the way, 'in the mail,' so to speak. One person in particular will be highly sexual and charged with creative ideas."

"Whew," Josie said, shimming her bare shoulders, "highly sexual, creative ideas—whoever he is, send him my way."

"You've got Adam. Besides, you don't like Derrick."

"It's not Derrick!" Josie said. "He's already here. She's talking about somebody else, somebody in the mail."

Caitlin laughed. "Maybe she just meant it's somebody male. Besides, she said he could already be here. I say it's Derrick. Although, he's not exactly creative." Caitlin's voice became wistful. "But he is sexy. He reminds me so much of David."

"Sara," Josie asked, "can you give us a handle on this guy's name? Does it by any chance begin with an M?"

Caitlin hit Josie's thigh. "Stop it. Don't listen to her, Sara, just go on."

The ice in Sara's water had long melted and the outside of the glass was wet with condensation. She took a quick drink and wiped her hands on her skirt. "Interesting. See how The Hanged Man is suspended, upside down, to a branchless tree? Being bound to the tree indicates dependency to the physical plane. However, the Hanged Man's upside down position indicates a complete reversal in this dependence. Notice how easily coins could fall out of his trousers; this symbolizes the rejection of materialistic values. Again, you're about to re-evaluate your values and way of life."

So much change being predicted. Caitlin's stomach churned at the thought. Fear or anticipation? Both, she quickly decided. On some deep level, Sara's words felt true, but Caitlin needed to touch and feel the truth, to see it with her own eyes. How could she make decisions without facts? This was all so...so...what...? Airy Fairy. That's what David would have said. And Steve. And Derrick. And Liz.

Sara dealt out five more cards, laying them over the other cards, almost in the shape of a cross. "Last part of the reading. How we doing? You okay?" Sara touched Caitlin's hand.

"I'm fine," Caitlin said. "I just need to sit back and sort out everything you've been saying."

"Very interesting," Sara said, studying the five cards. "There are some very specific messages here for you. We'll leave the middle one for last—that's basically just an overall statement. Each of the other four cards deals with a certain level of being—emotional, physical, spiritual, and intellectual. Let's start with emotional. That's this card here, to the left of the center one, the Five of Cups."

The card depicted a dejected man, his head bent, looking at three overturned cups with their contents spilled on the ground. Across the way, sitting high on a hill overlooking a body of water, was a crumbling tower. Birds were flying overhead, and behind the man were two more cups, standing upright, but he does not see them.

"Okay," Sara started, "the message to you here is to stop crying over spilled milk. You still have a lot of emotional fulfillment ahead of you, a lot of life to live. It's time to recognize the past, acknowledge it, and then release it. Let it go."

Caitlin took a deep breath. Was it time to let him go of David already? All his clothes still hung in the closet; his half-used toiletries continued to take up the bottom shelf of the medicine chest. A pipe, filled with smoked tobacco, still rested in an ashtray in the family room.

Sara looked solidly at Caitlin. "This next one is a warning." She was pointing to a card with the picture of a heart pierced by three swords, blood dripping from the one in the middle, the largest sword. "You have already had your share of sadness and grief, but you will have one last knife in the heart before your sorrow ends. You will have one more shattering of faith before the turmoil is finally over. This is what your husband has been trying to warn you about."

Caitlin caught her breath. The memory of David's face in the mirror—his dark eyes piercing hers—flashed in front of her almost as though it was happening all over again. Had he really been trying to warn her? "Is somebody going to...try and hurt me? Can't you tell me who? When?"

"You're in no physical danger. We're talking spiritual, karmic resolution. And being hurt emotionally. The shattering of trust can be as damaging as the breaking of a bone."

"Oh. Karmically." Relief washed through Caitlin's body and her voice carried a giggle.

"Don't discount it," Josephine said. "It's as important as anything else. And besides, Sara also said you'd be hurt emotionally. So keep that guard of yours up."

But it was hard not to discount the prediction. All this karma stuff was really beyond her. She wanted to know about this lifetime, forget about the others-- if there were others. Still, if any of this was even the slightest bit true, she probably should know more about it. After all, forewarned is forearmed, and she certainly didn't need any more heartache. David and Maryanne were enough. "Can you tell me who is going to hurt me; or at least when to expect it?"

"Soon. Definitely within the next year," Sara answered. "No, I can't tell you who, but it does feel like a man. I can feel him hovering over you, trying to take control. You're being warned, not to frighten you, but so you'll keep aware."

Sara smiled broadly as though she was personally responsible for the news being delivered. "Look at this. You will have heartbreak, that's for certain. But look at this other card with the man and the woman exchanging cups, looking into each other's eyes. Someone very special will share your life, perhaps someone you've known in another lifetime. He'll be a true partner, emotionally, intellectually, and spiritually, and you two will form a real commitment. This last card, here, and the middle one tell me that your guardian angel is in attendance. You will begin a new avenue that will bring you personal success and satisfaction, and you will learn to depend more upon yourself than other people for happiness. That's it. Any questions?"

Caitlin sat back in her chair and took a deep breath. She had the feeling she'd just been given the tour of a Chinese fortune cookie factory. All those pithy predictions. In the end they were just slips of paper stuffed into crescent-shaped confections. How could this reading, or anyone's for that matter, be any more accurate than a fortune cookie? And yet...

"No, no questions," Cailtlin said. "I may have a hundred tomorrow, but none right now."

Chapter Fifteen

What a fool he was. What a damn fool! Derrick continued pacing the length of his living room, drenched in sweat. He cranked up the air conditioning and poured another Scotch. Mostly ice. It was too hot to drink. Besides, he needed a clear head.

He couldn't remember the last time he'd been so upset. Probably not since Lucille, and that was nearly twenty years ago. He ran a hand through his hair, still expecting to feel thick, long strands. Instead, short tufts stuck out from between his fingers. Shit! He hated the way he looked—the length of his hair, the color, having to lighten his roots every few weeks. "Get a grip," he told himself, "you can go back to the old look later. Right now, concentrate!"

Friday night had been a major tactical error. Caitlin left for the Cape furious with him for bringing up that stupid Tarot card reading. How can I trust you with big things, if I can't even trust you with a small secret? Those were her exact words when he walked her to the door and tried to smooth things over. In fact, those were her only words. And she wouldn't take his calls the next day before she left. Man, what a mess. Who'd ever think Steve would take it so seriously, or react so strongly?

All Derrick had wanted to do was get Liz and Steve in his corner, figuring the three of them together could convince Caitlin to stay home, to stop looking for those answers she seemed so desperate to find. Who had answers anyway? Derrick had never been able to figure out why life deals the hands it does. You just had to roll with the punches and, if you were smart, make the most of it. Turn things to your advantage. That's all he'd tried to do Friday night, turn things around to his advantage. But it backfired.

He'd even called Steve the next morning, hoping a good night's sleep might have cooled him. But apparently he'd had anything but a good sleep, with Liz crying and carrying on all night. All that did was make him even more determined to hang tight. The only way out rested with Derrick, and the answer had to be in his notebook. Otherwise, what was the point of keeping it?

Hour by hour, he flipped through pages, examining the entries, reading all of his finely-written notes. He hadn't realized he'd collected so much information. Christ, he could write her life story from this one notebook. The answer was there, somewhere, if only he could find it.

As night came, Derrick became more frantic. He had to come up with a way, before she got back from the Cape. The longer she stayed mad at him, the easier it would be to do without him. Derrick was convinced of that. He hadn't won her over yet, not completely, and that's what he needed to do. Throughout the night, Derrick slept in snatches, tortured by images of Caitlin being pulled away from him. Faceless people were grabbing at her, leading her away while he stood helpless, unable to make her stay.

Dawn had barely broken through the windows when he got up and put on a pot of coffee.

He didn't care that Caitlin had gone away for the weekend. Not really. Although he hated any time that she was out of his sight. During the week was bad enough, with him in Massachusetts and her in Connecticut. But that was solvable. He was already thinking about asking for a transfer, or even changing jobs. In that respect, he'd have no problem; Derrick Secor was a hot commodity in the computer industry. No, his real problem was this alliance Caitlin had with Josephine. She was the real problem. If it wasn't for her, they would have never fought in the first place. There was no mistaking the fact that Josephine was pure trouble. He agreed totally with Steve and Liz on that point, although not for the same reasons. Derrick didn't give a damn about all that searching-for-truth stuff when it came to religion or any of Steve's high moral ground issues; he only cared about it in terms of how it might affect his chances with Caitlin.

Here it was now, Sunday morning and he still wasn't any closer to an idea. Unshaven, un-showered, with only a fresh pot of coffee to recharge his brain, Derrick grabbed his small leather notebook once again and sat down in a chair by the window, scrupulously examining each entry. The answer was there. It had to be. There was no other place to look. Late in the afternoon, he found what he needed. It had been there all the time, on different pages, in different forms. But it was there, and it would work.

He stood up and stretched, satisfied with himself and the plan that was beginning to take form. Then he remembered it was Sunday. All the liquor stores were closed. Stupid blue laws. He hated New England. Always did. Way too provincial. He'd have to call in a favor. But that's what it was all about. Lending enough money. Making enough contributions. Collecting the right chits. Derrick picked up the phone.

"Joe. Sorry to bother you at home like this, especially on a Sunday. How are the wife and kids?" He barely listened to Joe's response. Who the hell cared about his ugly wife's sprained ankle? Finally Derrick cut in. "Well, you know how women are," he laughed as though they shared a private joke, "just buy her something expensive. She'll be good as new. Listen, chief, I know this is inconvenient, but I need a big favor. Can you meet me down at your place in about an hour? I need a certain brand of champagne and it can't wait."

Chapter Sixteen

Aweekend at the Cape: romantic, therapeutic, filled with moonlight and memories—that's what all the songs and stories promised. But there had been none of that for Caitlin. All it had been was unsettling, filled with strange feelings and too many disquieting moments. Ending it with a Tarot card reading had definitely been a mistake. Maybe not from Josie's point of view; she loved stirring the pot, getting people to move in new directions. Josie had no tolerance for people who stood still in life, for the voyeurs of the world. She liked participants.

But for Caitlin, the reading had unearthed all kinds of uncertainties, including that nagging feeling she sometimes felt with Derrick, but had nothing specific to blame it on. He was wonderful and generous, almost to a fault, and fun to be with. He took charge, and Caitlin liked not having to make major decisions. She liked being protected. There was nothing wrong with that. So then why did she sometimes have the oddest feeling that everything was not as it seemed to be?

And then there was Marc. He had unsettled her in a different way, as though he could see right through her, as though he knew more about her than he had a right to know. More than she knew about herself. When it was finally time to leave, Caitlin could feel Marc's kiss even before it happened. After walking Caitlin to her car and saying yet another goodbye, Josie and Adam scurried back inside, feigning some excuse about Courtney needing them and leaving Caitlin and Marc alone in the warm, star-lit night. She immediately sat in behind the wheel of her car and closed the door, as though the layer of metal would somehow shield her from this impossible man.

Marc reached in through the open window and pushed down the lock. "Now, you'll be safe," he smiled. Caitlin shivered as he bent down and moved his face close to hers. She took a single deep breath, hoping it would calm her quickening pulse. It was as though a huge stop watch had clicked and, for just a moment, time had stopped, capturing Caitlin and Marc in a pose that was oddly familiar. Drawn toward the heat of his skin and the faint lingering scent of soap, Caitlin felt as if a long-forgotten memory was recreated, as though she had stepped into a piece of her past and was powerless to change what did happen or what was about to happen. As Marc's lips began to brush hers, Caitlin stiffened, but she didn't turn her head. She could have, giving him her cheek at the last minute, but she didn't. Instead, she remained cool and unyielding. For, although she was powerless to change the kiss or how much she wanted it, she could still maintain control over her response. Somehow, that seemed very important to her.

"I'll see you soon," Marc said.

"What do you mean?"

"I was serious about looking for land. You will help me, won't you?" His eyes took hold of hers until she finally stammered an answer.

"Well, sure, I guess. I mean, it is my business." Caitlin started up her car and immediately put it into reverse. "I don't mean it's my business." She was suddenly so flustered. "Whatever you do is your business, definitely not mine. I just meant it's my business, you know, my job." Hot blood rushed to her face. What a fool she was making of herself. "Well, bye, see you soon, I guess." She started to give him a half wave when he leaned in through the window and kissed her cheek.

"Real soon," he said, and then stood watching as she drove away.

Once she was on the road, Caitlin opened up the sunroof and all the windows, hoping the wind against her face would help to numb her mind. It was the same kind of quiet night as the one two months ago when she'd had what Josie still insists was an out-of-body experience. The black sky was sprinkled with millions of shimmering stars; the yellow moon, only a sliver shy of being full, seemed to be sitting on her shoulders, following her home. And, here again tonight, Caitlin felt oddly connected to the universe, to something larger than life or, at least, larger than the life she knew. Maybe Sara was right, Caitlin thought, maybe all we have to do is get up the courage to pull back that veil of illusion we create for ourselves, and we'd see the world as it really is, with all its levels of existence.

She laughed out loud. "Listen to me, I'm starting to sound like Josie. Levels of existence! Be real, Catie."

She played with the radio knobs until she found some easy listening music and then turned the volume up high, using the noise to drive out random images from her brain. But the music had just the opposite effect, mingling with the wind and the fragrant night air, knocking on the door of memories long forgotten. All the way home a montage of faces and images flashed before her, like cameras going off at a surprise party.

First there was David. Or was it Derrick? No, it was David, but then Derrick's face seemed to be superimposed on top of David's, like that silly book she had as a kid where you could strip pieces from one face in order to create another. You could end up with a mustached, curly-haired woman, or a round-faced man with a bald head, rosebud lips, and earrings. Caitlin's mind kept producing a person that was half David, half Derrick; and as hard as she tried to strip away the layers, she couldn't get back to the original. David and Derrick had blended in such a way that she could no longer sort out their separate parts. But she could still sort out experiences.

There was that weekend in Maine last summer, how painfully close she and David had felt. It was similar to that rainy weekend in Rhode Island when he insisted on buying her the cameo. They had always been happy with each other and with their marriage, but these two times stood out as special moments when they seemed to reach into each other's souls with a love so deep it scared them, so intense they felt the need to crawl into each other's skin. They tried satisfying those feelings by making love with a fervor that bordered on desperation.

Remembering those times set Caitlin's body on edge. Every nerve ached to be touched. She pulled the skirt of her sundress high on her thighs, letting the evening breeze caress her legs. On a night like this, David would have sensed her longing, would have pulled her to him, even as he drove, teasing her with the tips of his fingers by running them up and down her legs and across the thin fabric of her underpants. Caitlin took a succession of short deep breaths. She would be home soon. A long, cool shower would rid her of these unwanted feelings, of longings no longer satisfied.

Chapter Seventeen

What are you doing here?" Caitlin asked, arriving home shortly after midnight.

Derrick sat on the sofa in Caitlin's living room, a bottle of champagne and two of her crystal glasses on the coffee table in front of him. The room was enveloped in candlelight and the soft crooning of Sinatra.

"Sweetie, you look exhausted. Come here. Sit down. Relax."

Caitlin didn't budge. "I said, what are you doing here?"

"Don't be angry, Catie. I had to see you. I've been miserable all weekend, thinking I might have lost you." He walked over to her, slipped her purse off her shoulder, put it on the closest chair, and then reached out to hug her.

Caitlin stiffened and shrugged him off. "How did you get in?"

Derrick put one arm around her back and steered her toward the sofa. "I brought champagne. To toast your safe return home." He popped the cork and poured some into each glass.

Caitlin refused the drink in his outstretched hand. "I want you to tell me how you got into my house. Now."

Derrick smiled, smoothed down her hair, still ruffled from the wind, and pulled at her hand, until she finally gave in and sat down. "You're so tense, Catie. Here, take a sip and I promise to tell you."

Caitlin took one sip, and then another, eyeing Derrick the entire time. It tasted good. She was tense. "Okay, tell me."

Derrick put his glass down, licked a drop of champagne from his lips, and then put his hand on Caitlin's knee. She jumped at the unexpected intimacy, but did nothing to push him away. "Remember when I took your car, to put air in the tires? I had a key made. Don't get mad," he said quickly. "Here, let me touch up your drink."

Caitlin gave him a long, steady look, then closed her eyes, tilted her head back, and finished all the champagne in her glass. She was suddenly so tired. And so tired of feeling tired. Not sleepy-tired. More like beat up. It felt good to let go. She immediately felt giddy and flushed, enjoying the surge of warmth that flowed through her body. She liked the feeling of his hand on her leg, part of her wishing he'd move it up higher, touch her the way she knew David would have, the way she imagined on the ride home. No, she wouldn't get mad. She was tired of being mad, of being defensive. All she wanted was to be protected. And loved. She leaned closer to Derrick just slightly, her face tilted toward his, close enough for him to steal a kiss. "Why, Derrick? Why did you have a key made?" Caitlin's tongue was thick inside her mouth, and her body wanted to move under Derrick's touch. She used every ounce of control not to urge his hand upward.

"I only did it in case you needed me, to protect you, to get to you if I ever had to. I never intended to just come in like this." Derrick slid closer to her. She could feel the warmth of his breath on her face. His eyes held hers as he stroked her cheek, ran his fingers across her lips. He tucked her hair behind her ear and kissed her lobe. Gently. As soft as gentle breeze. His lips brushed hers in a kiss so light she thought she might have imagined it. She moved every so slightly, urging the hand on her thigh upward. "I missed you so damned much this weekend," he whispered. "I'm so sorry for hurting you."

The pleading look in his eyes, the gentleness in his voice, had as much an effect on Caitlin as the champagne. "Mmmm...this tastes so good." She ran her tongue across her lips. "And so familiar."

The room had taken on a little sway. Caitlin poured herself another drink. "Kristal. That's what David and I had at our wedding. And on every anniversary! It was a tradition. Our tradition." She examined the label, turning the bottle round and round, aware that she had crossed the line into tipsy, but not really caring. So what? Was David here to stop her? Chastise her? Take care of her? None of the above. To hell with control.

Derrick ran his fingers through her hair, sending shivers down her spine. "I want you, Catie. I want you so much." He kissed her again, and this time Caitlin kissed him back, her insides throbbing at his

108

Patricia Sheehy

touch. She pressed herself against him, willing his hands to run the length of her body, wanting his fingers to explore her flesh. He kissed her again and again, stroking her back, pulling her tighter toward him until she could feel his hardness, even through their clothes. Derrick gently moved his hand up Caitlin's thigh, caressing and rubbing until he was certain of her desire.

As he stopped to slip off his pants, he took another drink of champagne and gave one to Caitlin. In that split second, she looked up at Derrick as though he was a stranger. She pulled away from him and stood up quickly, horrified at what she'd almost done. She was a married woman. She brushed down the skirt of her dress and adjusted its straps, all the while backing across the room until her breathing became more even. She was wobbly and still slightly out of control.

Derrick watched her move away, his hands shaking as he pushed his hair back from his wet forehead. "What the Christ—?"

"Derrick, I'm sorry," Caitlin said. "I really am. I don't know what got into me. It's the champagne. It has to be the champagne. It always does something to me. That's why I never drink much...unless I'm with David." She covered her face with her hands. She felt embarrassed, because of what she'd almost done and because, deep inside, she still longed to be satisfied.

Derrick walked over to her and took her hands in his. "David's not here anymore, Catie. But I am, and I can take good care of you. I want to take good care of you." He kissed her roughly this time, his tongue exploring her mouth as he took her hand and placed it on his thigh, slowly moving it higher, encouraging her to feel his body. "Oh God," he moaned, as her fingers began to caress him. "Catiedid, I love you," he whispered in her ear. "Feel me. Feel how much I want you." He eased her onto the floor.

Catiedid, I love you. Blood pounded in Caitlin's brain as her body responded to the words—David's words—his private nickname for her.

"I love you, too, David!" she cried out, surrendering to Derrick as he masterfully handled her breasts, touching and sucking, making her want him with a desperation she'd almost forgotten. "Oh, my God, don't stop, don't..." She arched her back, feeling the heat of his passion as he entered her, feeling the intensity of her own passion, her body trembling as Derrick continued to move inside her, slowly at first, and then faster, harder, each thrust bringing them closer to fulfillment.

They held each other for a long time after, there on the living room floor, Caitlin's head cradled against Derrick's shoulder. Had she really called him David? Oh God, how awful. In fact, this whole thing was awful. "Derrick, I'm really sorry—" she started to apologize, but Derrick put his lips to hers.

"Don't," he said, stroking her hair, crooning softly, telling her not to worry about anything, ever again. "You're mine now, Catie. I'll take care of you. I'll make you happy."

Chapter Eighteen

Just as Sara and Janet Lee had predicted, the relationships in Caitlin's life were changing; new ones were coming in, old ones were leaving, and those that stayed seemed to take on a new form. Caitlin was still haunted by that disastrous lunch with Maryanne, feeling she could have handled it better, could have done something to preserve the relationship. Maryanne was the closest thing Caitlin had come to having her own daughter, and she missed everything that went with the territory—the sharing of confidences late at night, the shopping sprees, the messy room, even the fights over curfews and chores. She couldn't get up the nerve to call, knowing Brenda was doing everything in her power to solidify the breakup, but she had written Maryanne several letters over the past few months. None of them had been answered or in any way acknowledged. It was as though they'd been delivered into a black hole.

And while Steve's edict didn't end the friendship between Caitlin and Liz, it definitely strained their relationship. There were new boundaries that couldn't be crossed, unspoken rules that couldn't be broken. They had clandestine phone calls and quick visits during the day, but Caitlin could no longer joke about Steve's controlling ways, because Liz now felt compelled to defend her husband where once she would have laughed and agreed with Caitlin. And, because she couldn't freely share the details of her life—her friendship with Josie and Adam, her psychic readings, her questions about life and death — Caitlin became acutely aware of the holes in their relationship, holes that had probably always been there but were now made visible by awkward silences and half truths.

Even though Liz had no choice but to side with Steve against Caitlin and what he called her "mixed-up way of thinking," she tried desperately to get Caitlin back on track by pushing her in the direction of Derrick. Liz was convinced that he held the answer to all of their problems. He was ideal for Caitlin—for any woman, in fact—fun, rich, handsome, and generous; and if anyone could see to it that they were a foursome again, it was Derrick. Josie, on the other hand, kept encouraging Caitlin to date other people, Marc being one of the prime candidates in her mind, and to explore all possibilities.

But, little by little, Derrick's presence in her life made Caitlin forget she had options. Because he was so much like David or, over time, had become so much like David—Caitlin had stopped trying to figure out which was true—she still felt married. Very married. She had actually stopped grieving for her husband. It was hard to grieve for something she still had. Despite the not-quite-right feeling that continued to tickle her subconscious, Caitlin settled into a cadence with Derrick, pushing aside all thoughts of Marc, except for the few times she came across the scallop shell he'd given her at the beach. His peace offering. For some reason, instead of throwing it out, she'd tucked the shell into a corner of her jewelry box.

Whenever possible, Derrick insisted that they maintain her old lifestyle. In that way, he reasoned, Caitlin's pain over David's death would be minimized. "What did you and David love to do?" he would often ask, listening intently as she answered. And then he would recreate the experience.

The one thing they did that was different was throw a Halloween Party. It was one of those things she and David had always talked about, but never got around to doing. Derrick insisted that they have one, as a way of cementing their relationship, the way their making love had done.

Wanting desperately to attend, Liz told Caitlin to send an invitation to the house, hoping that enough time had passed and maybe, just maybe, Steve would let this be the ice-breaker they all needed. After all, he could save face by not being the first to give in, and yet be seen as gracious enough to accept Caitlin's extension of goodwill.

Three days before the party the phone rang. "Caitlin, this is Steve," he said, his voice maintaining an edge of formality. "I'm replying to your invitation."

"Steve, hi!" She hadn't realized until that moment how much Steve's approval and having Liz legitimately back in her life actually meant to her. "It's been ages. How's Liz? How are the kids?" She hated lying by omission, but in this case it was absolutely necessary. He could never know she and Liz had been deceiving him.

"Jason and Jessica are just fine. Thank you for asking. Liz is in bed with a headache right now."

"Nothing serious, I hope. You think it's her sinuses?"

"Actually, I think it's the beginning of another migraine. Mostly likely from stress. This invitation of yours has created chaos in our household."

"Oh?" Caitlin became immediately guarded. How like Steve to blame her for Liz's headache.

"Frankly, Caitlin, Liz really wants to come to this shindig of yours, and that's something given how much she hates costume parties. I told her we'd go only if that woman wasn't going to be there."

"What woman?" Caitlin asked, knowing perfectly well who he meant. Let him say it, she thought; let him actually verbalize his small-minded, pigheaded bigotry.

"That gypsy friend of yours. What's her name...Josephine?"

"Oh, Josie!" Caitlin said, oh-so-sweetly. "I don't know yet if she's coming. Although I did send her an invitation, her and her soul mate, Adam." Let him stew in that one, Caitlin thought. Of course Josie and Adam were coming.

The silence at the other end made Caitlin immediately sorry she'd been so flip. She bit her bottom lip and waited another few seconds. When he still didn't say anything, she broke the silence, her voice low and sincere. "I haven't heard from Josie yet, Steve, but does it really matter? Can't you and Liz just come regardless and have a good time? Derrick and I promise a really fun evening."

Caitlin heard a deep intake of air and then Steve's voice, hard and steady. "Look, the very fact that you invited her means that you're still involved with that woman. I can't condone it, any more than I know David would. And I'm surprised Derrick does. He's a pretty sensible guy. Coming to your house where she's an invited guest would be the same as sanctioning it. I can't do it. And I won't expose Liz—"

"But—" Caitlin interrupted.

"No buts. My wife is much too impressionable. Maybe by keeping Liz and the kids away from you, you'll realize the price you're paying for all this nonsense. You used to be such a good, sensible person, Caitlin. What happened?"

"I'm still me. I'm still that good-old-Caitlin who helped nurse Liz through pneumonia and watched your kids every year so you two could go on vacation."

"Good-old-Caitlin left with a band of gypsies."

"Steve, don't. Please? I lost my husband five months ago and now you're taking away my best friend. Don't do that to me—"

"You're doing it to yourself. I have to go. You take care."

"Wait! Steve. Don't hang up." There was silence at the other end, but at least he hadn't hung up. "Listen, don't make up your mind about the party. Give it some more thought. And come, even if it's last minute. You don't even have to call or anything, just come." Her words came in rapid succession, one tumbling out right after the other.

"Don't count on it. Goodbye, Caitlin."

* * *

Derrick handled nearly all the party details, including their costumes. He had intended to get something outrageous and dramatic, wanting them to be an infamous historic couple—Josephine and Napoleon, Anthony and Cleopatra, even Scarlet and Rhett. Instead, he had been drawn to the Western section of the costume shop. "Looks like we're nothing special after all," he joked, showing Caitlin the costumes, "just a couple of plain cowpokes. Except yours is a 'goin' out dress.' Couldn't put you in anything less."

Along with the costumes, he'd brought pictures of how they should look, and Caitlin spent over an hour trying to make her hair look authentic 1880's, pinning her silky strands back until they finally stayed tucked under the false chignon she placed at the nape of her neck. It was lighter than her natural hair, but with the hat on, nobody would ever notice.

When she was finally dressed, she twirled herself around in front of the full length mirror, feeling giddy and beautiful, as though she'd just stepped out of the pages of a Western storybook. Made of a satiny cotton, the top of the dress was sapphire blue, the high neckline trimmed with white lace, while the bottom was a checkered pattern of sapphire blue, strawberry red, and white. The form-fitting dress nipped in at the waist and hugged her hips, creating a classic hourglass shape. Using the pictures as a guide, Caitlin draped the overskirt just below the long, slenderizing darts in her skirt, gathering the excess material in the back and forming a small bustle. Derrick came into the room, strikingly handsome in his Stetson and bib pullover shirt. He wore brown leather boots and dark Levis studded with copper rivets. Around his neck was a large blue and red print neckerchief.

"Are we authentic, or what?" Derrick said. "Great choice, if I do say so myself."

"What about your glasses?" Caitlin asked, not having seen Derrick without them since that first night.

"Too modern. I put my contacts in." He laughed. "Like they're not modern. But I can see, and what I see is one gorgeous woman. You were born to wear that dress." He took her by the waist and spun her around. "You need a piece of jewelry, right here." He pointed to the lace around her neck. "What's wrong with me? I should have bought you something. To remember tonight by. Our first party. It makes us an official couple."

"Derrick, you can't keep buying and doing. You've done enough. And I appreciate it. I do. I'm not sure I tell you that enough." Caitlin rummaged through her jewelry box as she talked. "How about this?" She held up her cameo. "It's perfect, don't you think?"

"Yeah, it is," he said, and helped her pin it to the neck of her dress. Together they stood in front of the mirror, smiling at the image they presented. "The ideal Western couple, ready for a rip-roarin' Saturday night."

Caitlin laughed and, as she did, their image seemed to fade from the mirror as another one took its place. It was a scene, actually, from another time and place, but as real as they were.

Riding in an open buggy pulled by a single horse, was a young woman dressed strikingly similar to the way Caitlin looked tonight, right down to the cameo at her throat. Sitting beside her, driving the buggy, was a man with wavy brown hair, a moustache, and a small, deep scar on his cheek. The woman kept looking up at the man and smiling; every now and then he reached over and tenderly stroked her cheek. From behind them came a man in a leather jacket ridding aggressively, passing by them and then crossing their path as though deliberately intending to frighten them. The woman gasped as she saw the man, just as their horse reacted by bolting forward and dragging their carriage at a dangerous speed across the uneven terrain and down a slope toward the stream below. The man held the woman tightly, protectively, until the moment they crashed into a boulder. The man was thrown against a tree. The woman was pinned under the overturned carriage. The man in the leather jacket was at the woman's side snapping his fingers in front of her face, "Molly, Molly, can you hear me, are you alive? Molly, talk to me ..."

"Catie, Catie, are you all right? Catie, can you hear me? What's wrong? Talk to me." Derrick continued snapping his fingers in front of Caitlin, calling her name until she finally responded. The image in the mirror disappeared as quickly as it had appeared. She blinked rapidly and tried clearing her dry, dusty throat.

"What the hell just happened?" Derrick asked.

"I don't know. What do you think?"

"What do you mean, what do I think? You blanked out on me."

"Didn't you see it?"

"See what? What are you talking about?"

"Nothing...I...I don't know." Caitlin rubbed her right thigh, acutely aware of the searing pain that had crept in over the last several minutes. She looked up at Derrick. "It's Halloween. Anything's possible..." she said, laughing briefly. "For a minute I actually imagined—"

The doorbell rang, announcing their first guests, and Caitlin never did tell Derrick what she saw in the mirror.

Chapter Nineteen

Derrick was right. In many ways, this was their coming-out party. Since all of Derrick's friends lived out of state, only a few were invited and only one couple actually came. Most of the people were Caitlin's friends, people she and David had gotten to know over the years. Many of them were people she hadn't seen since David's funeral. Now it was time for them to see her with Derrick, to place his image over David's and begin the process of accepting them as a couple. Caitlin was pleased with the way she and Derrick hosted the evening, circulating the room, making everyone feel at home. It was as though they'd been doing it all their life—he fit so easily into her established patterns, into David's way of doing things. And more than one person that evening commented on Derrick's uncanny resemblance to David.

"Maybe he's a walk-in," Josie commented, a sly smile on her face, when she heard Lauren booming about the likeness between the two men.

"I mean, he even smells the same!" Lauren laughed. "I always thought David had a distinct, kind of classy smell. And I don't mean B. O., honey." She slapped Caitlin on the back. "It was definitely the smell of expensive cologne."

"Oddly enough, they both use the same after-shave," Caitlin said, and then turned to Josie. "What's a walk-in?"

"Ah ha. And I thought you were ignoring me. I should have known better." Her turquoise eyes twinkled. "Simplistically speaking," Josie hushed her voice and darted her eyes back and forth to see who else might be listening, "the soul of a dead person occupies the body of someone already living."

"Right." Caitlin laughed. "So...David is inside Derrick?"

"Could be. David dies in the car accident. Or rather, his body dies. But he's not yet ready to leave this earth plane; he still has some unfinished business or something important to contribute to the world. Then there's someone named Derrick Secor, depressed or ill or whatever, but at any rate, ready to vacate his body. He wants to leave the earth plane. So, here we have David—who wants to stay but can't because his body is giving out—and Derrick—who has a perfectly good body, but wants to leave. In order to spare David all those years of growing up, if he were to reincarnate through the traditional birth process, Derrick lets go—dies—and lets David use his body. David walks into Derrick's body. It's all done with free will and the knowledge of both parties."

"You're nuts," Caitlin told her.

"Don't discount it," Josie said. "It certainly would explain the extraordinary way Derrick has transformed into David over these past months. Either that, or he's one great con man. That's another possibility."

Lauren threw her head back, taking a long gulp of Scotch and soda. "Josie, you are a hoot and I don't believe a word of it, but it's a great story, especially on the night of the All Dead, or whatever Halloween is supposed to be."

"I'm with Lauren on this one." Caitlin laughed, refusing to let Josie goad her into defending Derrick. "Great story, interesting theories, but I'm not buying them. Either one."

* * *

Ever since Derrick started spending weekends with Caitlin, he routinely slept in the guest bedroom. Sometimes Caitlin would lay in bed next to him, leaving his bed for her own only after he'd fallen asleep. Other times, she would tuck in next to him in the morning, bringing a pot of coffee and the newspaper with her. They nearly always made love when he stayed over and while she never again called him David, sometimes, when her eyes were closed and she inhaled his scent, she could fool herself into believing she was making love to her husband. It was understood right from the beginning that Caitlin preferred to fall sleep in her own room, and she could not share David's bed with any other man, not yet and maybe never. Caitlin was relieved when Derrick respected her feelings without challenge or reprisal.

In the early morning hours after their Halloween party, however, Derrick left the guest room, slipping quietly and uninvited into Caitlin's bed. When she rolled over and felt the warmth of his body, she thought for one brief moment that David had returned. Or that he had never left, that she was finally waking from a very bad dream, maybe even a coma or some kind of extended fugue state. All was restored. David. Liz. Maryanne. Her life was back to normal.

Hazy and half asleep, Caitlin reached over and ran her hand across Derrick's bare chest, reaching upward to feel the contours of his face before giving him a kiss. Her eyes opened wide with fright. Something in the way this man felt told her immediately it wasn't David.

Who was this stranger laying on her husband's pillow, occupying his side of the bed? She tried to sit up, to focus herself, but the man's arms were around her, pulling her down, his warm, damp breath covering her face as he pushed his naked body tightly against hers.

Fighting him off, she was finally able to switch on the small light on the table next to her bed. She grabbed the phone, trying frantically to dial 911. He took the phone from her hand and placed it back on the receiver. Only then did she look at the man's face. "Derrick! On my God, Derrick. I was so scared. For a minute...I didn't know who you were...I thought..."

"It's me, Catie. Only me." He reached across her and turned out the light, his hand stopping to caress her thigh.

"What are you doing here?"

"I missed you. Tonight was so wonderful. We need to be together."

"I can't, Derrick. Please go. You scared the life out of me. Don't ever do that again."

"Catie. Catie." He began caressing her. He kissed her, gently at first, and then deeper. She pushed at his chest and turned her face. "No, not tonight, not here."

"Sweet Catie. It's just you and me. Let me love you."

Why not? David was gone. Derrick was here. And she was so tired. Explaining her feelings, pushing him away—it all took too much energy. Caitlin let Derrick make love to her. But this time she couldn't pretend it was David. This time, she was making love to a stranger. She was making love to a stranger in David's room. And David was somewhere in the room—in their room—watching.

Long after Derrick had turned over and fallen asleep, Caitlin lay awake, staring into the darkness, horrified that she'd made love to Derrick, here in David's bed, and embarrassed that she given in so easily. Every muscle was on alert, every nerve ending on fire. Where was he? She was certain that David was there. She could feel him. She could almost see him: there, no there...in that swish of air...there...in that beam of light that just danced across the room from...where?... outside somewhere. "I'm sorry," she cried silently. "David, I'm sorry." Tears streamed down her face as she remained perfectly still, watching for signs of her husband.

As the first rays of morning began to sneak into the room, Caitlin panicked, knowing he would leave with the light. She had to find David now, before he disappeared again. Heart pounding, she crept out of bed, tugging and grasping at the air, as though she was making her way through layers of dense fog, convinced that if she kept reaching out, kept exploring vapid corners and pockets, that one time it would be David and not air that she held in her hand.

Chapter Twenty

From the moment he saw her, Marc felt as if he'd met Caitlin before. He ran through a mental list of everybody he could recall meeting, no matter how seemingly insignificant, of everywhere he'd ever been, trying to find the time and place she'd first touched his life. For a while, he became obsessed with the need to know, but coming up blank time and again, he finally attributed it to a misplaced sense of deja vu.

Marc was all set to call Caitlin the day after she left Arcadia, but Josie told him to cool it. "She already thinks you're too intense. Don't scare her off. You'll be throwing her right into the arms of this Derrick character." To his mind, waiting when he didn't want to wait, was playing games. And when you played a game, someone always lost. But he was also smart enough to realize that timing could be everything. He didn't want Caitlin to rebuff him simply because he was out of sync with her needs.

Josie finally gave him the green light. "Things don't seem to be slowing down with Derrick. If anything, he's weaseled himself into her life even more. You'd better make your move before he has a permanent foothold."

That was all Marc needed to hear. He was on the phone that same day asking Caitlin to line up some land he could look at. It was time for a new development.

* * *

Caitlin couldn't say why she was anxious over seeing Marc, but there was no doubt she was. Every time a gust of wind blew outside, she looked up, certain that the door was about to open. When he finally did walk in the front door of Colonial Realty late in the afternoon, she was unprepared for the jolt she felt at seeing him again. There he was, good looking in a windblown sort of way, appearing out of place in the delicate, antique-filled room.

He was dressed in faded jeans and a blue and white plaid cotton shirt. A brown suede jacket hung casually from his lean frame. Lumbering under the weight of what he carried in his arms, Marc spotted Caitlin as soon as he entered the room and immediately headed for her desk, throwing her his half-smile.

"For you," he announced as he set his gift smack in the middle of her desk on top of papers and open files. "Happy Halloween."

"Is that wonderful, or what?" Debra exclaimed before Caitlin could respond.

"Or what is more like it," Caitlin said, laughing at the outrageously large pumpkin with its happy, acrylic face. "You do know we're into November?"

"Okay then happy *belated* Halloween.

"Did you do this yourself?"

"Sure did. Like it? Most men bring flowers or candy. I tend to scoff at the conventional."

"Apparently." Caitlin smiled. "But most men don't bring their agents anything. They tend to think the commission is sufficient."

"This really is good. Very good," Debra said, running her fingers across the shiny face. "Do you paint? Other than pumpkins, I mean."

"I used to. Not any more." Marc answered softly. "Except for a pumpkin now and then," he added lightly.

Amelia walked over to examine Marc's gift. "Gallagher," she mused out loud. "The builder?"

"Guilty," Marc answered.

"How'd you know?" Caitlin asked. "Marc, meet Amelia and Debra. Ladies, this is Marc Gallagher."

"His signature." Amelia pointed to the name almost hidden in the creases of the pumpkin's face.

Square block letters, small and precise, were so carefully printed that they actually became part of the art work. Painted thinly in red, it simply looked like part of the mouth. Caitlin studied the signature and then looked back up at Marc. She'd seen that name before, painted in exactly the same way. But where?

"Shall we go?" Caitlin asked. She stood up and put on her coat. "You guys take good care of him for me," she said, patting the top of the pumpkin.

"Your car or mine?" Marc asked once they were in the parking lot.

Caitlin was about to say she'd drive, as she did with most clients; she'd learned early on that driving was an important, subtle, way of maintaining control. But when she spotted the forest green Jaguar, she couldn't help herself. "Is that yours? I didn't see it when we were at the beach."

"It was in the shop. I hitched a ride with Adam. Why, would you have been nicer to me if you'd seen it?"

"Maybe. It's absolutely my favorite car. And, my favorite color. Do you mind if we take it?"

"On one condition." Marc tossed his keys to her and headed for the passenger side. "You drive."

Twilight had already started to set it. Nightfall in New England always came too early in November, so as much as Caitlin wanted to cruise around town, getting the feel of the Jag, she took Marc directly to the Winslow property.

They walked through the wooded acreage as far as the brook, dried leaves crunching beneath their feet. It was sunless and damp, and Caitlin shivered in her thin trench coat. "It's not officially on the market yet. There's been a lot of controversy around the property. But it was all settled last week and it's now ready to sell. A friend of mine knows the family. If you're interested, we should act fast."

"It seems perfect, Cate. How many acres? Wetlands? And what kind of controversy?"

"Thirty-five, some, and it's a long story." Caitlin's teeth were beginning to chatter.

"You're chilled right through." Marc put his arm around her and headed toward the car. "I happen to know a little place about ten miles from here with the best homemade soup. You can tell me everything over dinner."

The restaurant was what Caitlin would expect to find in England, or maybe Ireland—a small, dimly lit room nearly overpowered by the largeness of the dark booths, the wood gleaming from decades of lemon oil. The aroma of freshly baked bread permeated the air, and Caitlin found herself hungrier than she'd been in ages.

"So tell me about the property," Marc said as soon as their

minestrone soup was served.

"Well, if popularity is important to you, this is not the piece to buy. The people in the area don't want to see this land developed. All of Riverside's farms are disappearing. The farmers keep selling off the land and new subdivisions are taking their place. You can't blame them, the landowners, they just want the best price for their property and the only way they're going to get it is if it's approved for development."

"That's understandable." Marc broke off a piece of bread and dunked it in his soup. Such an ordinary action, yet something about it gave Caitlin a rush. Eating with him like this felt so natural...she shivered and drew her coat tighter around her shoulders.

"You still cold?" Mark asked, touching her hand.

"Just a shiver. The soup's helping." Caitlin let the spoonful of warm liquid and vegetables work its way down her throat before continuing. "Anyway," she said, "this Winslow property was the proverbial last straw for a lot of people in town. Mr. Winslow—he has to be eighty-five if he's a day and all he wants to do is sell his farm and move to Florida—well, he went in for a zone change. He knew he wouldn't get what the property's really worth unless it could be developed. He had a buyer all lined up. The neighbors went wild, fought it every inch of the way. It's been two years now. The original developer backed out, bought another piece. But Mr. Winslow kept at it. Finally, he got all the approvals. Wetlands was the final straw. He agreed to preserve ten acres of what he considered perfectly good developable land in order to get their stamp of approval."

"So it's on the market now?"

"Not officially. It's been a long battle. He's roaring mad because nobody in town lifted a finger to support him and now some developer is going to walk in and profit from all his trouble. Obviously, he'll profit too, but that seems to be beside the point. I think he'd be happy selling to someone from out of town. He'd see it as poetic justice."

"It's a great piece. Let me do some research. Look at it again in the daytime. Meanwhile, see what he wants for it."

Caitlin smiled. This would mean a hefty commission if she could pull it off. And then maybe Marc would list the houses with her when they were built.

Marc interrupted her thoughts. "So, how have you been? I've thought about you. A lot."

"You have?"

"I have." He smiled at Caitlin. "There's just something about you. I felt it the first minute I looked up and saw you, at the beach, digging your toes into the sand. Something vulnerable. And familiar. But then Lady Ice made her frigid appearance."

"Sorry about that." Caitlin reached over and touched his hand. "I'm just going through a rough time. Or at least, I was. Things seem to be better now. I don't mean to be that way. Lady Ice. It's not the real me, if you know what I mean."

"Well that's good," Marc said. "So...how's Derrick?"

"Okay. Why?" Why did he have to go and spoil the mood?

"Just asking. You still seeing him?"

"I'm not exactly seeing him." Why couldn't she just come out and admit she was dating Derrick? That's what she was doing, wasn't it? Dating. Seeing. Making love to him. Letting him move into her life.

"You're not?"

"Well, yeah, I guess I am. He's nice. He reminds me of David."

"So I understand," Marc said. "According to Josie, a little too much so."

Damn Josie, Caitlin thought. She should mind her own business. "That's a hard thing for her to judge," Caitlin said, "seeing as she never knew David. And I probably exaggerated. You know, added a little drama to the whole thing."

Marc studied her for a minute, his cobalt eyes piercing her veneer. "I doubt it. Anyway, be careful." Marc hesitated a minute and then plunged in. "Is there enough room in your life for another interest?"

Caitlin knew exactly what he meant. She could feel the last few minutes building to this point. "There's enough room for a friend," she finally answered.

"Friend is fine," Marc smiled. "It's certainly a good place to start."

Caitlin wrapped her hands around her hot mug of coffee. She didn't need the complication of Marc Gallagher in her life. And, yet, she hadn't said no.

Chapter Twenty-One

Only two weeks into December and already Connecticut had been paralyzed by a major snowstorm. The Farmers Almanac was predicting the harshest winter New England had seen in eleven years. Piled high against buildings, the soft fresh snow seemed embracing, even protective, reflecting all that was right with the world. But then it became crusted and dirty, dotted with sand and bits of black grime, an ugly reminder of how life could play cruel jokes, of how quickly things could turn around. New cover was needed for Christmas.

As usual, the holidays were frenzied and everyone complained how impossible it was to get everything done. Everyone but Caitlin, who found that this year there were too many hours in each day and not enough ways to keep busy. Work had all but come to a halt and the Christmases she'd known in the past had virtually disappeared. There would be no spectacular Christmas Eve dinner for family and close friends—she couldn't even imagine hosting such a dinner this year—and there was no need to shop herself silly, looking for those perfect extra gifts that always turned out to be the hit of her gift-giving. There was no David or Maryanne to fill the house with noise and anticipation. No Jessica or Jason to buy extravagant toys for. And barely a Liz to keep her up on the latest gift trends and who should be expecting what from their husbands. Although Caitlin had fooled herself into thinking her grieving had passed, there was no way to fill the chasm that David's death had created. The greatest evidence of that was the return of the large brown package.

When the UPS truck arrived, Caitlin's spirits soared. An unexpected gift was always fun. But when she saw her own handwriting on the brown wrapper and the impersonal stamp that read Refused--Return to Sender, Caitlin felt as though a knife had sliced through her heart. Even though Maryanne hadn't answered any of her letters over the past months, Caitlin still held out hope for their relationship, praying that a Christmas gift might melt Maryanne's resistance, if even just a little.

She sat in the living room for hours, until the light in the sky grew dim and the house became dark, clutching the unopened package, remembering last Christmas. She and Maryanne had become collaborators, trying to surprise David with a new desk and chair for his study. He was always so hard to surprise, so aware of all that was going on. They giggled for weeks, trying to come up with an elaborate scheme to keep him out of the house while the furniture was being delivered on Christmas Eve, and then out of the room until Christmas morning.

Caitlin would never know for sure if David was truly surprised, but she and Maryanne believed he was as they opened up the door to his study on Christmas morning and witnessed the startled look on his face. And believing was enough.

All their gifts to him were joint—a desk set, stamp holder, pen and pencil holder—anything and everything for his desk, including gold-colored paper clips. They'd had weeks of laughter and secrets between them shopping for the man they both loved. It was one of the most special times in their relationship. Could Maryanne really just walk away from her now, from what they had begun to build and share? The returned gift said she could.

In so many ways, Derrick was a real comfort to her this Christmas. At times Caitlin truly believed she was in love with him and that she could be happy again with him by her side. But other times, his very presence only served to heighten her sense of aloneness. He was too much like David, and, yet, not enough like him. The occasional dark moods, the blaze of anger when challenged, the secrets he seemed to harbor—all of these were specific to Derrick Secor. Sometimes he frightened her. But because the fear was hard to tap into, too difficult to identify, she generally just brushed it away.

Strangely, during the entire Christmas season, the closest she came to feeling a real part of the holiday spirit was the one afternoon she spent with Marc. He called her at home on the Wednesday before Christmas.

"How are you doing?" he asked. "I was sitting here thinking about you. I know how rough that first Christmas alone can be."

"I'm all right, really. But it's nice of you to be concerned." She kept her voice distant, impersonal. It was the only way she could lie effectively.

"It's okay to let yourself feel the pain, Cate. As a matter of fact, it's good. Feeling it makes it real and then you can put it aside. Finally, eventually, you'll get over it. Not completely, but enough."

How unlike Derrick, Caitlin thought, who wants me to pretend there is no pain, no lost past. "Really, I'm doing okay," she said. "By the way, Mr. Winslow seems agreeable to your new terms. I'm sure he'll sign after the first of the year."

"That's great, but I didn't call on business. This is the holiday season. Time for good cheer and helping others. Business can wait. Are you up to the true spirit of Christmas, and can you spare a few hours tomorrow?"

"I think so. On both counts." Caitlin answered cautiously. "But exactly what am I getting into?"

"The spirit of Christmas. You'll see. Make sure you wear jeans, sneakers, and a warm sweater."

"Are we playing Santa Claus?" Caitlin's voice perked up at the expectation.

"Not exactly," Marc laughed. "But close enough. I'll pick you up at your house, eleven sharp."

* * *

"Where's the Jag?" Caitlin asked the next morning as Marc held open the door to an outdated station wagon brimming with large boxes.

"The lady loves me only for my car!"

"I don't love you at all." Caitlin tossed him a smile. "But where is it? What's this?"

"This," Marc said as he started the ignition, "is a station wagon."

"No, really? I couldn't exactly identify it. A little beat up, isn't it?"

Marc laughed, a deep, hearty laugh. "Just slightly," he said, poking his finger through a slit in the upholstery. "I use it for hauling stuff. Sometimes one of my guys will borrow it. It's the extra car."

128

"And what are we hauling today?" Caitlin asked, turning around to look at all the boxes.

"Food, non-perishables. For St. Anne's House in Hartford. That's where we're going. To work in their soup kitchen. They're always short-handed around the holidays."

St. Anne's House was little more than a store front in the city's north end. The street was deserted except for a few men huddled in doorways, trying to stay warm. Marc pulled up in front, careful to avoid the broken glass near the curb.

"The guys in the kitchen will haul the boxes in later," Marc told her. "The doors to this place are going to open any minute, so let's get going. You'll work harder in the next two hours than you've ever worked in your life. And you'll never feel more satisfied."

The small kitchen was filled with the aroma of homemade vegetable soup. "Meet Gus," Marc said, nodding toward a burly man stirring the contents of a huge metal pot. "Gus used to cook for the army. Now he only cooks for 150 people every day. I can't remember the last time he took any time off. And this is Eddie. He's been with St. Anne's about three years now. Guys, this is my friend, Cate Saunders."

Gus wiped his hands on his clean white apron before grabbing Caitlin's hand and sharking it vigorously. Eddie continued cutting bread, filling all of the small wicker baskets in front of him with an equal number of slices. He nodded at Caitlin, his black face gleaming with sweat.

"Almost time," Eddie said to Marc.

It seemed to Caitlin that they were waiting for a play to start, all props in place, curtain about to rise.

"You'll get the hang of it," Marc said, taking Caitlin by the hand, leading her into the outer room, which was cold and only slightly larger than the kitchen. There were four Formica-topped tables, each with four wooden chairs; the counter sat an additional twelve people.

"We can only feed twenty-eight people at one time," Marc explained. "When one person leaves, we let another one in. Sister Agnes, here, keeps things organized and moving. Maria," he nodded toward the small Puerto Rican girl wiping down one of the four tables, "will work the tables and we'll work the counter. When she calls for a set-up, Sister Agnes will bring out a bowl of soup, followed by a sandwich, and you'll give Maria the drinks. Plus, you'll work this end of the counter. I'll work the other end. As soon as one person leaves, clean off their space and start again. We close the doors at 1:45 sharp."

Caitlin saluted him. "Aye, Aye, sir."

"And don't let any of them take advantage," Sister Agnes ordered. "Only one drink, no matter what they say. We've got chocolate milk today. They can have it, but they can't have a hot drink, too. Only one! And no exchanging desserts." She waddled back into the kitchen, her wide girth barely fitting through the door frame.

Eddie came out and unlocked the door.

Twenty-eight people filed in noiselessly and sat down. Only a few talked quietly with each other. They'd been lined up outside in the cold; now all they wanted to do was eat. As she began serving drinks to the men at the counter, Caitlin had to keep from reeling under the stench that came from the man sitting directly in front of her. He wore mismatched gloves and a torn army jacket. His auburn beard was long and knotted; a striped wool hat kept his long hair back off his face. The creases in his face were filled with particles of grime. He ate slowly and with impeccable manners. When he finished, he folded his paper napkin as though it was made of precious linen and placed in neatly on top of his Styrofoam plate, nodded at her, and left.

"Chocolate milk," said the 40ish curly-haired man who immediately slipped into the vacated spot at the counter. "Haven't had one of those since I was a kid." Caitlin handed him the small carton and a paper cup. His hand shook as he pushed the cup aside. He opened the carton, put it to his mouth, and drank its contents in one gulp, leaving a small moustache of brown on his upper lip. "That was real good." He winked at Caitlin. He couldn't have been more than thirty-five. "I'm real cold, though. How about a cup of coffee while I'm waiting for that hot soup?"

"I'm not supposed to," Caitlin stammered, backing away from the counter, hoping distance would help her be callous enough to refuse him. "Only one drink to a customer."

The man laughed. Not a cruel street laugh, but a light, gay laugh as though something really was funny. "Well, now, I'm not exactly a customer. I think you have to pay to be one of those, but I really would like coffee. The Sister will never know, she's in the back ladling soup."

Caitlin looked around. He was right. She poured the coffee and slid it in front of him. "Merry Christmas," she said and then turned to the next man, giving him his choice of dessert.

"Are all these people homeless?" Caitlin asked Marc when they had a moment to catch their breath. "Some look as well dressed as us, like that guy over there in the ski jacket."

"We don't ask any questions. Anyone who comes in that front door gets fed."

"The women bother me the most," Caitlin said. "Maybe because there are so few of them, it just seems sadder." She was thinking about the two black women who had just left the counter. One in particular was well-dressed, makeup expertly applied to her smooth skin. She sat down, her shoulders slightly stooped, her eyes never looking up. She nibbled on a piece of bread, sipping the hot tea. "I'm so embarrassed." Caitlin heard the young woman tell her friend. "I never thought I'd come to this." The women's words haunted Caitlin. She wanted to take her home, make life right for her again. Instead, Caitlin gave her a bowl of hot soup and tried not to stare.

At exactly 1:45, Sister Agnes shooed the last person out and locked the door. Buckets of hot water bubbling with Lysol seemed to appear out of nowhere. Clean-up included wiping down tables, walls and counters with the disinfectant. Maria took a paper napkin to wrap up the few stales donuts that were left on the desert tray and tucked them inside her coat pocket. "My kids love 'em," she grinned. "They have sweet teeth."

By 2:30, Caitlin and Marc were on their way home, every bone in her body aching for a hot bath. "You look beat," Marc said as he pulled into her driveway. He touched her hair gently. "I didn't really prepare you for today. Are you okay?"

"Yeah...I am," Caitlin answered slowly. And she really was okay. "This was good for me. Thanks. I'm always giving lip service to how we should contribute, help others out. This gave me a chance to do it. You dropped me into the middle of a world I barely knew existed. Intellectually I knew it existed. But not emotionally. You know what I mean?"

"Yeah, I do. That's exactly how I felt the first time. The experience grows on you, gets under your skin. You can come with me any time you want."

Caitlin looked at Marc a long time, trying to sort out her various impressions of this man. "You know," she told him haltingly, "when I first met you, at the beach, I thought your intensity, that way you have of probing, of poking a stick right through the thin part of a person's skin, was meant as a sneer, a way of mocking others." She looked at him questioningly, wanting him to confirm her next thought. "I think I read you wrong."

"That you did," Marc said, stroking Caitlin's hair again, moving closer to her. "It's just that I hate walls. More than anything, I hate those defensive, defiant walls people build for themselves and then hide behind. Knocking them down takes so much effort."

"And you have no walls? No secrets?"

"Ah, she wants to know my secrets," Marc said in a feigned Russian accent, twirling an imaginary handlebar moustache. "My secrets aren't walls, because I know that they're there. And besides, my walls have doors, so I can go back and forth at will. And sexy comrade can come in if she pleases."

"I think that was a wall right there," Caitlin smiled. "Humor won't let you off the hook."

"You're right," he said. "I'm much better with other people's barriers than I am with my own. But I am trying. Josie says it's my 'karmic challenge this time around,' whatever that's supposed to mean. I shouldn't joke. I know exactly what that's supposed to mean. And, believe it or not, I think she's right."

"Well, the only thing I believe in right now is a long, hot bath." Caitlin buttoned her coat and opened up the car door. "See you." She waved, walking toward the front door.

"Wait!" Marc hollered. He jumped out of the car and grabbed a large burlap bag from the back of the station wagon. After unlocking the door, she watched as he struggled up the walk with the awkward bundle, pushing past her to deposit it in her foyer. Gently, he lifted off the brown fabric to reveal the largest white poinsettia she'd ever seen. Caitlin laughed out loud, touching the small green balls hanging from the stems.

"I thought you might have forgotten to get a tree this year."

"Didn't want one."

"So...this'll put a smile on your holiday. Enjoy your bath." He kissed her on the cheek and left.

An hour later, the phone rang. "Feeling better?" Marc asked. I wanted to bribe you with the poinsettia before asking you to help me out again. Are you game?"

"I don't know." Caitlin was surprised at how good it felt to hear his voice again. "What now?"

"I'm working on a deal that would mean shelter, nice shelter, for homeless folks. If it comes through, it'll mean a lot of hard work from a lot of talented people. All gratis. We'll be refurbishing an old hotel, and we'll have to have it done a year from this spring to meet all of the funding requirements. I thought maybe you'd like to be in on it. It'll mean a lot of scut work. Maybe you could also help with some of the design work."

"Are you trying to bribe me with the design part? It sounds exciting, but I couldn't. I'd only make a fool of myself. I have no formal education, only have a few good ideas, once in awhile."

"Ideas are what we'll need, Cate. Good, fresh, practical ideas. Leave the technical stuff to me. Say you'll do it."

"I'll think about it. If your funding comes through. And I hope it does. Even if I'm not involved."

"But you will be. Merry Christmas, Cate."

Marc hung up before she could answer.

Tripping over her terry cloth robe, Caitlin struggled to move the poinsettia into a corner of the family room. She would surround it with presents, she decided, glad once again she refused to let Derrick talk her into a Christmas tree. The poinsettia was perfect. It did make her smile. And so did the ornament she tucked among the lush leaves—a small, perfectly shaped scallop shell.

Chapter Twenty-Two

Caitlin would have liked to let Christmas slip by unnoticed, but at the last minute she decided to fill up some of the empty space on Christmas Day by having a brunch for Derrick, Adam, Josie and Courtney. It was something different from the big dinners of Christmas past and a perfect solution for the five of them, each looking, as they were, for a way to normalize the holidays during a time when their lives were anything but normal.

Derrick arrived early and surrounded the poinsettia with brightly wrapped presents, teasing Caitlin about how it was a poor excuse for a tree. He never knew where, or who, it had come from. "I bought so many gifts," he laughed, "just so everyone would focus on them and assume there's really a tree here. You know, pile the presents real high and pretend they're blocking a small tree. I even bought some pine-scented spray!"

As soon as everyone was there, they sat on the family room floor opening up gifts. While Derrick had spent some time with Josie over the past few months, mostly when she'd stopped by to see Caitlin, he'd only met Adam a couple of times, and never Courtney. Still, he purchased gifts for everyone, showering them with expensive items he knew they would love. For Josie there was a silver bracelet inlaid with turquoise stones, and a sterling rope chain to hold her crystal. "It's a beautiful crystal," Derrick said "but that chain doesn't do it justice. Hope you don't mind my saying so."

"How could I mind when you've replaced it with something so lovely?" Josie crossed the room and kissed him on the cheek. "Thank you, Derrick. It was really thoughtful."

He had scoured the shops for Courtney, buying her everything on a teenager's list, from a watch to CDs and DVDs to a pair of long triangle earrings handmade in sterling silver. For Adam, there were Broadway tickets he and Josie could use during the college's Christmas break, and a pair of leather gloves lined with cashmere.

Derrick seemed to have tremendous fun watching everyone open their gifts, especially Caitlin. He sat at her feet, beaming, watching her open each beautifully wrapped package, like a young boy waiting for approval. His last gift to her was a twelve-inch crystal Christmas tree. Hanging delicately from its branches were miniature glass ornaments, hand blown in a myriad of pastel colors. "Much better than a poinsettia, don't you think?"

"It's beautiful, Derrick. Everything is beautiful. You've been unbelievably generous." Caitlin smiled at him.

"Catie, do you think that's all I'd give you? A bunch of clothes and a crystal tree. Look at it closely," he ordered. "Go ahead, look."

When she looked again, Caitlin couldn't imagine how she missed it the first time. Woven across the branches like a strand of garland, Caitlin discovered a diamond and gold bracelet.

"Oh, Catie!" Josie gasped, "it's gorgeous, absolutely gorgeous."

Caitlin held out her hand so Derrick could fasten the bracelet on her wrist. Tears filled her eyes. "Derrick, I've never in my life owned anything so beautiful. But I feel bad. You've given us all so much, especially me, and my gifts are so small by comparison, a fountain pen, a tie—"

"I love my gifts," he said, "but, mostly, I love making you happy. And you are happy, Catie, aren't you?"

Before Caitlin could answer, Josie stood up and practically shouted, "Derrick! How could I forget? I have one more thing for you. Catie, where's my purse? I put the gift in there."

"Finding the purse will be one thing," Adam chuckled. "Finding something in it will be quite another. That thing should have wheels."

"Here it is," Josie said, handing a small, beautifully wrapped package to Derrick. "From the three of us." She smiled over at Adam and Courtney and then watched carefully as Derrick opened his present.

"What the—? Well, this is very nice." Derrick's voice was careful and controlled as ran his hands over the rich, black leather. "Thank you."

"Catie says you're always jotting things down in a notebook—or checking out what's already there—she's not quite sure—and I figured maybe it was time for a new one. I hope it's the right size. Is it? Let me see yours. Let's compare."

"I...I don't have it with me."

"Yes, you do. I saw you slip it into your pocket this morning," Caitlin said as she picked up stray pieces of wrapping paper and stuffed them into an empty box. "Maybe he's some kind of spy," she said, winking at Courtney.

"Maybe I just like a little privacy." Derrick stood and started helping Caitlin clean up ribbon and paper and stack presents around the poinsettia. "These women, they have to know everything," he said to Adam. "Can't have a private thought with them around."

"You're right about that," Adam smiled, putting his arm around Josie and planting a big kiss on her cheek. "But then again, what would I do with my own thoughts?"

"Write them down in a little notebook and turn them into your memoirs? That could be hot." Josie pinched Adam's behind.

"Mom!" Courtney squealed. "Stop it. You're always embarrassing me." She slipped a new CD into her portable player, stuck the headset on, and tucked into a corner of the couch, tapping her feet to the beat of music only she could hear.

The atmosphere in the room was charged with tension as the adults finished cleaning up, all the while making small talk about the weather, such a beautiful Christmas, wonderful presents, thank you so much...

"I'll get the food, while you all finish what you're doing," Caitlin said.

"I'll help," Josie said following on her heels. "Ouch," she said once they were alone. "He was touchy—"

"You shouldn't have done that."

"What? Give him a present."

"You know what, Josie. You were goading him."

"Well, don't you want to know the secret of the little black book?"

"Yes, but..."

"Is it really in his pocket?"

"I saw him put it there."

"I think we should knock him out and read it and see what all the mystery's about."

"Let's just have a nice day," Caitlin warned. She shook her arm slightly so that her new diamond bracelet fell back down against her wrist. "It's beautiful, isn't it?"

"It is, Catie. I just hope it's worth the price."

"Josie—"

"I'm sorry," Josie said, making a zipping motion across her lips. "Truly. I'll behave."

As it turned out, they actually had a good time over brunch, which lasted for hours. They sat around the dining room table telling silly stories from their past, Courtney begging for one tale after another, taking pleasure in the fact that these seemingly together adults had gone through the same adolescent agonies she was beginning to face. Eventually, the stories wore down; their faces were tired from smiling, and their stomachs hurt from too much laughter and much too much food.

Adam was the first to stand up and stretch. "If we don't move from this table, I may just fall asleep right here, with my face flat down in the few remaining crumbs."

"There are no crumbs remaining on your side," Josie laughed, patting his round belly. "You're a healthy eater, dear, that's what I love about you."

"How about a game of Monopoly?" Caitlin asked after they'd all pitched in and cleared the dining room table. "We could light a fire in the living room and play on the floor." It was something she and David used to do on long winter nights.

"Sounds great," Josie said. "Adam you get the wood. Courtney, you start rolling newspaper, do it nice and tight, so the fire will catch."

Adam stood up at her command and saluted. "Yes, Miz Josie. Right away, Miz Josie." Then he looked at Courtney and winked. "Why do we take this abuse?"

Courtney giggled and started crumpling up pieces of newspaper.

"Monopoly?" Derrick said. "That's a kid's game. Why would you waste time playing that?"

"I thought it'd be fun, a nice way to finish off the day." Caitlin shrugged, feeling slightly silly. "David and I used to—"

"It's no kid's game," Josie said. "It's a game of power and money, for people with grit. And I'll beat your pants off." She rubbed her hands together and assumed an evil grin.

Derrick didn't even seem to hear Josie "So, was good ole' Dave any good at the game?"

"Why? Does it matter?" Josie asked as Caitlin went to look for the game.

"It was just a question," he said between tightly set teeth. "Don't make anything more of it."

Josie would have probably pushed further, but her attention was drawn to the painting over the mantel. When Caitlin returned, Monopoly game in hand, Josie looked at her inquisitively. "Catie, all the times I've been here, I've never been in this room."

"I know. It's kind of like an Irish parlor, off to the side and used only when the priest comes calling. David and I used it a lot in the winter, because of the fireplace. I don't know why they didn't put one in the family room."

"It's a wonderful picture," she said, her eyes riveted to the painting.

"Isn't it? I love it."

"How long have you had it?"

"I don't know. I was still single when I bought it. David and I were married eight years—so maybe, ten years ago—I bought it at one of those summer art shows in Mystic. Why?"

"Just wondering. It's beautiful work. Tempera. It's a difficult medium. Did you buy it directly from the artist? Was he at the show?"

"I don't know. I can't remember. Why?"

"Just wondering. Think hard. Try."

"God, Josie, I don't know. I'm sure I did. All the artists are usually there, hoping to sell. I fell in love with the painting right away. It touched some childhood chord in me...the girl on the pond, sitting there on her sled watching the other kids skate, the dog prancing around, the snow flakes drifting down...and look, now I live on water just like that. When the kids are out there, I feel like my painting has come to life. Maybe the picture was foretelling!" Caitlin poked Josie in the ribs. "Maybe it was leading me toward my destiny!"

They all laughed. "Mom would go for that one," Courtney said. "According to her, nothing is an accident."

"Maybe is right," Josie added. "Maybe more than you think."

"Are we going to play Monopoly or discuss paintings all day?" Adam interrupted before Caitlin could quiz Josie on her last remark. "Fire's lit and I'm ready to go." He settled himself on the floor and began setting up the game.

Outside, a soft dusting of snow was coloring their world white. Every now and then a gust of wind rattled the windows and Caitlin would look up to assure herself that she was safe, and then she would inch a little closer toward the fire. She looked at the friends around her. New people in her life...in her new life. They'd found a way to belong--

to make lemonade, as Josie would say, out of lemons. No, it wasn't Christmas Past. But, still, it was good. The afternoon passed quickly.

Caitlin took the game seriously, buying up property and hotels whenever she could. Before they knew it, she was the major landlord and they we all paying her rent, including Derrick, who was intent on winning and kept making trades with Adam. The men had just decided to change the rules and go into partnership when Josie looked at her watch.

"Holy Christ," she exclaimed "Cow, I mean cow, sorry. I'm trying hard to watch my language. It's going to be my New Year's resolution, so I might as well start now." She jumped up and grabbed Adam's hand. "We have to go. I promised Greg I'd bring Courtney home by six. Boy, will he be pissed. Look at the time. And it looks like the snow's getting heavy. Let's go guys. Now!"

Adam looked at Courtney. "You heard the woman, let's move it. By the way, Josie dear, will pissed still be an acceptable word after the first of the year?" He laughed his deep laugh. "Courtney and I will take bets on how long this resolution lasts." He turned and wrapped his short, solid arms around Caitlin. "Goodbye, Catie dear, thanks for having us to your beautiful home and for sharing your holiday. I love Christmas. Always have. Could never understand why my parents didn't have the same sentiment!" He reached over and shook Derrick's hand. "Derrick, good seeing you again. And you're one hell of a game player. Remind me never to bet against you."

Derrick said his goodbyes and closed the door behind them. "I thought they'd never leave." He put his arm around Caitlin's waist and kissed her hair. "Mmmm. Smells good. You always smell good. I could eat you up."

Caitlin wriggled out of his hold. "Why don't you like Josie? She's such a neat person."

"Who says I don't? Look at the gifts I bought her. Besides, it's Josie who doesn't like me," Derrick said. "I've certainly tried. I've turned on the charm, high voltage, but it doesn't seem to make a dent."

"She loved your gifts, and I know she really appreciated everything you did, especially for Courtney. But you're right, charm doesn't work with Josie. Especially if she thinks you're trying to be charming. She likes real. Just be yourself."

"Yeah, sure." Derrick shrugged. "Anyway, forget Josephine, forget everything. Except me." He nuzzled her neck and then pulled her over to the sofa. "Sit here. I have something for you. I've been waiting all day for a private minute with you. I thought we'd have more time this morning, but they got here so early. Close your eyes," Derrick ordered. "I'll be right back."

In the minute he was gone, the door bell rang. Of all people, there stood Liz, draped in an ankle-length mink coat.

"Liz! Merry Christmas. I never expected...how'd you get away?"

"Steve brought the kids to his sister's. I told him I felt a headache coming on. It wasn't really a lie. I'd definitely have one before the end of the night if I had to go there. I waited until I saw her leave. I hope you don't mind, my being here. Can I come in?"

"Of course you can. I'm really happy to see you, just surprised." Caitlin backed away from the door.

Liz shivered and wrapped the coat tighter around her body as she stepped into the house. She looked small and vulnerable and extremely uncomfortable. She shifted from one foot to the other and then thrust a small silver box toward Caitlin. "Here. I just couldn't let Christmas go by...it's a silk scarf..."

"Oh, Liz...thanks." Caitlin slipped the ribbon off the box and opened the gift. "It's beautiful," she said, draping the emerald length of silk around her neck. "I have something for you, too. I bought it...well, you know...just in case."

She took Liz's gift from the bench in the hallway, where Maryanne's package still sat. "Open it later. You can hide it for a while, and then you can tell Steve you got it yourself, on sale or something."

They both stood awkwardly, hating the distance between them. "So...can you stay a while? Can I get you some tea? Some juice?"

"No. Thanks. I can't. Steve could be back any minute."

"It's beautiful, Liz," Caitlin said, fingering the mink coat.

"Thanks."

"Okay, open your eyes," Derrick announced, coming into the room with a small package and a vase filled with white roses. He stopped suddenly. "What the—? Liz? Well, I'll be. You're a sight for sore eyes." He put down the vase and stuck the package in his pocket. "Great coat." He touched the fur approvingly. "Female pelts. Look at the sheen. Big bucks! Santa was certainly good to you. I hope you're going to be good back."

"I'm always good. That's why I got it. Do you really like it, Catie?" Liz whirled around.

"I do. It suits you. And it's just what you've always wanted. I'm very happy for you."

"Catie, I have to go. I miss you. I miss you so much. So do the kids. We've got to work things out, get them back to the way they were.

Derrick, see what you can do." She gave Caitlin a quick hug and went through the motion of kissing her on the cheek. But the kiss landed in the air, as it always did.

"That was exhausting," Caitlin said after Liz breezed out. "I almost don't know why she bothered to come over, she was so uneasy the whole time she was here."

"Isn't it obvious? She had to show off that coat of hers. It was eating her up alive, enough to chance the old man's fury. I don't blame her; it really is some coat!" Derrick said.

"That can't be the only reason. I'm sure she misses me as much as I miss her. This whole thing with Steve really frosts me."

"Well, you know what the terms are. And they certainly wouldn't bother me. I'd pick Liz over Josie any day. That woman's no day at the park."

"See, I knew you didn't like Josie. But I do. And I'm not going to choose between them."

"Whatever," Derrick said impatiently. "It'll all work out. And I just might have the solution right here." He patted his pocket. "Catie, please, come over here. Sit on the sofa next to me."

Caitlin sat down and buried her nose is the vase of flowers. "The roses are lovely, Derrick, thank you."

Derrick took Caitlin's hand and gently pressed it to his lips. "Catie, I've never been happier than the time I've spent with you. I don't want it to end. I want to be with you always. I want to love you and protect you and take care of you. I want you to be mine. I want you to marry me." He pulled the box from his pocket and handed it Caitlin.

She was too stunned to move.

"Open it," Derrick smiled. "Go ahead, open it." He began to remove the bow and red wrapping.

"Derrick, I can't ...I'm sorry...it's too soon."

When she wouldn't open the box, Derrick opened it for her. "Four karats, total, Catie. Only the best for you."

"It's stunning," she whispered, looking at the large oval diamond with six channel-set diamonds on both sides. She was almost afraid to touch it. David had never bought her an engagement ring. They'd decided to put the money toward a house instead. Her wedding band, sprinkled with small diamonds, had always been enough. More than enough.

"Put it on, Catie. Say yes and marry me."

"I can't." Caitlin got up and walked across the room. "I'm not saying no. I'm just not saying yes. I'm too confused, too tired." She ran her fingers through her hair. "You shouldn't have done this. Not today, not on my first Christmas alone."

Derrick walked over and pulled her to him. "I only wanted to make you happy. And I know I can, Catie. I'd do anything for you. Anything. You wear this while you think about it. I know your answer will be yes." He went to slip the ring on her finger. "But you'll have to take this one off." He touched her wedding band, and put his engagement ring in her palm. "You can't have it both ways."

Caitlin took a deep breath and wiped the tears from her eyes. "I can't deal with this. Not tonight. You shouldn't have done this." She fingered the band of diamonds encircling her wrist. "The bracelet was enough."

"You're tired." He told her. "Let's go to bed. Things will look different in the morning."

They undressed silently and climbed into bed, Caitlin wishing now she'd never let Derrick start sleeping in her room. It'd been a gradual shift, ever since Halloween when he'd climbed in uninvited. And now, on this Christmas night, when the world outside was blanketed in freshly fallen snow and the heat pumped rhythmically throughout the house, Caitlin did not want this man beside her. She felt cold and empty and horribly disloyal. And it was on this Christmas night, when sleep came fitfully and she cried silently for the life that was lost to her, that she had the dream for the first time. Each time it came in the succeeding weeks, it became more real, until Caitlin actually came to believe that she took nighttime journeys to the past, with David as her guide.

Chapter Twenty-Three

In her dream, David would come for her just as she was about to fall asleep. Or was she already asleep? It was hard to know. Her heart would quicken as she sensed someone in the room, feeling a presence at the foot of her bed; but her body was so heavy, she couldn't move no matter how hard she tried. She would open her eyes, ready to scream. But no sound came from her mouth. And then she would see David, his hand outstretched.

It was always the same.

"Don't be afraid, Catiedid. Take my hand and come with me."

"You look good, David," she told him each time. "Is heaven a nice place?" And he always gave her the same answer. "Real nice, Catie. You'll like it when you get here. It helps prepare you for the next time."

"What next time, David? What next time?" This part always made her anxious. She wanted to know. She wanted answers. But he wouldn't give her any. He just held her hand tightly as they walked through time.

"Shhh. Watch now, Catie. Watch and remember."

They walked through what seemed to be a long hallway of rooms, each separated, not by a door, but by a thin veil, a gossamer curtain, through which only shadows could be seen. At David's request, Caitlin pulled back the first curtain. Everything behind it could be seen clearly now. And what Caitlin saw seemed to be characters acting out a specific life event. Except they weren't characters. And they weren't memories. It was real life, her life. Curtain after curtain, Caitlin walked through pieces of her own past, as though she was walking down the continuum of life, back to the beginning.

She saw segments of the life she and David shared together. There was Maryanne the day she came to live with them. Bold, defiant Maryanne, who needed so much love, especially from her father. Then she saw Maryanne wave goodbye and fade from view. Like a play, she watched the enactment of various scenes: there she was in tears, hiding in the bathroom, crying alone. She didn't want David to know how sad she was. It was the day she'd finally agreed not to have any children. She would never have a baby of her own. Oh, look, Caitlin thought, turning to view another scene—there's the pillow fight we had one night after a stupid argument. Another scene: there they were walking along the beach at sunset, she couldn't quite tell where it was...and then their wedding. How happy they both looked.

She walked through the dimly-lit spaces, looking at the scenes on both sides of her, as though riding a conveyor car through a Disney World exhibit. At the end of each segment, she pulled back yet another curtain. There was Trevor, her high school boyfriend, leaving for the army, and, over to the right, there she was giggling with the girls at Cape Cod. And her mother--there was her mother, sitting on the porch all alone. She was dressed in black. And then Caitlin saw the hearse. "Oh my God, that's when Daddy died."

It seemed like she was moving backward in time, seeing her life in reverse order.

She pulled back the next curtain and there she was, a young girl with long braids. Sitting on a small stool, she was watching her father work. He was making a chest for her dolls to sit on. Why did he look so concerned? He was looking at her—not at the child, but at the adult. It was as though he could see her now and was desperate to tell her something. Why couldn't she hear? He was waving his fist in the air, talking to her, but she couldn't hear his words. "What's he saying?" she asked David frantically. But he didn't answer. "Daddy...Daddy..." Caitlin cried out as she passed the scene of his workshop.

The next curtain revealed an even earlier time. They were all sitting around the dinner table. It must have been a Sunday afternoon. They were still dressed in their good clothes and they were saying grace. Her father raised his wine glass in a toast, and her mother looked across the table at him and smiled. Caitlin remembered that time. He'd just gotten a raise and they were going to spend the money on a real vacation. They were going to take a cottage at the beach for two whole weeks.

Another scene flashed quickly in front of her. Her father was crying. He was holding her and crying as though his heart would break. She was just a baby. She'd caught pneumonia and the doctors held out little hope. That was the night Caitlin had almost died.

Just ahead, she saw her mother lying on a table, bright lights overhead. There were other people in the room. A doctor. And nurses? Her mother's arms remained outstretched until those other people placed something on her chest. Oh, look...it was her. It was Caitlin. She'd just been born.

And then came the last curtain. It looked heavier than the rest. Caitlin reached out to pull it back, just like she had with the others. But she couldn't manage. It was too heavy. "Help me, David. Help me!" she would cry out.

He always let go of her hand, right then, and she imagined he was going to help her push back the curtain. But that's when he would fade away, his words echoing in the room: "Remember, Catie. Remember..."

Alone, without David, the curtain petrified her. She couldn't move and she couldn't pull it back. She always woke up with a start, her heart pounding so hard she could feel it in her throat, his words burning in her head.

Remember what?

Chapter Twenty-Four

Marc called two days after New Year's, insisting that Caitlin meet him at the old Bond Hotel in Hartford.

"Now? Today?" she asked. Somehow it seemed too soon. Mentally hung-over from the holidays and the dreams she'd been having, she was too drained to get involved in anything else.

"Now! Today!" Marc echoed. "We have to start this project right away or chance losing the funding."

"I don't think it's for me. I'm sure you can get someone else to help."

"I'm sure I can, too. But I don't want to. You're perfect for this project. And I think it'd be great for you. Something new to take your mind off your troubles."

So, Josie had been talking to him again. Probably told him all about Derrick's proposal, her problems with Liz. The Dream.

"What troubles? I don't have any troubles to speak of."

"Okay, Lady Ice. I don't mean to tread—"

"So don't."

"All right. Here's the deal. I'll be strictly business. No personal talk, unless you say so. Meet me in an hour?"

"Oh, for Pete's sake," she sighed. "Two. I'll be there in two hours. But no promises. I'm just humoring you." She hated herself for being such a wimp. Why couldn't she just say no?

* * *

"Well, what do you think?" Marc asked as soon as she walked in.

Moving from room to room, it was hard to know what she thought. Doors—where there were doors—were barely on their hinges. Broken windows were haphazardly covered with cardboard and tape; nearly all of the paint was peeling like badly blistered skin, and the small porcelain sinks in each room were stained the color of clay. Yet, it had promise. She could see that.

"We're going to call it Esperanza. It means hope," Mark told her.

"That's nice." You're nice is what she wanted to say. "It could work. It really could." She looked around at the deterioration. "But it's going to take so much..."

"I know. WORK. And lots of it. Loving hands and strong backs. We need as many of them as we can get. We're having a major clean-up party next week to sweep out all this debris." He kicked a beer bottle into a pile of old papers. "By then, Jake Fisher will have a detailed report on the heating system. And Paul will have the bad news on the electrical—Paul Peterson—you'll meet them both, along with the others."

"It really is exciting," Caitlin said as they moved into the huge kitchen area. "My God, this looks pre-war. The question is, which war?" She opened one of the old wooden cabinets, screamed, and jumped back, landing on Marc's foot. A cockroach had crawled out from the dark recesses to claim its space. Marc put his arms around Caitlin's waist in an effort to steady them both, holding onto her a minute longer than necessary.

As Caitlin moved away, a ray of sunlight poked its way through a high transom-style window and bounced off the diamond ring on her right hand, sending rays of color across the ceiling. Marc took hold of her hand and examined the ring. "It's beautiful, Caitlin. David had excellent taste. But, then, why should I be surprised?"

She pulled her hand away and shoved it into the pocket of her slacks. After a week of arguing, Caitlin had finally agreed to wear the diamond on her right hand. She wasn't ready to remove her wedding band, to consciously strip away her marriage to David. But she didn't want to lose Derrick, and he made her feel that that was exactly what would happen if she didn't give in. "It's not from David," she said quietly. "Didn't Josie tell you?"

"Tell me what? Josie and I don't talk that often. And when we do, she makes it a point not to tell me things about you, even when I ask. She believes in self-discovery, or some such nonsense. So what should she have told me?"

Caitlin focused on a large grease spot across the room. "It's an engagement ring. From Derrick." Her voice was low, almost apologetic. She quickly got mad at herself. Why should she apologize? What she did was nobody's business but hers. And Derrick's, of course. She squared her shoulders and forced herself to look directly at Marc, but his face was unreadable, his eyes impassive. An instant later, he was giving her a smile and a gentle kiss on the cheek.

"Well, congratulations. I thought maybe you'd wait for me. But apparently you're in a hurry."

She relaxed her shoulders, unclenched her fists. "No, not really. Derrick is, more than me. But I told him I wouldn't do anything until after June. It's only right. David will be gone a year, June tenth."

"I hope he makes you happy."

They were quiet for a few minutes, not knowing what to say next. Outside, a gang of boys walked by, pushing at one another, joking about girls and what was going to happen next Saturday night.

"Well," Marc said, rubbing his hands together, "it's getting late. And I promised, no personal talk. Why don't we finish the grand tour and get out of here."

As they walked around examining various rooms, Marc talked about the project. "It's the most important thing I've ever worked on. St. Anne's House will own Esperanza. Once we do the design and renovations, we're out of it. The state will help subsidize it. Without government funding, we'd be lost."

"How will it work?" Caitlin asked. "Who will stay here?"

"Women, mostly. And their kids. We'll have some men. The smaller wing will house them. And families. We're going to design four family-style rooms. The goal is to give people a fresh start. To get them back on their feet. They can't be on anything while they're living here: no drugs, no alcohol. If they have a problem, they have to agree to counseling programs. And there'll be random weekly tests. The longest anybody can stay will be eighteen months."

This would be the first residence of its kind in the Hartford area and Marc was determined to make it happen. A safe place for women and children. Maybe when it was done, he'd finally have peace.

"The place will be run totally by the residents," Marc continued. "They'll cook all the meals, keep the place clean, do all the repairs. And they have to get a job within the first three months. That way, after the eighteen months, they should have enough saved to go out on their own. A unique thing about this program is that there'll be childcare. That's a huge problem for homeless women. There's no place to leave their kids while they work. And if they can't work, they can't break the cycle of homelessness. The other great thing is that a couple of the rooms will be turned into classrooms. They'll focus on basic life skills, math, reading, managing money, looking for a job. The folks who live here will have a chance to turn their lives around."

"It sounds wonderful, Marc. Count me in, whatever I can do."

"You'll do plenty, believe me. This is my favorite area. We came in through the side door, so you missed this grand entrance." Marc stopped and let Caitlin take in the full glory of the once-splendid lobby. "We're going to keep as much of the original work as possible," he explained, running his hand along the intricate woodwork. "This will be one of the main living spaces, like a huge family room where everyone can gather."

Marc's words became distant, as though coming at her though a dense fog. Caitlin's mind traveled the length of the huge staircase that led to the rooms upstairs. She held onto the mahogany banister as pictures flashed in front of her face , pictures of the Bond Hotel, the way it used to be in the early 1920s. She saw fashionable ladies in long-waisted silk dresses, with skirts that grazed the mid-calf. For a brief moment, Caitlin felt that she was one of those ladies. She started to climb the stairs, compelled to follow the faint pictures flashing in her mind. The higher she got, the stronger the images became. There seemed to be two men on the stairs, directly in front of her. How did she know them? They began to argue—

"Caitlin, don't go up there." Marc's hand covered Caitlin's, stopping her from taking the next step. His voice pierced through the mist and disjointed pictures as he led her back down the staircase. "These stairs aren't safe yet. Be careful."

She looked at him, dazed. "The oddest thing just happened. For a moment, I actually felt like I'd been here before...on that staircase." She shook her head and laughed. "Now I know I'm becoming a nut case. Either that, or it's a case of too much Josie."

"Maybe neither." Marc winked at her. "Maybe it was a real memory. Now wouldn't that be interesting?"

Chapter Twenty-Five

I told him August," Caitlin said. "We're going to pick an exact date next week."

"What?" Josie demanded, waves of coffee sloshing across her mug and onto her skirt. She reached for a napkin and tried blotting up the brown stains already setting in. "Oh, the hell with it." She tossed the napkin aside.

Winter was sliding into spring and the two women were sitting on Caitlin's back porch enjoying an unseasonably warm morning. They'd decided to play hooky from work and go shopping for spring clothes.

"This August? Why would you do that?"

"Don't bug me, Josie. I'm tired of arguing with him about it. And I don't want to argue with you. If we're going to get married, we might as well just do it."

"That's a great attitude. Maybe you should check in with your inner self on this one, if you get my drift. You know, trust the gut!" Jose said, hitting her stomach with her fist and imitating Sara's deep voice.

Caitlin played with the diamond ring still on her right finger, twisting and turning it, holding its sparkle up to the morning sun. But then she found herself touching her wedding band, finding comfort in the feel of the thick, cool gold. "You need to just let this be, Josie. Be happy for me."

"I want to be. Honest I do. Okay, new topic: any more dreams?"

Caitlin was so relieved that Josie had changed the conversation, she fell into the trap of talking about her dream, the dream where David seemed to being warning her, begging her to remember what she could not. "It's always the same one. Not every night anymore. But a lot. It's exhausting. It's been going on since Christmas."

"I know. I can't imagine...what do you think he's asking you to remember?"

If I knew that then I know, right?"

"Right." Josie played with the stains on her skirt. "They're probably in there for good. Oh well...Think he's warning you about Derrick? Maybe you should give yourself more time."

"Josie, please. The truth? I like having a man in my life. It's not easy finding a good one. You know that."

"Yeah, but it's even worse being with the wrong one. By the way, Marc tells me you've been working day and night on the renovations. Now, there's a good man."

"Don't push, Josephine," Caitlin said. "Marc and I are friends and that's the way both of us want it. Derrick's a wonderful man, you just don't know him like I do."

"Do you? I mean, really know him? Just don't rush into anything. It's a lot harder to undo than do."

Before Caitlin could respond, a blonde head peeked around the corner.

"I had a feeling you'd be out back here. I didn't see your car leave at the usual time this morning, and then I saw hers pull up." Liz nodded toward Josephine. "I almost didn't come over," she said haltingly. "But I had to." She walked in through the screen door, letting it slam behind her, and burst into tears. "You're the only one I can turn to, Catie, the only one I can trust."

Liz looked as though she'd been crying for days. All the blood vessels in her eyes seemed to be broken, and her ivory skin was covered with red blotches.

Josie stood up, coffee mug in hand. "I'll make myself scarce."

Liz waved one hand, dabbing at her swollen eyes with the other. "Don't bother. It doesn't matter. Nothing matters." And then she burst into tears again, trying to talk between gulps of breath. "Steve's having an affair."

"Are you sure?" Caitlin asked. Josie immediately went into the kitchen to make Liz a cup of tea.

"Of course I'm sure. You'd think I'd make something like this up?"

Liz sank into one of the overstuffed wicker chairs. "I caught him. Red-handed. I'm a cliché. My whole life is a cliché. What am I going to do? I can't deal with this. I just can't deal with it!"

"Maybe you just misinterpreted things?" Caitlin suggested tentatively.

"Misinterpreted, huh!" Taking the tea from Josie, she gave her a small, thankful smile. "That creep, that self-righteous creep. Lying to me all this time, and me so sorry for him about having to work late so much for this new corporate client. Asshole. I was feeling so sorry for him..." Liz blew her nose with a ragged tissue and took a sip of tea. "So sorry that I baked my special peach cobbler—and Catie you know how many hours that takes, it's such a complicated recipe—anyway, I baked it, brewed a pot of coffee, and while it was still warm, fixed up a picnic basket and went to his office."

"Oops," Josie said, exchanging glances with Caitlin.

"Oops is right," Liz said. She blew her nose again. "There was no one around, the whole place was deserted, so I figured, poor Steve, holed up in his office, working alone with no support, and I quietly went down the hallway until I got to his office. I was so excited about surprising him that I didn't even knock. I just opened the door. So quietly, he didn't see me at first. He was sitting on the couch next to that...slut, playing with her long bleached hair, running his hand up and down her leg. She had on these four-inch heels and no stockings. Then his hand disappeared up her skirt and the slut started to groan. That's when I gasped and dropped the picnic basket."

"Oh, God," Caitlin said. "Oh my God."

Liz started to laugh, a hysterical, high-pitched laugh. "They both stood up and tried to look formal, as though maybe I would believe that it was all a mistake, that I hadn't really seen what I saw. There she was, trying to smooth down her leather skirt, and there he was with this big bulge in his pants and a wet spot the size of a quarter. I couldn't say anything. I just picked up the basket and left. God only knows how I got home."

"Where were the kids?" Caitlin asked.

"Home. In bed. I don't usually leave them. They're still too young, but I couldn't call you, you know. So I just told them to be good, read books or something, and I'd be right back. And I locked them in with the security system. What could happen, really?"

Caitlin didn't want to deal with the what-could-happens. Liz was upset enough. But it was hard to believe that calling her to watch them was worse than leaving them alone. "So then what?" she asked.

"Steve was practically right behind me. He must have left that little trollop without so much as a backward glance. We fought all night. All I can say is thank God I was the one who found him and not somebody else. I mean, it would be all over town. I'd never be able to hold my head up."

"Maybe he's not really having an affair. Maybe it was just a one-time mistake. You know, too many long hours, too much temptation," Josie offered.

"That's what he tried to make me believe. But I knew he wasn't telling the truth. I could see it in his eyes."

"Could you really?" Caitlin asked, knowing how little emotion ever seemed to show in his gray eyes.

"I could tell," Liz said, nodding her head. "And I was right. Finally, about three in the morning, he admitted it. There have been others this past year. Nothing permanent. I guess that's good, right? It means he's not in love or anything. It's just been for sex. He says things just haven't been the same between us, that we've become too married. Can you imagine that, too married? What does that mean anyway? He says we should just forget about everything. Let it be."

"And what do you say?" Jose challenged.

"Well, maybe he's right." Liz sat up straight and squared her shoulders. "I haven't exactly been Miss Sexpot or anything like that. And I have put on a few pounds since the kids. Maybe he did need more than I was giving."

"Oh come off it!" Josie said.

"Liz, really," Caitlin said, "don't turn this into your fault. Don't let him off the hook so easy!"

Liz look surprised. "Catie, you're the last person I'd expect to be vindictive."

"I just think you should stand up for yourself, that's all. I mean, can you really just forget about all this?"

"No, never. I'll never forget this. I mean, how could I? If I forget, then he'll forget, and then he'll never even know how much he hurt me."

"So what, then?" Caitlin asked.

"I don't know. I have to think about it."

"Don't do anything rash," Josie said. "Take your time and think about what you want. Being a single parent, a divorced mother, isn't a walk in the park. So just make sure."

"Single parent? Divorced mother?" Liz looked genuinely surprised. "Why would I ever want that? No," she said thoughtfully, "I'll make

him pay. I'll just add up the pain and suffering and make him pay."
Liz's eyes took on a gleam.

"You know," she continued, "he bought me that mink at
Christmas...that had to be a guilt gift. I'd really love a killer diamond
bracelet. Not some small trinket like I have now. I mean, look at you,
Catie, you have one and you're not even married. And then we're
going to plan that cruise he keeps promising me. Of course, he'll have
to take an AIDS test. If that comes out okay, then we can just go back to
normal. I'm also going to insist that you and I can be friends again,
Catie, although you probably still won't be able to take the kids out
until... well, you know. Sorry, Josie, no offense meant, but I only have
so much leverage, even in this situation. And I don't want to push it. I
mean, he might think leaving home would be easier and then where
would I be?"

"Independent?" Josie asked. "Oh, and no offense taken. I know
where it comes from."

"Why in the world would I want to be independent? I have
everything I want right now. I have no interest in going to work or
compromising my lifestyle. I just want everything back to normal."

"Liz," Caitlin said, concern rippling through her voice, "can things
really go back to the way they were? Will they ever really be normal?"

"If I make it that way." Liz stood up to go, looking more confident,
less frightened than when she had come in. "I don't want to be a single
person. That would be the worse thing possible, unmarried with two
children. I like being part of a couple. I like having a social place. You
don't have that as a single. You two should know that. Steve says the
most important thing is that we act like nothing has happened, and
pretty soon it'll be true...or just as good as true. And I think he's right.
But first he'll pay."

"What about love?" Caitlin asked, putting her arm around Liz's
shoulder and walking through the back yard with her.

"Love?" Liz shrugged. "It's there. It's just different. But I don't
really want to think about that. I just want to get back to normal. I don't
want to be like you, looking for a new life, looking for answers that
don't exist. I just want to be happy."

Caitlin hugged Liz and watched her walk back down the street to
her gray and white colonial, a wave of sadness sweeping over her
body. She and Liz could be friends again, out in the open, thanks to
Steve's indiscretion. But things would never be the same. They'd
walked too far down separate paths. And in such a short time.

Back on the porch, she told Josie how she felt and how sad it made her feel.

"Did you really expect anything different?" Josie asked. "How could things ever get back to the same between you two? Too much has changed."

"You're right. You're always right." Caitlin sighed deeply. "It's hard to understand why Liz wants to go backward instead of forward. She's always holding onto yesterday, afraid to let go."

Josie was quiet for a few minutes, then she said, "Isn't that just what's going on with you and Derrick? Aren't you trying to hold onto the past through him? And isn't he trying to recreate that past at every turn of the bend? And isn't that just a little bit scary?"

Caitlin didn't say anything, but a shiver went through her body. Derrick was trying to recreate the past. But what past? Hers and David's? Or another past, one behind that curtain she saw at the end of her nightly journeys with David but was too frightened to pull back?

Chapter Twenty-Six

Working on the renovations of the Bond Hotel filled Caitlin with a renewed sense of purpose. Marc had been absolutely right about the healing power of hard work done in the service of others. She joined the key project members in carving out as much time as possible from jobs and daily routines, knowing how quickly the deadline for completion would arrive. And if she wasn't exactly happier these days, she was definitely more content than she'd been in the months since David's death.

Before she realized it, March had turned into June, the first anniversary of David's death. Getting to that time in one piece had been her private touchstone for survival. She had made it. And because she had made it, she went into a period of mourning and self-doubt. How could she have gone on so easily without David? Maybe she hadn't loved him enough after all. Maybe she was incapable of the kind of love that makes you committed to someone forever, even in death. How could she have planned another life so quickly, agreed to marry Derrick so readily? What kind of a person was she after all?

Derrick had no tolerance for her renewed period of despair. Eager to get on with their future, he seemed to be through with wanting to keep David alive for her, and he continually brushed aside his name whenever Caitlin brought it up. In the end, it was Marc who helped her, who visited the cemetery with her and held her when she cried. She'd always assumed Marc had been married and divorced. Then one day, sitting on the grass in front of David's grave, he told her that his wife and only child—a daughter—had died a few years ago. An accident, was all he'd say. Someday...he'd said...someday he'd tell her everything. What he did tell her, however, is that he understood her self doubts and recriminations. He understood the need to relive things, over and over again, that carving out valleys of pain in her heart was a way of remembering, of holding on, of not forgiving herself.

"I know it's impossible to believe right now," he said, "but one day the pain will dull. It'll be as though soothing water seeped in during the night and healed the sores. You'll have scars. And all the memories. But it won't ache the way it does now. Honest."

Marc had been the best kind of friend during that time. Until the second week in July.

The Bond Hotel gang decided to meet at Marc's house in Mystic one Thursday evening , an off-campus planning meeting they called it. They sat on the floor eating pizza and drinking Merlot, discussing timelines and strategy, and batting around design ideas. Marc had started a fire to ward off the chill coming from the ocean. He kept all the windows open so it wouldn't get too hot, and so they could hear the crashing of the waves as they hit against the rocky shoreline.

"This reminds me of the old days," Beth said, a heavy-set woman with long brown hair and thick bangs. By day she worked as a social worker in the inner city, and by night she continued that dedication by getting involved in projects to aid the homeless. She got up and removed a candle from one of the brass candlesticks on Marc's glass-top sofa table and stuck it into an empty wine bottle. "Except then we drank cheap Chianti. Or Wild Irish Rose." She leaned back against the sofa, hugging her knees to her chest. "Remember those days? Some cheap wine, a joint or two, and great music. We'd sit around philosophizing, convinced that eventually we'd come up with the answers to solve the woes of the world. We were so young, so naive, we didn't even know the questions! But here we are, folks, still trying to come up with answers."

Marc turned on the radio and songs from the past filled the room. "It's an oldies station, Beth. It's the best I can do."

"Way old," Beth said, listening to Elvis croon Are You Lonesome Tonight? "But cool. Keep it on."

"You know what the difference is now?" Jake said. "It's that we can make a difference. Not a global one, but a difference anyway. That's why we're all here, doing what we're doing. We have resources, connections. In small ways, we know how to make the system work for us."

"The system!" Beth scoffed. "I work with that system every day of my life. The damned thing needs to be trashed. A bunch of rules that have gotten so convoluted, they're based on an illusion of how the bureaucrats think things are. They're not based on reality at all. I think every legislator and congressman should be made to live just like the people they're making the rules for. Then maybe, just maybe, they'll see what really needs to be done, how the money they're so stingy with really needs to be spent."

"Okay, Beth!" Don lifted his wine glass in a toast. "On with the bandwagon, but unfortunately, the only wagon I'm getting on right now is my SUV. We did some good work tonight, but I have to be in court bright and early tomorrow. I'm outta here."

The rest of them stood up. "Looks like we're all going," Paul said. "And I was just getting comfortable. I could get into a place like this. Beats city living. Next time, I'll drive; and you, Don-old-boy, can snooze all the way home. That way we can stay later." He put his arm around Don's shoulder as they all walked out.

Caitlin smiled as Marc closed the door behind his friends. "I really like them. Thanks for giving me this chance, for believing in me. Everyone is so dedicated, so interesting. Well, I should go..." She picked up her purse and began looking through it for her car keys.

"I hope you include me in the interesting part," Marc said, walking toward her. He took the purse from her hands. "Please don't go yet. Let's take a walk on the beach."

Just feeling Marc close to her, without anyone else in the room made Caitlin heady, disoriented. She should leave. Right now. "All right, a short walk, to wake me up for the drive home."

"Great, I'll get you a sweater. The beach'll be chilly."

Marc took her hand, leading her down the deck stairs, across a small grassy area and then down a dozen concrete stairs to the sand. As soon as her bare feet were planted safely on the sand, she let go of his hand. "Wow, that's cold," she said, feeling the fine, cool grains between her toes.

"Are you sure you don't want to put your shoes on? I'll run back up and get them."

"Pumps on the beach? I don't think so," she laughed. "I'll get used to it. Actually, it feels kind of good."

They walked down to the water, the night breeze blowing their hair in different directions. "Thanks for the sweater," Caitlin said, closing her arms around her chest. Wearing it made Caitlin feel as if they'd become intimate. Strange, how familiar it all felt, wearing Marc's sweater, being close to him like this, talking in almost hushed voices. It was the same kind of feeling she had at the Bond that first day, when she saw the lobby and grand staircase.

"Cold?" Marc asked, putting his arm around her shoulder.

"A little. Not really." Caitlin let his arm stay, not shrugging it off as she'd started to do. "What a wonderful place to live, Marc. Is this where you've always lived? As an adult, I mean, with your wife and daughter?"

"No, I bought this place afterward. I wanted to get away. I lived like a hermit for the first couple of years. You've done remarkably well this past year, Cate. Remarkably well."

"Thanks."

"Except for Derrick. I know it's none of my business, but in some bizarre way, I think he's your way of holding onto something you really need to let go of. I can't even tell you why I think that—"

Caitlin stiffened. "Josie talks too much. Derrick and I are just fine. He's my future, not my past. Let's not even talk about."

"You're right. Sorry. It really is none of my business. Anyway, about the house. When I bought it, it was in a shambles, never updated from the fifties. I threw all my energy into recreating a new space from the existing one, using glass and stone and capitalizing on the natural setting. I found out I was good at it, so I came out of hiding and went into development."

"What did you do before?"

Caitlin could feel his hand go rigid on her shoulder. She looked up and saw the sudden tightening of his jaw. "I'm sorry," she said. "I didn't mean to pry."

"It's not prying, Cate. I'm not keeping secrets...it's just painful. Let's leave it for another time."

They stopped walking and let the cold water lap around their feet. Marc touched Caitlin's cheek and then gently pushed her windblown hair away from her face. It seemed to her that the whole world was dark except for the spot where they stood, moonbeams casting a spell around them as their eyes locked and their bodies began to touch. She stood on her toes, ready to meet his kiss, but as Marc's lips brushed across hers, she backed away, nearly falling into the cold ocean water.

He reached out and caught her, but not before she got wet. "Why did you do that?"

"I'm engaged, you know that. We're going to be married in August. This can't happen." She dropped his hand and headed up toward the house.

Marc gave her a few minutes and then caught up with her on the deck. Quietly he took her hand and led her inside. The lights in the house were still low. The radio played soft tunes.

"I have to go," Caitlin told him.

"Your slacks are soaked. You'll catch pneumonia if you go home like that. Stand by the fire until you dry off, at least a little. We'll have a small glass of sherry to take the chill off and then you can go."

She cast him a doubtful look. She felt her clothes. She was soaked. But she couldn't stay. Not for another minute.

"I'll keep my distance. I promise."

In the end, she agreed. They both stood by the fire, keeping an adequate amount of space between them. Room enough for the Holy Ghost, as the nuns used to say. Sipping her sherry, Caitlin looked at the photographs on the mantel. "Your daughter?" she asked. "Great photo. Were her eyes really that violet?" The little girl was blowing bubbles, her eyes wide with delight as she popped one in mid-air. Long, fine blond hair framed a cherub face.

"That's Jenny. She's five there. Yeah, her eyes really were that color. The violet from a box of Crayolas. I would have expected her to have deep blue eyes, like mine. I don't know where they came from."

"Her mother?" Caitlin asked, spotting a picture of the three of them, all hugging a huge teddy bear in front of a Christmas tree. "Is that you, with a beard?"

"Yep, my scruffy days. No, Sheila's eyes were green. Like yours. Except that yours have more golden specks." He moved closer, to inspect the color of her eyes.

Caitlin turned back to the photos. She touched the crystal frame that held Jenny's photo. "You must miss her terribly."

"I do. But I hold the image of a five-year-old. She'd be fifteen by now. I wonder a lot about what kind of teenager she would have been. She had this strawberry mark—heart shaped—on her left check; you can't see it in the picture, her face is turned. She called it her love mark, a kiss from God. I wonder how she would have felt about it later on, as she was growing up. The doctors told me that if it didn't fade, they could do something to lessen the brightness."

"I'm sure she would have been fine."

"Probably, but I always worried. Even after...after the accident. I kept obsessing about Jenny and her birthmark, as though she was still growing up, just somewhere else, without me, and I needed to worry about how she was managing."

Caitlin reached out to push back stray pieces of hair from Marc's forehead, wanting to comfort him, feeling warmed by the fire and the sherry, and the sense of belonging she felt standing in the room with him. From the radio came a song from the Lettermen.

It seems we stood and talked like this before
We looked at each other in the same way then
But I can't remember where or when...
Some things that happen for the first time
Seem to be happening again
And so it seems that we have met before
And laughed before
And loved before
But who knows where or when

When the song was over, Marc took Caitlin in his arms, kissing her deeply and knowingly. When they finally broke apart, they locked eyes and Caitlin found her mind repeating the phrase, at last...at last...

What did that mean? At last, what?

"I'm sorry," she said, stepping back from Marc.

"Don't be."

"But I am. You have a very seductive atmosphere here, Mr. Gallagher." She tried laughing but it sounded forced. "The sound of the ocean...the music...the fire...Anyway, I am sorry."

"Cate..." Marc reached out, to touch her arm, but she backed away further.

"I have to go."

Without another word, she headed out the door.

Chapter Twenty-Seven

Marc didn't try to stop Caitlin from leaving his house that night. He knew the kiss had upset her, had taken them beyond the boundaries of friendship they'd so carefully constructed over the last several months. The question now was what would she do about it? Anything he did now would only scare her away, make her even more determined to honor her engagement to Derrick, and Marc knew in the deepest, quietest part of his soul that it would be a huge mistake. For all of them.

There was no doubt in Marc's mind that Caitlin would now do everything in her power to avoid being alone with him. But he also knew she took her commitment to the project very seriously. He'd still see her. Maybe he'd even be able to catch her alone. For what? To apologize? To talk some sense into her? He wasn't quite sure. Only the moment—if it ever happened—would tell.

True to form, Caitlin showed up for all of their meetings and work sessions, but she made a point of keeping distance between them and always having someone else in the room when they worked together. Now they never exchanged anything more personal than "a nice day out," or "how are you?" Words you would say to a stranger. Sometimes she would show up at the hotel at an odd time, knowing

Marc wouldn't be there, do her assigned chores and leave before she ever saw him. But he always knew she'd been there. Over sawdust and paint and turpentine, her presence lingered in the air.

On a Saturday morning near the end of July, they were all in the lobby discussing design details. Plans were spread out across an old door set on two sawhorses. Each of the group had long ago brought a stool or chair from home, and they now sat around the makeshift table on unmatched chairs.

"Well, what do we all think?" Marc asked, excitement in his voice. The renovations were at a turning point. The gutting was done, and now they could start building. With a little luck, they would meet their deadline.

"Well, I, uh, have a couple of ideas," Caitlin said, "but they might be silly."

"If it's real stupid, we'll let you know." Jake winked at her. "But you should know by now, nothing's silly. Except maybe Beth's earrings. Where did you get those, anyway? And why?"

Beth fingered her long owl earrings made of pink papier-mache. "They go with the outfit. Besides," she raised her chin indignantly, "they make me wise. You should all be wearing owls. It just might help."

Jake balled up a piece of paper and threw it at her, grazing her shoulder. "What's your idea, Catie?"

"Well, I was just thinking—" She crossed one leg over the other, feeling ten eyes on her at once. "You know, some of the women, they'll be young mothers and, well, what happens if they're downstairs in the family room, or doing kitchen duty, or maybe taking one of the classes at night?"

"What do you mean, what happens?" Marc asked.

"If they have kids, and if they're in the bedroom, say asleep, how will the mother know if there's a problem? It's not like a real house, where you can hear them. It's too spread out. So I was thinking, what if we install intercoms in each room—I don't know if this can be done, exactly. But one intercom would be labeled A, for instance; another one B, and so on. And then the receiving end of the intercom would be in central parts of the house, say the family room and kitchen, with a corresponding A, B, C, et cetera, that could be turned on if the mother was away from the bedroom. It would have to be turned on at both ends, bedroom and central living area. That way privacy wouldn't be an issue. And if one person couldn't listen for her child, another could. Maybe it could even be one of the assigned chores."

"Paul, can it be done?" Don asked. "Personally, I think it's a great idea. It could prevent some disasters. Can't believe none of us thought about it until now."

"I'll figure out the wiring involved and let you know. What's your other terrible idea, Catie?" Paul asked.

"This one's more whimsical. I was in the kitchen the other day, standing inside that old pantry. There are no tall buildings to block the sun, and the light hits the building from mid-morning to late afternoon. So what if we knocked out part of the wall, replaced it with three glass walls, and turned it into a greenhouse? We don't really need the space for storage with all the new cabinets. Just think," Caitlin's voice became excited, "the residents could grow herbs, maybe even flowers, to keep the place cheery. Unless, of course, it really is a stupid idea. I mean, maybe they're all too busy surviving to be bothered with something like that."

They were all quiet. Caitlin looked over at Beth. She, of all people, knew the souls of the people who would soon be living at Esperanza.

"Catie, I think it's better than a good idea," Beth said finally. "It's a great one. What could be more hopeful than a garden? It's great therapy. Can we get some prices and figure out how to make it happen?"

"Sure can." Marc practically beamed. "Looks like we're done," he said, rolling up the plans. "Anyone up for lunch?"

Before anyone could respond, the front door opened with such a force it seemed that a gust of wind had blown it open. Derrick stood in the threshold, arms crossed, surveying the large room and its occupants.

"So this is where you've been hiding." His smile was charming as he came toward the group. "Hi, I'm Derrick Secor, Catie's fiancé." He shook hands all around and then walked over to Caitlin and put his arms around her. "Did you forget we planned to pick out flowers today?" He turned to the group. "Our wedding is less than five weeks away and we have tons to do." He tucked his hand under her elbow, so that she would stand. "I'm sure you understand—"

Marc stood up. He was about two inches taller than Derrick, who immediately backed up onto the staircase so he could look across at Marc, rather than up at him. A trickle of fear ran through Marc's body. Derrick's movement had triggered some alarm in a corner of Marc's mind, although he couldn't for the life of him determine why. The moment passed and Marc took a deep steadying breath.

"We were just talking about lunch," Marc told Derrick, keeping his voice calm and polite. "Why don't you join us? We could fill you in on the project. You'll see why Cate's spending so much time here."

"Sorry, chief, count us out. Lunch is definitely on the agenda, but some place quiet and romantic. You know how it is," he laughed. "Thanks anyway. But I do look forward to seeing all of you again. Perhaps at the wedding. Catie here has told me so much about all of you."

As Derrick pushed past Marc, the two men locked eyes; it was only for a split second, but long enough for a palpable flash of anger to pass between them.

"Well, if we're going to eat, let's eat," Beth boomed in a louder than normal voice.

"Yeah, let's get out of here," Marc said, tucking the rolls of plans under his arms. "I'll make those other revisions we talked about and run them by Lawson on Monday. How about Arch Street Tavern? Meet you guys there." He locked the front door and they each went to their separate cars. Marc, who had hauled tools and lumber to the site that morning, climbed into the driver's side of the old station wagon while Derrick slid behind the wheel of his silver Mercedes.

* * *

Caitlin had been unable to leave the Bond under her own power. In fact, she felt as though she might have remained permanently glued to the floor if Derrick hadn't wrapped his arm around her back and steered her out. She was horrified by Derrick's behavior—and just as much by her own passiveness. How could she have stood by and let him bulldoze her friends like that? So smug, so arrogant.

They drove the entire way without talking; the easy-listening music coming from the radio was louder than normal.

When Derrick pulled into the parking lot of a small restaurant tucked away in the woods by the Farmington River, he took her hand, "Let's not fight, Catie. Let's have a nice lunch."

Caitlin pulled her hand away and silently followed him into the restaurant, waiting until they were seated before she spoke. "Derrick..."

"Thanks," he said, looking up at the waitress and accepting the menus. "Stay right here; we'll order right away. My fiancée is so hungry, she's cranky, aren't you, darling?"

"What is wrong with you?" Caitlin hissed as soon as the waitress left with their order.

"What? What do you mean?" He tried to take her hand, but she pulled it away.

"How could you say that to the waitress? Even if I was cranky—which I'm not—it's none of her business."

"Well, you're something."

"Try mad."

"Because I wanted to take my fiancée out for a special lunch? Because I'm excited about our wedding?"

"No. Because you're rude."

"Rude? You spend all your time with that group of...whatever... instead of with me, and I'm rude? I don't think so, Catie. I think you have your priorities screwed up."

Caitlin pushed her chair back. "I think this lunch was a mistake. Maybe this whole thing is a mistake. Take me home."

Just then the waitress delivered their wine. "Your lunch will be out in a few minutes," she said.

Derrick reached over and placed his hand on Caitlin's. "Stay, please. I'm sorry if I upset you." His voice was smooth and seductive. "Let's start over. I'll even apologize to your friends if you want. Come on, Catie. It's just that I love you so much. We have a wedding to plan. And a honeymoon. Come on, please."

Caitlin settled back into her seat, but she didn't say another word until they were nearly finished eating.

"Derrick, this project is so important to me. I feel like I'm really making a difference. It's the closest I've ever come to my old childhood dream of becoming an architect, of using talent--my talent--to help somebody else. If you can't see that, if you can't support that..." Her thoughts were taking shape as she spoke "I guess what I'm trying to say...if you can't support me in this now, how can I trust you to support me in anything once we're married?"

"Oh for Christ's sake. You're making too much of this."

"I don't think so. You were rude to my friends. But it's about more than that—"

"Catie, Catie...you're right," he interrupted. "I'm an ass. I'll admit it. I just love you so damned much. I don't want anyone or anything taking you away from me."

Tears slid down Caitlin's cheeks. Derrick reached across the table and used his napkin to blot them up. "Don't let me being an idiot upset you so much. Let's salvage the day, shall we?"

"Derrick, you have to give me room—"

"I will. I promise. So, now, let's talk wedding plans. Did you get the invitations out yesterday? Do we have that appointment with the florist later today?"

When she shook her head, answering no to both questions, Derrick took hold of her left hand. "Catie, it's only five weeks away. What's going on here?"

"I know. I just want it to be low-key. It feels strange, having another wedding. I just wish we could be married without all the fuss. Maybe we should hop a plane to Vegas. Besides, how could I get the invitations out? You haven't given me any names yet. Who do you want to invite? I've never even met any of your friends, except for George and Marie Dawson."

"We've been through this already. I want to invite my dad, of course. But he'll probably be too weak to make it. The Dawsons. And my boss, since I'll probably still see him even after I transfer here to Connecticut. But once I'm living here, I'll never see any of those people again, so why bother?"

"Of course you will. Friends are always friends. Massachusetts isn't the other side of the world."

"There's nobody. So let's drop it. We'll work on the invitations tonight, together, and get them done. By the way, I stopped by and saw Steve this morning. I've missed our little foursomes. That's going to change though. He's really happy about our getting married, thinks it'll stabilize you, bring things back to the way they used to be. Don't get tense on me," he said, seeing her shoulders tighten. "You can be and do whatever you want, as long as it works for us. But we can make Steve happy at the same time, can't we? We'll just let him think whatever he wants."

"Thanks but no thanks. That's how he and Liz live—in the land of delusion. Count me out. He either accepts me the way I am, or forget it."

"Lighten up, Catie. Life's too short. Don't start getting ruffled over nothing. The old guy's still licking his wounds. That little diversion of his cost him plenty, and my guess is he's not done paying. Anyway, the whole purpose of bringing up Steve is that I asked him to be my best man. And I think you should ask Liz to stand up for you. I kind of hinted as much, so she'll probably be expecting a call. Surprisingly, Steve was agreeable. Though it would be a good way to break the ice."

"Damn you!" Caitlin hissed between clenched teeth. "How could you? I was going to ask Josie. You know that. She's been there for me all through this past year. I wanted her by my side, not Liz who deserted me as soon as things got rough."

"Catie, she didn't desert you. She just took her place by her husband in a controversy. Which is exactly the way it should be. Besides, that's all water over the dam. Liz has been your friend for years. I think you should ask her. I think it would be a big mistake to have Josie. You can invite her, though. And Adam, too.

"Geez, thanks. Is there anything else before we end this terrific lunch?"

Derrick hesitated, almost as if he was going to change his mind about something, but then he lowered his voice to a soft, smooth tone. "There is one thing that's really bugging me," he said, stroking Caitlin's hand. "This." His fingers stopped on her wedding band. She still hadn't taken it off. "It's time to take it off, Caitlin." He wrapped his fingers round the gold band and began sliding it off.

"Don't!" Caitlin nearly shouted, feeling as though her finger was on fire. "Don't," she said again more softly, tears caught in her throat. "Not yet."

"When? On our honeymoon?"

"Just trust me, Derrick. I'll take it off. But when I'm ready. And not a minute before." She put her napkin on the table and stood to go. "I'm out of here. Take me home now, or I'll find a ride."

They were both quiet on the way back. Things would work out. Caitlin was sure of it. People were always tense before weddings, fighting about stupid things. In five weeks, they would be married and all these petty problems would disappear. Caitlin leaned back against the head rest and tried clearing her mind, but she found herself touching her lips, tracing the outline of a kiss. Marc's kiss.

Chapter Twenty-Eight

My mother's definitely coming up for the wedding," Caitlin told Josie. They were lounging around in Josie's living room, wearing shorts and tank tops and sucking on Popsicles. It was one of those humid late-July evenings without a whisper of a breeze, where gnats and mosquitoes clung to human skin, and being inside was the only reasonable choice. With all the windows open and the overhead fan working at full speed, this small room, decorated in cool white and celadon green, was almost comfortable.

"And this is, what? Good? Bad?"

"I don't know. Good, I guess. But she's difficult."

"Whose mother isn't?"

"Not like her. She's got it down to a science."

"What does she say about all this?"

"All what?"

"Oh, well, the fact that you're tense, anxious, unfit for human company. Not exactly the stuff brides are made of."

"I am not! Besides, I don't get into stuff like that with her. She's happy for me. I know she is. But mostly, she seems to want to know why I found somebody, especially so fast, and she never did."

"Yikes."

"I know. There's always been...I don't know, friction, competition between us. Dad was constantly grooming me to be this 'perfect' lady—which I'm far from, by the way. I think it made her feel inferior, like she wasn't good enough. Actually, I think she was jealous. And then he died, and she was lonely. She criticized me constantly after that. It was almost as if she blamed me for his death. But in her own way she loves me. I know she does. She was devastated when David died."

"Hmmm...and now Maryanne blames you for David. Sounds like some karma being worked out here."

"Don't even go there." Caitlin said.

"Then how about this for conversation: doesn't it say something to you, that it's only weeks before the wedding and you still can't remove David's ring? And there's something else bothering you, I can tell—"

"I can't explain it. Marrying Derrick—it just feels inevitable. Like all roads have been leading to this. I'm not having doubts exactly. I don't know...it just feels strange. Maybe too quick? That's all. It just feels out of my control—if that makes any sense. Call it destiny. You do believe in destiny, don't you, Josephine?"

Josie just smiled. "Do I detect too much protesting going on here?"

"That's because you drive me to it."

"What about Marc?" Josie asked. "Now there's a man in love—"

"Why? What did he tell you?" Caitlin asked, sitting up straight. She'd never mentioned the kiss to Josie. Had he?

Josie raised her eyebrows. "Such a reaction from someone who doesn't care."

"I don't," Caitlin answered. "But, still...what did he say?"

"Not a word, Catie dear. But I can see love in his eyes. I hear it in his voice every time he says your name. And he tries to say it as often as possible. By the way, he's very impressed with your ideas. Feels you should go back to school, get a degree, pursue the career you were meant to have, instead of peddling houses. But I'm sure he's told you that already."

"At least a million times," Caitlin smiled. "He really thinks I'd be good in some area of design, if not architecture per se."

"And he's probably right. He also thinks Derrick's a first-class you-know-what. I think asshole is the word he used."

"Stop, Josie, right now. Please. This is the way it is: Marc and I are friends. We both like it that way. I'm going to marry Derrick Secor. And that's that. I'm just having pre-wedding jitters, that's all."

"Yeah, right. And I'm the Queen of England. You're having gut reactions, and I say you should listen to them. Isn't that what Sara told you to do? Listen to the gut. And remember what Janet Lee said, about people not being what they seemed? Switch the masks, isn't that what she said?" Seeing tension creep across Caitlin's face, Josie held up her right hand. "All right, I know when I've gone too far. Not another word. But I can't stop worrying. If you want to talk, or if you change your mind, even at the last minute, I'm right by your side, ready to ward off the enemy!" She rose to her feet and feigned a sword fight with her Popsicle stick.

Caitlin laughed. "You are so dramatic. I don't know why we didn't appreciate you in high school."

"That's because I was light years ahead of my time. Too progressive for the little people." Josie sat back down on the floor. "Listen, are you sure you still want me to be your maid of honor? I'll back out if it makes things easier on you."

"Absolutely not!" Caitlin said. "Derrick can have Steve or anyone else he wants for his best man. And I get to have who I want. That's you! But," she laughed, "it does mean you and Steve will have to be on your best behavior. Think maybe there's a little karma going on there?"

Josie threw a pillow at her. "Thanks. Seriously, what about Liz? She'll be furious if Steve stands up for Derrick and she's left out."

"That's not my problem. Derrick should never have tried arranging things behind my back. I'm still pissed. I told him to fix it or call the wedding off."

"Whew...the girl does have balls."

"When I need them —"

"So," Josie said, "if he doesn't straighten things out, the whole thing's off?"

"Not the marriage, dope. Just the wedding. It's making me crazy anyway. I'd rather go to Vegas and elope." She looked at her watch. "It's late. I have to get home."

"I'm with you, no matter what you do," Josie said softly.

"I know. Thanks."

By the time Caitlin got home, the night air was filled with the electricity of a summer storm. She climbed into bed and listened to the wind whipping through the trees. Cracks of lightening sliced through her bedroom window. Thunder crashed and clapped, blotting out all other sounds. Finally the rain came: huge, heavy beads of rain that quickly turned into a steady downpour, seducing her into a deep sleep. Once again, David came for her, guiding her through the various stages of her life. This time the dream was at its most intense.

Walking through the corridor of curtains, Caitlin was no longer afraid, as she had been those first few times. Now, she viewed each scene with curiosity, trying to read the expressions on everyone's face, trying to relive the emotions. As always, each curtain pulled aside with just a gentle touch, as though a light breeze had stirred, helping to pull it back. Once again, she walked through the scene of her birth and once again she came to the last curtain, the one that felt leaden, too heavy for her to pull aside on her own.

Tonight, David didn't leave her side. When she reached out for the edge of the curtain, his hand moved with her, helping her to pull back the massive drape. Suddenly, it felt as light as all the other curtains. Caitlin's heart beat wildly. She was about to see what lay on the other side.

As soon as the curtain turned light to the touch, David removed his hand from Caitlin's, leaving her with the full burden. She felt the brush of his lips across her cheek as he began to disappear. "Remember, Catie. Now you can remember."

The words echoed in her brain as her hand remained on the fabric. With David gone, it felt heavy once again. But it was manageable. She could look beyond it now, on her own, if she chose. She pulled it back just far enough to catch a glimpse of brightness on the other side. Unable to make herself move forward, Caitlin stood absolutely still, gazing at a steady stream of light. There seemed to be a whole other world, beckoning to her, calling out for her attention. If she stepped across into the light, would she ever return? Caitlin clutched the edge of the curtain, knowing instinctively that the decision to walk through would change her life forever. Would it end her life? She dropped hold of the curtain, as though it had become a hot iron in her hand. As she did, Caitlin heard the faraway sound of a large crash.

As she fell into a deeper sleep, David came to her again, this time as her lover rather than as a guide. She could feel his presence, even though she couldn't yet see his face. She could feel his hands caressing her body, his fingers running through her hair and then moving down to trace the outline of her face. They were in some old-fashioned room, far away, bathed in the glow of candlelight. David was kissing her breasts now and her body was moving beneath him, responding to his love, to the memory of his love.

But something was not quite right.

Caitlin looked at herself more closely now, through the mist of her dream state. It was her, but not her, not the same Caitlin she saw in the mirror every day. The Caitlin in her dream had a rounder face. Her lips were naturally red and bow-shaped. Her brown hair was thick and wavy and, unpinned now, it cascaded down her back. She took a closer look at David, at the man lying on top of her, touching and caressing her naked body, trying to distinguish his features. "I love you. I always will," he was telling her.

A deep chill ran through Caitlin's body. The man that lay on top of her, loving her, burning a hole in her heart with the intensity of his passion—this man had a moustache and a deep scar etched in the cheek of his otherwise handsome face. This man was not the David that she knew. Yet she knew, without a doubt, that it was the David she loved.

Chapter Twenty-Nine

R ain pelted against the windows all the next morning as Caitlin wandered around the house, unable to shake off the effect of the dream. It was so real: those images of David and herself, looking so different, yet being the same people. She knew it was just her subconscious at play, but still, it seemed her mind was trying to get her to remember something in her past that she'd long forgotten or deliberately buried. David's words—Remember, Catie, remember— echoed in her head as she studied photographs of family and friends, framed and scattered throughout the house.

Caitlin was momentarily stunned when she reached the living room. So that loud crash hadn't been part of her dream. Her favorite picture, the oil painting Josie admired at Christmas, had fallen off the wall and crashed onto the tile hearth, cracking the frame in two places. It seemed the wire had come lose. But the picture was intact.

Well, now she had a reason to get dressed, to push aside the depression she felt coming on and move into action. She'd taken a few days off from work, to take care of all the things she'd been pushing aside, but she didn't seem to have the energy to tackle any chores. But the picture—she could take care of that. It had to be re-framed and hung before the wedding, before anyone came to the house, if for no other reason than to cover up the spot over the mantel, the only space on the painted wall that was still its original deep sage color. The rest of the wall had faded over the past eight years, and she'd never even noticed. She looked around with new eyes, realizing that the house was becoming worn. Like me, she thought, like all of us. Life is just passing by, and we're getting a little more tired each day.

Dressed in a raincoat and matching hat with a large floppy brim, Caitlin stopped by the Bond to check the work schedule and then ran back to her car, jumping over huge puddles in the pot-hole filled parking lot. She was halfway into the car, when she heard Marc's voice.

"Yo, Cate, wait up."

"Marc, hi," Caitlin called back, talking to him across the roof of her Infiniti. They could barely hear each other over the pelting rain. "What's up?"

Marc ran up to the car, his raincoat pulled over his head. "Mind if we sit inside for a minute?"

Caitlin hesitated for only a minute. They couldn't stand outside and talk. "Sure. Hold on." She pressed the button to unlock his side.

They sat inside, listening as the rain beat against the car. The water formed an invisible shield against the windows, creating a cocoon in which there was only the sound of their breathing and the smell of damp fabric.

Marc broke the silence. "Cute," he laughed, flipping the water off Caitlin's large-brimmed hat. "I can barely find you under there."

"At least I'm dry! Don't you believe in hats, or umbrellas? You're soaked to the skin." Forgetting herself for a minute, Caitlin reached over and pushed Marc's wet hair back from his forehead and began blotting droplets of water from his cheeks. Their eyes met and Caitlin quickly pulled back her hand.

"So. What's up?" Caitlin asked.

"I just haven't seen much of you."

"I know. I've been busy, with the wedding and all. But I get my work done around here. In fact, I was just checking out my schedule for next week."

"I know you do. That's not what this is about. Damn it, Cate. Do I have to spell it out for you? I miss you."

"And I miss you too. But...well, you know...it's just not...it's just not smart right now, to spend time together. You know what I mean."

Marc took hold of her hand. "You mean you might discover that Derrick isn't the one for you after all."

"Don't. You'll just spoil things."

"I don't want to upset you, Cate. I just want you to be happy. I had the oddest feeling on Saturday when Derrick walked in...like I knew him from somewhere...but I don't. It was bad energy, if you know what I mean."

"You sound like Josie. Listen, sometimes Derrick has that effect. I want to apologize for the way he acted. I was really embarrassed. Sometimes he comes on too strong, or something. He doesn't mean to. He's just upset because I'm spending so much time here and not enough planning our wedding."

"That should tell you something. About yourself, at least, if not about him."

"Marc! Whether you mean to or not, you're making me choose sides. Please don't. I'd have to choose Derrick. I am going to marry him."

"Oh, Cate—" Marc moved toward her, his eye catching sight of the painting she had placed in the back seat. With a sharp intake of air, his face turned red and then almost immediately drained itself of all color. "What are you doing with that?"

"That picture? It fell off the wall last night, and at the oddest time. I was in the middle of this recurring dream—"

"What are you doing with that picture?" Marc's eyes riveted to the winter scene, his left hand reaching through the front seats to stroke the broken frame.

"That's what I'm trying to explain," Caitlin said slowly. "It fell down on the hearth and broke, right at a crucial point in my dream."

"Forget the damn dream! Where did you get the picture? What are you doing with it?"

"Marc, what's wrong? Why are you acting this way?"

He didn't answer. It was more like he couldn't answer her. His gaze remained on the oil painting, but his mind seemed to be miles away.

"The picture is mine, Marc. I bought it years ago at an art show. In Mystic. Please, tell me what's wrong." She put her hand on his arm.

His blue eyes, filled with anger, moved from the picture to Caitlin. "How could you?" he asked. "How could you know and not say anything?" Marc took a long, deep breath. "I have to get out of here."

Caitlin could barely see him through the windshield as he walked away from her, wind and water whipping around his unbuttoned raincoat. She wanted to run after him, to ask what had just happened. But she didn't dare. She knew instinctively that knowing would draw them closer. And Caitlin couldn't afford that right now. Whatever he thought about her, whatever he imagined she did, or didn't do, would simply have to be.

Chapter Thirty

Gloomy weather hung on for nearly two weeks, making everyone edgy and irritable. It seemed that a permanent grayness had descended upon the northeast, calling an early halt to the warm, nourishing days of summer.

It was easy for Caitlin and Marc to avoid each other during that time. She made quick visits to the Bond at off times, and even when Marc was there, he seemed preoccupied. His face had a glazed look; his actions seemed rote and disinterested. It wasn't until Caitlin picked up the newly-framed picture and hung it back over the mantel that she began to uncover the secret of that puzzling afternoon.

She called Josephine immediately. "Josie, why didn't you tell me? You could have saved everyone a lot of heartache."

"Or created more," Josie countered. "I was actually sorry we spent Christmas in your living room. I might never have seen it otherwise. I didn't know what to do, Catie. I agonized over it. Finally Adam stepped in and told me to stay away from it and let things unfold naturally. Which, apparently, they did."

"You could have told me. I feel like such an idiot not having noticed it before. And I wouldn't have flaunted it in front of Marc if I had known, especially if I'd known it was going to cause him such pain. What's the story with it anyway?"

"That you have to get from him. Honest. It's not mine to tell. And I'd hardly call what happened flaunting it. I think Adam was right. This whole thing is unfolding naturally. Like destiny. There was no real reason for Marc to see that you had the picture, except that it seems to link the two of you. If that link wasn't meant to be, the picture probably wouldn't have fallen, and you wouldn't have had it in your car, and he wouldn't have seen it and reacted. Now the next step is for him to open up and tell you why. I'm probably the only person outside of his family who knows what happened. He's still so tormented by guilt. When he does tell you, it means he really trusts you, Catie. It means he's giving you his heart."

"You mean if he tells me. The thing is, Josie, we were good friends and now everything's strained. Not just because of this. I really miss talking with him. I want to reach out, but I don't dare."

"Why?"

"I don't know."

"Yes you do. It's because you're afraid you'll realize you're making the wrong decision, marrying Derrick and not giving yourself time to fall in love with Marc."

"Josie. I warned you about that. I'm getting married next Saturday. Either you're with me or against me on it. You can't be half way."

When they hung up, Caitlin went back to the living room and studied the picture. The young girl was perched on a sled, her knit hat slightly askew, on top of finely spun blonde hair. She was off to the side, on the fringes of the frozen pond, her dog by her side. A wistful look was on her face as she watched the older children skating. Snow fell in huge, fluffy flakes. Pinecones were nestled in already fallen snow by the base of a large tree. The artist's name was embedded in the trunk of that tree, in artfully constructed block letters so that it became part of the bark. Once again Caitlin ran her fingers over the artist's name: M. Gallagher.

Chapter Thirty-One

When the delivery boy handed her the long florist's box, Caitlin assumed they were white roses from Derrick. She was unprepared for the rush of emotion that swept across her when she opened the box and discovered a bouquet of irises in a purple so deep and so lush they seemed to be made of velvet. The message was written in Marc's large scrawl. I'm so sorry. Please let me explain. Meet me at the Bond at three. She knew she shouldn't go; she had way too much to do. After all, tomorrow evening she was getting married and leaving on a three-week honeymoon. The last thing she should be doing is meeting Marc Gallagher. Still, she was burning with curiosity. And didn't she owe him the courtesy of an explanation?

"I don't have much time," Caitlin announced as she walked into the old lobby, pushing her bangs back off her head. "Hello?" she called out. "Marc?" The entire place appeared vacant. Why wasn't anybody working? Maybe she'd misunderstood the message. Maybe he hadn't meant today. She felt momentarily let down, when he appeared in the doorway to the dining room. He looked like his old self once again, a windblown handsomeness about him that Caitlin found endearing.

"Hi," Caitlin said. "Where is everybody?"

"Hi yourself." He smiled. "I sent everyone home early. I wanted a little time alone with you."

"Oh?" Caitlin's stomach fluttered. "Well, I really don't have much time. Tomorrow's the big day, you know, and I have lots to do. I'm sorry I didn't invite you to the wedding. It's going to be small and, besides, somehow I just though it would be awkward—" She put her hands to her cheeks, as though the action itself would stop the red from traveling up her neck and filling her face with color. "I talk too much sometimes."

Marc leaned against the threshold between the two rooms, giving her one of his half-smiles. "Calm down, Caitlin. I'm not going to bite, I promise. I have a wedding gift for you. I just wanted a few minutes. alone to wish you well. And, well, to apologize." He held out his hand and beckoned her to follow.

The large hotel dining room was dark and cool. It was a windowless room, with heavy wood and ornate paneling. Across an aluminum folding table, Marc had spread a lace tablecloth, and on the table were silver candlesticks, the flames of the candles flickering with their movements. Marc filled crystal glasses with champagne and handed one to Caitlin then lifted his toward her. "To you, Caitlin McKenna Saunders, may happiness follow you all the days of your life."

"Thank you, Marc." She took his hand. "You really are a good friend."

They stood quietly, holding hands, in a room so still it seemed to Caitlin that she could feel the beating of Marc's heart in his fingertips. Her own heart raced as their hands gripped tighter, as though afraid to let go, afraid of what might be lost when they did. Caitlin shook her head in an effort to break the trance.

Marc swallowed hard and took a deep breath. "Well," he said.

"Well," Caitlin said back, taking a small sip of champagne.

"Here." Marc pulled a box out from under the table. "A wedding present. From me to you."

"Oh, Marc," she said sadly, fingering the white paper and huge silver bow. "Do you want to come to the wedding? You can, you know. I just thought, well, you know—"

"I know. And you're right. I just wish you'd given us more time. But you didn't, so the best I can do is wish you happiness. But my being there...you were right, it wouldn't work."

Caitlin kept her eyes down, unable to meet his gaze. She kept running her fingers across the smooth wrapping paper and textured ribbon, not knowing quite what to do with herself.

"Don't be sad. You should be happy. And if you are, I'll be happy for you. Go ahead, open the present."

She threw him a thankful look and then began opening the gift. "Oh, Marc, it's gorgeous." She held the crystal vase up to the candlelight. It was brilliantly cut with flowers engraved in each of four oval panels. Above and below the panels were chains of diamond-shaped etchings, so fine they captured even the candlelight and bounced color back into the room. It was about twelve inches high with the top fanning out wider than the base. Perfect for a bouquet of irises.

"I turned the antique shops upside down looking for just the right one," Marc said. "See the S surrounded by a wreath here on the bottom? That means it's an authentic Sinclair and it's exactly the kind of vase they would have used in this room in the twenties. I wanted you to have it, as a reminder of our work together. Of the Bond the way it used to be. But you didn't have to get married to get it." He smiled. "I would have given it to you at the end of the renovations, as part of the celebration."

"I don't know what to say."

"Don't say anything. And listen, if you ever need a friend, if you ever need anything at all, I'm here for you. Day or night, you understand?"

Caitlin nodded, unable to trust her voice. Marc moved closer, until she could feel the warmth of his breath on her face. She looked up at him knowing how it would feel to have his lips on hers. She didn't back away. Instead, she moved a little closer. Marc took her face in his hands and traced the outline of her lips with his fingers. "We've been connected from the moment we met." His voice was husky. "Why couldn't you wait? Why couldn't you give us time?"

"I can't explain it..." Caitlin stammered, wanting Marc to kiss her and so afraid that he might. "It just sort of happened with David and me. I mean Derrick...Derrick and me. It just seemed to unfold. I don't even remember making a conscious decision."

"Oh, Cate," he pulled her to him, hugging her tightly against his body, the top of her head coming just to his shoulder. The moment for kissing had passed.

They stood for the longest time, arms wound around each other. Caitlin was the one to pull away. "Marc. I have to go. I'm getting married tomorrow." Standing there in the flickering candlelight, she needed to remind herself of that fact, as much as she did him. "I have a lot to do."

"You can't go yet. I have dinner, right here." From a small cooler, Marc produced tuna sandwiches and salads. "Cooler food. It's the best I could do."

"Picnic food," Caitlin corrected. "How can I resist? But I have to leave as soon as we're done eating." She sat down and unwrapped her sandwich. "Reminds me of that first afternoon you came to the cemetery with me."

"Cate, I want to explain. About the picture and all."

"You painted it."

Marc nodded. "Seeing it in your car like that really threw me. Set me back ten years. Somehow, I blamed you for how I felt. Irrationally, I assumed you knew all along...maybe Josie had told you that the painting was mine, and now you were taunting me with it. I really am sorry. I know that isn't true. I knew it then. I just needed a place for my anger, and you were there."

"But why?" Caitlin asked. "Forget about me. Apology accepted. Why didn't you ever tell me you're an artist? And why does that picture upset you so much?"

"It was the last one I ever painted. Although I didn't know it at the time. I loved that picture. Selling it was difficult, but you paid good money for it. Two month's mortgage, to be exact. I wish I could remember you. I've been wracking my mind trying to place you there, buying my painting. And now look at us, here today, ten years later."

"This is what Josie calls destiny," Caitlin said. "It's funny. I remember that day very clearly now. The Mystic show was filled with artists, up one street and down another. I was with a girlfriend. Neither of us were in the market for artwork, not really. I saw the painting from across the street. I almost got killed getting over to it, panicked that someone would buy it before I had a chance. I ate peanut butter and jelly for a month afterward, trying to balance my meager budget. But I never regretted it. It's odd, but I'd forgotten all about this. Your eyes, they haunted me for days afterward. I wanted to go back to Mystic, to find you. Eventually, I shook the feeling and got on with my life. Maybe that's why you seemed so familiar that day Josie introduced us on the beach. Remember how unsettled I seemed? Couldn't meet your eyes, digging my toes in the hot sand?"

"I remember." Marc laughed. "You were a pistol that day. That whole weekend in fact. Lady Ice!"

"Selling the painting must have felt great. So why did seeing it in my car upset you so much?"

"It wasn't the painting so much, as what it reminded me of. I've spent the past ten years trying to push down the memories, and they all came flooding back that day in your car. I sold three paintings that Saturday in Mystic. I was ecstatic. To my mind, it validated me as an artist. If that kept up, we'd be comfortable. It meant I could make a living at art and things would become right between us again. Sheila and I had been fighting a lot. She wanted to quit her job, have another baby. And her parents, particularly her father, were always on my back to get a 'real job' and support my family the way a man should. The pressure was getting to both of us. All of that was going through my head as I drove home Saturday night. I couldn't wait to see Sheila, to tell her the good news. Who knows? Maybe I'd sell a couple more on Sunday. Everything was going to be fine. Except when I got home, there was no Sheila. No Jennifer. And it was all my fault."

"You don't have to do this, Marc. You don't have to tell me any more."

"Yes, I do. It's time. No walls. No secrets."

"No walls. No secrets," Caitlin repeated, taking hold of his hand.

"I was twenty-five when I married Sheila," Mark continued. "She was pregnant. She knew painting was my life, and I was determined to make a name for myself. As a wedding gift, her father gave us enough money for a down payment on a handyman's special. It wasn't much of a house, but it was a start, and by putting in more windows, I converted one of the upstairs rooms into a studio. Meanwhile, Sheila worked full time—we needed steady income—and she still had the energy to turn the house into a real home. I hate to say it, but I barely noticed.

"The only thing outside of my painting that I didn't ignore was Jennifer. She was the light of my life, with that blonde hair and those violet eyes. I felt I had to give her lots of love, to make up for that strawberry birthmark on her face. It became my personal crusade. I gave her a miniature oil painting set, and from the time she could walk, she spent hours with me in the studio painting on large sheets of brown paper. Actually, I feel bad about all that now. On top of everything else, Sheila must have felt left out.

"By the fourth year, we began to fight regularly. I'm not sure if we even loved each other any more by then. You know what they say— when poverty knocks on the door, love goes out the window, or something like that. We needed more money coming in just to break even. The house needed a new furnace. The wiring was old--we were always blowing fuses. She was tired of wearing cheap, outdated clothes and eating hamburger three times a week. I couldn't fault her. I sympathized with her...but not enough to stop painting. I was convinced things would turn around. And by the fifth summer, they'd started to. My paintings were finally being recognized, and I was starting to make some real money.

"The weekend of the Mystic Art Show was hotter than hell."

"I remember that," Cailtin said. She got up and moved around the room, unable to sit still, feeling the heat in the room, just as it had been back then. "The weather hadn't broken in weeks. Every day was more of the same: temperatures bordering one hundred and the air saturated with humidity."

"That exactly right," Marc said. "Sheila had been putting bowls of ice in front of the fan to cool her off at night, but nothing seemed to work. She finally went out and bought an air conditioner for the bedroom on credit. It sat there for two days before I got around to putting it in early Saturday morning, just before leaving for the show. As soon as I turned it on, the fuse blew. Those damn fuses, they were always going. And I was in a real hurry.

"I went down to the basement and rummaged through my box of fuses. It called for a fifteen amp, but I knew if I used that, it would keep blowing; and besides, I didn't have any more. It would mean a trip to the hardware store. So I popped in a thirty amp. I told Sheila to keep the air conditioner on all day, so the room would be really cool when she went to bed that night. Obviously, she did. She had Jennifer sleep in bed with her that night, so they'd both be comfortable. Little did anyone know that all day the wiring had been heating up. With the thirty amp fuse, it never blew; instead, the wiring inside the walls just got hotter and hotter. With the door closed and the air conditioner going full blast, the room must have been like an inferno when the fire broke out. The fire chief said they probably never even knew what hit them."

"Oh Marc..." Caitlin took his hand again and held it tightly while he continued talking.

"Everything was destroyed in the fire. Everything. Forget my paintings. I'd give anything to have one of Jennifer's right now. My selfishness, that's what destroyed them. I vowed never to paint again. The most I've ever done since is a pumpkin now and then for some church fairs, and that one for you."

"Marc, it was an accident. To give up your painting...you're so talented."

"I had to. It was the only thing I had of value. I had to give it up. The one thing we had was insurance money. Sheila's father was in the business, so he saw to that. It must have killed him to see the check issued. It was sent to me by an anonymous clerk. It felt like blood money. I almost didn't take it. But I did, and for two years I had the closest thing I could imagine to a nervous breakdown. I bought the place at the beach and spent every waking minute renovating it, wearing myself out so I'd fall into a stupor at night. Eventually, the work and the sea air, and enough time, made me whole enough to begin a new life. I discovered I enjoyed creating space, developing land. I used what was left of the insurance money, plus some bank loans, to build a couple homes on spec. The rest, as they say, is history."

"And you do things like Esperanza."

"It helps. Giving back. Trying to make a difference."

Caitlin stroked Marc's hand and then slowly, gently, lifted it to her lips, kissing his fingers, then the palm of his hand. He reached over with this other hand and brushed away her tears, his eyes never once leaving hers. It was hard for Caitlin to know how much time passed before she took at deep breath. "Marc..."

"Don't. Don't go."

"I have to."

"You're always leaving me." He stroked her hair and leaned in to kiss her.

Caitlin started to pull away and then stopped. She kissed him back and then picked up her things, wiping tears from her eyes. "Marc, I'm really sorry. I have to go. I'm getting--"

"Married. I know."

Chapter Thirty-Two

Derrick arrived at nine the next morning, suitcases in hand, beaming an infectious smile. "Today's the day. Are you going to finally let me move in?" Derrick joked. "I would have been here at daybreak, but I knew you'd kill me for waking you so early." He kissed Caitlin and carried his bags straight to the bedroom. "Don't panic. I'm not a heavy packer. Only one's for the trip," he said. "The rest is stuff I'll need immediately, when we get back. We can pack up my condo later, once we sell it. God, Catie, am I happy. The happiest I've ever been in my life." He whirled her around until they were both so dizzy they fell onto the bed.

"I am too, Derrick. When David died, I don't know, I thought my world had collapsed around me. And then you showed up, out of the blue. You filled all the empty space." She played with his short strands of hair. If she squinted enough to blur Derrick's features, she could still actually fool herself into thinking she was with David. It was the haircut, and the glasses. And his smell. She could close her eyes and feel David next to her. It was disconcerting and comforting all at once.

"I'll make you happy, Catie, I promise. I'll never let anything make you sad again. You believe that, don't you?"

"I believe you'll try," she answered softly. "But sometimes sadness isn't within our control."

"This is too serious," Derrick stated, attacking Caitlin under her arms, making her double over in giggles.

"Stop, stop!" she cried out between laughs, trying hard to get back at him, but Derrick was stronger and quicker than she was.

Finally he stopped and gave her a warm, lingering kiss. "I'd love to make love to you right now. We have the entire day ahead of us." He jumped off the bed quickly. "But I'm going to make us both suffer and save it for tonight, when you're officially Mrs. Derrick Secor."

"Are you sure?" Caitlin asked seductively.

"No." Derrick held out his hand to help her off the bed. "But let's try. Besides, I'm starving. Cook me some eggs, woman."

The day passed quickly. They both had hundreds of last-minute things to do to get ready for their evening wedding and small reception, and all the last minute details necessary before an extended trip. They buzzed around the house like two children getting ready for the first day of school, scared and excited all at once.

"Only three more hours," Derrick warned Caitlin at exactly three o'clock. "You better start getting ready, unless, of course, you plan to marry me in that get-up. Which, by the way, wouldn't bother me a bit. Any way is okay, as long as you become mine."

"I think I'll fix up a bit," Caitlin said, pulling at her flat hair. She was wearing old denim shorts and a tank top. "As soon as you leave, which better be soon or I'll never have enough time."

The plan was that Derrick would get ready at Liz and Steve's. He would drive himself to the church and they would pick her up about five-thirty. Josie and Adam would meet them at the church. Getting Caitlin to the church—seeing her before anyone else—helped to soothe Liz's hurt feelings over not being maid of honor. Caitlin wondered how Derrick had gotten Steve to be so agreeable, given his feelings about Josie, but decided she was probably better off not knowing. She suspected it involved some promise to get things "back to normal"—the way they used to be. But that was never going to happen. Caitlin had a new normal by which to measure her life. Marc and Josie had seen to that. For the first time in her adult life, she was seeking answers beyond her comfort zone and looking for ways to change and grow. Her plan, once she and Derrick were settled into their married life, was to go to college and get her degree. She figured their honeymoon would be a good time to discuss her ideas with him. He'd feel confident about their relationship once they were married and would support her decision.

As soon as Derrick left, Caitlin went upstairs and took a long cool shower. She got ready slowly and calmly, not letting herself think about anything except the secure, happy life that lay in front of her. Then she took her dress from the closet and removed its plastic covering.

Caitlin had insisted that both Josie and Liz accompany her on the shopping excursion, giving them each private instructions on how to behave. "Liz is Liz," she warned Josie, "she's doing what's best for her. Don't ride her about it and don't make her feel like a loser because of her decision to stay with Steve." And she reminded Liz that while Josie may dance to the beat of a different drummer, she was a warm, loving person and a good friend.

They went to one bridal store after another until they found The Perfect Dress. It had to be ivory, or some shade of ecru, Josie insisted. And it had to be something absolutely feminine, in a tea length, Liz stated. Remarkably, they all agreed on the same dress, made of ivory Italian silk and adorned with fine embroidered flowers of the same color. It had an illusion neckline, dropped waist, and a trim of lace at the hem and sleeves. And it looked stunning on Caitlin.

She stepped into the dress, glad she'd decided to get ready alone, in the privacy of her own bedroom. Now...just a few finishing touches. Caitlin secured a sprig of Lily of the Valley to her hair with her grandmother's mother-of-pearl comb, and then pinned her cameo to the inset of lace at her neckline. Looking at herself in the full-length mirror, Caitlin felt like a bride from another time and place. For just an instant, she felt a rush of air beside her and an overwhelming sense of not being alone in the room. She turned quickly toward the door to see if someone had come into the room. When she turned back to the mirror, there was David, standing beside her, dressed for their wedding day. Caitlin reached out to touch his face. As her hand got closer, the image faded until there was only Caitlin, looking back at herself, hand outstretched. Smoothing out the skirt of her dress with trembling fingers, she turned away from her lone reflection.

Just nerves, Caitlin told herself. And guilt. She couldn't help but feel a pang of guilt at the one thing left to do. It was time to remove her wedding band.

She was about to slide off the ring and place it in David's leather jewel case next to his wedding band, when she noticed Derrick's glasses on a corner of the tall bureau. Caitlin went over and picked them up. He was so excited, he'd probably forgotten them. Unless, of course, he'd decided to wear his contacts. But that would be almost out of character; he'd never worn them after that first date. Except for the Halloween party. She'd call Liz and have Steve run over to pick them up. Derrick wouldn't be able to drive without them.

Absently, she held the glasses up to the light of the window, examining them for no particular reason except that they were Derrick's. They were a part of the man she was about to marry.

"Oh my God—" She dropped the glasses on the bureau as though they'd turned hot in her hand. She looked at them, puzzled, and then carefully picked them up again. The lenses. They were made of glass, plain ordinary glass. He didn't need them at all.

She sat down on the bed, all dressed and ready to go, feeling like a jilted prom date. Because of a pair of glasses? Don't buy into Josie's suspicions. There's an explanation. We're only talking about a pair of glasses here. Or are we?

She looked at the clock on the bureau. There was only a half-hour before Liz and Steve showed up. Caitlin stood, shaking her hands and arms, urging the blood back into them. She knew what she had to do.

She began searching every inch of bureau and closet space she'd given to Derrick over the past months. Piece by piece, she had removed David's belongings so there would be room for Derrick's. Piece by piece, he had invaded David's space. At least that's how it felt now. Like an invasion. Finally. There it was. Tucked in the back corner of a drawer, under the lining of paper, she found what she was looking for: Derrick's small black notebook.

Turning page after page, Caitlin read all his notes, meticulously written in black ink. Dated entries. One after the other. Starting a week before that first date and ending with their engagement.

When the doorbell rang at exactly five-thirty, she wiped the tears from the corners of her eyes and walked down the stairs, clutching the notebook in her hand.

Liz and Steve looked like the perfect couple—Ken and Barbie is all Caitlin could think—faces gleaming, all dressed up in fancy clothes, ready for the wedding. "So, what do you think?" Liz asked, turning 365 degrees so Caitlin could inspect the movement of her pink silk dress. "And look at these earrings." She pointed to the diamond studs in her ears. "Two karats each. Wait until Sylvia sees these. Tell me she won't die."

"My last payment," Steve snarled. "Guilt doesn't run cheap these days."

"Neither does infidelity," Liz cooed, slipping her arm through his. "But we're going to forget all about that. Things are getting back to normal."

"The wedding's off," Caitlin announced, clutching the book in her hand.

"What?" they said in unison.

"The wedding's off." Caitlin grabbed her purse from the table in the foyer and pushed her way between Liz and Steve. "I won't let him manipulate me again!" she shouted over her shoulder. "Not ever!"

Chapter Thirty-Three

Caitlin had no idea where she was headed as she got behind the wheel and sped away from the house. Anywhere, as long as it was away--away from the church, away from Derrick and the strange control he seemed to have over her.

"David, I'm so sorry. So sorry," Caitlin said out loud. She was overwhelmed by guilt, realizing how easily she'd been willing to supplant David with Derrick, to let an imposter move into his space, take over his memory. "It just seemed so right."

The word again burned in her mind. What had she meant by that? She wouldn't let Derrick manipulate her again. Those were her exact words as she ran away from Liz and Steve. It was as though he'd done it before, that this was a repeat of some past experience. But that simply wasn't so. Or was it?

Remember, Catie, remember. David was speaking those words to her now, as she drove the car. Caitlin could see his face, right in front of her, blinding her to oncoming cars. Then she saw Derrick's face, laughing, mocking her. Suddenly there was a group of faces, all versions of David and Derrick, all faces she didn't recognize. And then there was Marc's face, off to the side, as though waiting patiently for her to recognize him. But it wasn't really Marc. Yes it was. He just looked different. But it was Marc. She'd know those cobalt eyes anywhere.

There was a blast of light and the sensation of a cool breeze. The last curtain was being pulled back for her. Caitlin sensed her father's presence on the other side, ready to be her guide down this forgotten path. She felt less afraid, knowing her father was there — he would never harm her, never lead her into dangerous territory. It would be good to be with him again, if only for a while, to discover the meaning behind all this.

Caitlin smiled, ready to begin the journey, when suddenly, she was enveloped in darkness. Like a cruel practical joke, the curtain became unbearably heavy once again; it dropped with a loud crash before she could cross the threshold into the bright light. All she could feel now was pain.

* * *

Caitlin opened her eyes to see her mother standing over her. She was dressed in blue chiffon and rhinestone jewelry, her hair meticulously coifed and sprayed. She looked as though she was going to a wedding. Oh my God, she is, Caitlin realized. My wedding.

"Catie, dear, you're okay. You're going to be okay." She smelled of Shalimar—her "good" perfume—and her voice actually had the soothing, lilting quality she reserved for only the most tragic of circumstances. Caitlin couldn't remember the last time she heard her mother's "comfort voice"—not even at David's funeral. Yes, she remembered now...she was twenty-three—

"You hit a tree." Josie's voice was coming at her from a corner of the room, cutting into her thoughts. Caitlin turned in time to see Josie flash her a wide grin and a thumbs-up. "But you're going to be fine. Your mother doesn't lie. Miracle of miracles, a few scratches and a couple broken ribs —"

"What's this?" Caitlin asked, her voice raspy, filled with pain. She was pointing to the tube coming out of her chest.

"Oh, that." Josie was trying hard to sound casual. She was by Caitlin's side now, patting her hand. "Well, you didn't get out of this wedding the easy way. One of those ribs you broke punctured a lung. But everything's going to be okay. Honest. They put that tube in there to re-inflate your lung. In twenty-four hours, you'll be good as new; but they'll probably keep you in a few days, just to make sure. Not to worry. Honest."

"What happened?" Caitlin asked. "Do you know what happened?"

"We thought you'd tell us," Josie said. "All we know is that you hit a tree. You were a block away from the Bond. I called Marc. He's on his way over."

"No, don't. I don't want to see him. I don't want to see anyone." Caitlin put her hand to her head. The pain...she was in so much pain... what had happened? That's right...she remembered now. The brightness...the loud crash...and then blackness. She had thought the curtain to the past was closing on her again, that maybe she wasn't going to remember after all. Instead, she had hit a tree. Too many faces in her way. Too much light. She couldn't see the road.

"It's a done deed, Catie. I already called Marc," Josie said. "Besides, you couldn't keep him away."

Liz burst into the room. "Catie, Catie! Are you all right? Is she all right?" She walked over to the bed and grabbed Caitlin's hand, nearly pushing Josie aside. "We've been worried sick about you. Steve's downstairs turning thirty shades of green. You know how bad he is with hospitals. When you ran off like that, I just knew something awful would happen, and it did. I can feel a migraine coming on."

"I'm fine, Liz. A bruised ego, more than anything. I can't even run away from a wedding in style." Caitlin tried laughing, but it hurt too much. She gripped the metal bar on the side of the bed until the sharpness of pain subsided. "Go home, take care of that headache."

"In a minute," Liz said. "But you have to tell us why you ran away." She spotted Caitlin's dress soiled and torn, rolled in a lump on one of the chairs. "Your beautiful dress. You'll never be able to wear it now."

"I don't intend to. Please, everybody, leave. I'm so tired. I need time alone."

"She's right," Nora McKenna said, asserting her motherly authority. She kissed Caitlin's head and beckoned for the others to follow her out of the room. "We'll figure things out tomorrow. A new day, a new perspective. Have a good sleep, Caitlin."

"She will once we've talked." Derrick's voice seemed to bounce off every wall in the room. He stood in the doorway, dressed in a black tuxedo, a single white rose pinned to his lapel. His face was tight with rage.

The women all stopped mid-stride, but Caitlin dismissed them with the sweep of her hand. "Go. Please. He won't be here long."

As soon as they left, Derrick closed the door. He began pacing the length of the small room. "How could you do this to me? To yourself? Look at you, all bruised, broken ribs. That horrible tube coming out of your chest. Why, Catie, why?" Then his voice softened and he knelt by her bedside, stroking her hand and arm. "Catie, you look so hurt, and so sad. Why were you leaving me, Catie? I love you so much."

"Where are your glasses, Derrick?"

"You cancel our wedding and nearly got yourself killed and you want to know where my glasses are?"

"Where are they?"

"At the house, I suppose."

"So, how can you see? You say you need them. You wear them all the time. They're a fairly strong prescription, aren't they?"

"What is this, Catie, what's the point?"

"Just answer my question."

"All right. I'll play your silly game. Yes, they're a strong prescription. You know they are. I'm wearing my contacts. So I'm vain. You caught me. Hang me by my thumbnails."

"Take them out, Derrick."

"What?"

"You heard me. You're wearing contacts. Take them out."

"For Christ sakes, Catie. I am not going to take out my contacts."

"I said, take them out!"

"I can't! All right? I can't because I'm not wearing any. And I don't need glasses either. Satisfied? You know my deep, dark secret. I'm a fraud. I don't wear friggin' glasses. And for that, you sell me down the river?"

"Not for that," Caitlin whispered. She could barely talk now, but she had to finish this. "Give me my purse." She was sure she'd thrown it into her purse as she ran for the car. Derrick watched as she struggled with the clasp. "For this," Caitlin said, producing the small leather notebook.

Color drained from Derrick's face, fear replacing rage. He sat down next to her. "I meant to throw that away months ago. I never meant to hurt you. Give me another chance, Catie. I love you. I really do." He started to stroke her left hand, until he saw that she was still wearing David's wedding ring. He pulled back as though hit with a blast of frigid air. "I didn't know I'd fall in love with you. I just didn't know."

"Just tell me why. You owe me that. And then I want you to go back to my house and remove every last one of your things. I don't want any evidence of your ever having been there."

Derrick took a deep breath. "Don't do this to me. Please." He looked more boy than man right then, beaten and vulnerable, and Caitlin had to steel her resolve to keep from feeling sorry for him. But then her fingers tightened around the leather notebook and she knew that nothing would ever be right again.

"I don't know where too begin," he said.

"Begin right here." Caitlin opened up the notebook. "With the first entry." She was groggy and in pain, but she needed to know. "White roses. Callahan's Florist. Whiting House, by the Connecticut River. Everything in here is about me, about what I like; about David, his after-shave, the kind of shoes he wore...And Catidid! Here it is, catalogued under nickname. My God, Derrick, you seduced me with that name!"

Caitlin kept flipping through the pages, her voice becoming shrill and excited. She wiped her damp forehead with the edge of the sheet. It was as though some force outside herself was giving her the strength to continue. "Here --" She thumped the small page with her index finger. "Our champagne. Kristal. I'd wondered how you could have bought that same one simply by coincidence. Nothing was by coincidence was it, Derrick? It was all designed to make me fall in love with you."

She threw the open-paged book at him. It hit his thigh and bounced to the floor. "Sick. You're sick. You spent all this energy trying to recreate David. For what? So I could fall in love with you? I don't even know who you are. You're just some sick imitation of a dead man! I don't love you. I hate you." She wanted to cry, but it hurt too much. The sobs remained stuck in her chest, making her breathing labored and uneven.

"Catie, let me explain. Maybe I can make you understand. This whole thing just got out of hand. But by then, I really loved you and I didn't know how to stop. I just decided to let things go on the way they were. After all, we were happy, weren't we? And I didn't mind being a little more like David. In a way, it's what I always wanted. It started to feel natural. I almost couldn't tell where one of us ended and the other began."

"You were good, Derrick. Neither could I. Just tell me why."

"Okay. But then give me another chance, Catie. I'm really not so bad."

Chapter Thirty-Four

As Derrick began to tell Caitlin his story, he was once again back in high school, the insecure senior who couldn't hold a candle to David Saunders, the one who always stood in David's shadow waiting for an invitation to tag along, waiting for the girls David would magnanimously hand over when he was tired of them.

Chance had thrown them together all through school. Or Fate. Their last names kept them in the same homeroom and sometimes the same classes. But it was something else that bonded them as friends. It was their need: Derrick's need to learn from David, and David's need to be revered.

They were the same age, about the same build, and they had nearly identical coloring. That's what always baffled Derrick. They were so much alike, yet David had that something extra that made him popular, that made the girls stand in line for his attention. Coming from the right side of town helped, as did having pocket money, even on a Monday when everyone else was generally broke. Derrick had none of that going for him. His father was a laborer, not an attorney like David's, and Derrick's family lived in a modest clapboard house way across town. Beyond everything else, though, it was David's sense of being that attracted people: his easy smile, the way he had of always saying the right thing. And that's why Derrick hung around, in his shadows. He wanted to learn from David. He wanted to be just like him. And David liked having Derrick around----somebody who wouldn't steal the show, somebody who would be grateful for crumbs of attention, somebody who would continue to be loyal and faithful and always remind David how special he was.

For all his gifts, David's flaw was that he knew how good he was. And he used that knowledge for his own gain, often in ways that hurt others. For Derrick, the big hurt came the summer of his senior year. For once, he'd gotten a girl on his own. She wasn't one of David's cast-offs or someone's "nice but plain sister." She was a girl from Holy Academy. Her name was Lucille. She was a quiet girl, beautiful, with long, blonde hair and sea-blue eyes. For the first time in his life, Derrick was in love. And for the first time, Derrick had something of value, something that was his and his alone.

Derrick didn't even see it coming. He didn't suspect all those times when they'd be out together and David ended up sitting on the other side of Lucille, rather than next to his own date. Or when David would tag along, offering to drive and then he'd pick Lucille up first, or drop her off last. Derrick didn't even suspect anything when David announced he was going to spend July and August in Europe and Lucille cried for days. To his mind, she was a sensitive girl who cried over lost puppies and friends who went away.

"Don't worry," Derrick had consoled her, "he'll be back before you know it and the three of us will do all the old things." Meanwhile, it was a glorious summer for Derrick. He took Lucille to the beach, brought her on picnics with the family, and won stuffed animals for her at local fairs. If Lucille held back a little when he kissed her, if she seemed reluctant to do more than hold his hand and cuddle a little, that was okay. She was his and they were falling in love slowly. They had their whole life ahead of them.

And then David returned, married to Brenda. It'd been a whirlwind courtship through France and Italy. He'd forgotten all about Lucille, about his secret promise to marry her when they returned, if she really was pregnant. She'd only suspected when he left.

"It was just too much for her," Derrick told Caitlin. "A small town. Three month's pregnant by now. And I never even suspected. When I found out, I offered to marry her. I wanted to marry her. I didn't care whose child it was. A week later she swallowed a bottle of sleeping pills. I left town the day after. Didn't even stay for the funeral."

"You're lying!" Caitlin cried. "You're lying. That's not the David I knew. He could never be that callous."

"Maybe it wasn't the David you knew. Maybe being married to Brenda and having his own child made him grow up. But it was the David I knew—"

"You're lying. He was nothing like what you're telling me. Besides, what has that got to do with what you did to me?"

"I hated David after that. I blamed him for everything. Even my two failed marriages. If it wasn't for him, I would have been happily married to Lucille. If it wasn't for him, she'd still be alive. And then David died. My dad called and told me."

"That was you, at the cemetery?"

"Yeah, it was."

"Watching me?"

"Getting to know you."

"Whatever. You were spying."

"At first I was just curious. Then this plan, small at first, began to unfold. Before I knew it, it had totally taken over my brain. It was like I had no control over it. There you were, David's wife. Something of his I could take. But I knew you wouldn't fall for me. No more than Lucille had. I knew I had to become David. It was the only way. I was crazed, Catie, I know that. But the thing is, I don't want you because you're David's. Not any more. I want you because you're you."

Caitlin could feel bile build up in the back of her mouth. Waves of sweat passed over her body. She had to wait until the nausea left before she could speak.

Derrick took her silence as a sign of hope. "Catie, please. We can still make it work. I won't cancel our trip to Hawaii. I'll just postpone it until you're out of the hospital. Forget about having a wedding here, it was a lousy idea. We'll get married there. The sun and air will do you good. Help you to heal faster. Please, Catie. I can't lose you. I just can't."

What a tragic story, Caitlin thought. Even if it wasn't all true — it was his perception of the truth, and that made it just as real. Maybe he could make her happy. That's all she wanted, a little happiness. Losing Derrick would be like losing David all over again. Maybe it could still work. "Oh, Derrick..." she heard herself say in a small, forgiving voice.

Derrick's face filled with anticipation. But as he leaned in closer to Caitlin, the muscles just beneath his skin froze his face into a look that sent chills of warning down Caitlin's spine. It was the look of a man who'd finally won the battle; it was the look of a conqueror.

As difficult as it was to breath, Caitlin forced herself to inhale deeply. A small kernel of strength began to form, giving her the courage she needed. She struggled to take her engagement ring off her swollen finger, pain slicing through her with each movement. When it was off, she unclasped her diamond bracelet and pitched both pieces of jewelry into Derrick's hand. "It's over, Derrick." Caitlin told him. "It's finally over."

Chapter Thirty-Five

Derrick tightened his fist around the jewelry, gold and diamonds burning their imprint into the palm of his hand. The muscles in his neck and shoulders throbbed as he worked to contain his rage. He would win her back, but only if he maintained control. Taking a deep breath, he slipped the jewelry into the pocket of his tux, and then kissed Caitlin softly on the forehead, pushing strands of wet hair back from her face. Running the back of his thumb across an ugly bruise on her cheek, he truly wished he could erase the damage.

"I never meant to hurt you. I only wanted you to love me."

"Go, Derrick. I mean it."

"Catie..."

"Go!"

"We can make it work, Catie. Start over again—"

"I said go." Caitlin wiped her forehead with the already damp sheet, and reached for the buzzer. "I'll call for the nurse if you don't leave."

Derrick stared at Caitlin for a long hard moment calculating his options. Essentially there were none. He realized that now. Without another word, he stormed out of the room, allowing himself to feel the fury coursing through his veins. There had been nothing more he could say. She'd turned to stone in those last few seconds. Damn it! She'd almost forgiven him. Derrick had seen in her eyes; he heard it in the sad tone of her voice. But, somehow he'd played his cards wrong in that room; he'd done something to make her change her mind. But what?

He barged through the glass double doors of the hospital's front entrance, and in a final, grand gesture, tore the single white rose from his lapel, crumpled it in his hand, and threw it at one of the building's brick columns.

Then he saw Marc Gallagher coming up the walk and blocked his way. "She's not seeing anyone."

"Out of my way, Derrick. You're in no position to be calling the shots here."

"I said she's not seeing anyone."

Marc put his hand on Derrick's arm as though to push him aside.

"Don't touch me, man. Touch me and you're dead!" Derrick shouted, knowing he was losing control of the situation. Lose control and you lose. That was the motto he lived by, and he was blowing it. Out of the corner of his eye, he saw a security guard coming toward them. "Look, chief, I'm sorry," he told Marc. "I've had what you might call a bad day." He straightened his jacket, ran his fingers through his hair, and left before Marc could respond.

Derrick's next stop was Caitlin's house where he packed up all his belongings. He might as well clean out everything; it'd be a while before he was back and he'd need some of this stuff. Going from room to room, collecting various items now scattered throughout the house as if he really belonged there, he felt the kind of emptiness he'd known only one other time in his life. The day Lucille died, the day he left town and never looked back.

In the family room, he spent a long time looking at his favorite photograph of him and Caitlin on a carousel. They'd gone to a local carnival with Adam, Josie, and Courtney, and it was Courtney who had captured the moment on film. Strange, he thought, how things work out. He'd only set out to win Caitlin over, not to fall in love with her. There were to be no emotions at stake. She was simply going to be the final prize, the pawn that settled an old score. The real irony was that he'd had to be more like David than himself in order to win. And he would have won, if she hadn't found that stupid notebook. But, just like every other time, the real Derrick Secor took second place.

When the last box was loaded into his car, Derrick slammed the trunk and took one final look at the house. He was going to miss coming here...but he'd be back. Somehow he and Caitlin would end up together, he had to believe that.

Just then, Liz came running over. Oh, Christ, he thought, the broadcaster of the year. He didn't need her right now. But then again, maybe he did, if she was still in his corner.

"Derrick, hi," Liz said. "I'm really sorry about what's happened. I just wish I understood it all."

"Not much to understand, Liz. She dumped me."

"I guess that's what I don't understand." Liz dabbed at her eyes with a tissue. "She couldn't do better than you. Tell me what really happened. You know I won't breathe a word of it. I won't even let on to Caitlin that I know, if you don't want me to."

"Not much," Derrick said, leaning back against his car. He'd changed into a polo shirt and chinos. At least now he could let his hair grow and get back into some of his real clothes. That was definitely an up side to this mess. "I guess I tried too hard to please her. I kept notes about what she liked and disliked. She found that offensive."

"That's it?"

"As far as I can tell."

"I know she was curious about that notebook of yours. She mentioned it a lot. And about how you sometimes seemed too much like David. But to call off a wedding, for that? As far as I'm concerned, she could look far and wide before finding someone as wonderful as you. I really mean that." Liz grabbed hold of his hand. "This is just so awful. What will you do now? You're not going to give up, are you?"

"I'm not quite sure what I'm going to do. Give her some time."

"That's a good idea. Stay away and she'll see just how much she's missing. You know, absence makes the heart grow fonder. I bet she'll actually be calling you inside of a month. I'll put a good word in for you whenever I can."

"Thanks, Liz. I knew I could count on you." He kissed her on the cheek before getting into the car. "I'm sure, then, this isn't goodbye." Derrick put the key into the ignition and was ready to drive off.

"Oh, God!" Liz turned pink and threw her hands up to her cheeks. "I almost forgot, Derrick, I'm sorry. I hate to do this, but Catie called me from the hospital...and asked that I make sure and get the key from you. You know, the key to her house."

A wave of heat washed over Derrick's body. She wanted the key back? That made everything too permanent. He coughed before speaking. "Are you sure?" he asked, locking eyes with Liz.

"I'm sure," Liz said, her voice filled with pain.

"Maybe you forgot to ask me," Derrick suggested, stepping on the gas pedal so that the engine revved. "Maybe I just drove away before you remembered. That's really what almost happened anyway." He flashed Liz his most disarming smile.

"I'm sorry," was all Liz could say. Her eyes averted as she held out her hand. "She'll just change all the locks. And be furious with me."

Derrick dug deep into his pocket and held the key hard inside his fist before turning it over to Liz.

She hadn't even backed away from the car when Derrick put his Mercedes into gear and drove away. He couldn't get away from this place fast enough. A bunch of boring, middle-class people, living boring, middle-class lives. Who needed it? It's exactly what he'd had with his other two wives. Saved by the little black book!

Before he reached the end of the block, Derrick had formed a plan for himself. Europe. He had lots of time coming. After all, he was supposed to be on his honeymoon. Italy and France. That's where the women were. He'd find somebody who really appreciated him. He'd call his boss, tell him he didn't need the transfer after all. Everything would fall into place. In fact, it'd be better than ever.

He checked his image in the rear view mirror. For the first time that day, he was pleased with himself. By the time he finished wooing Europe, he'd be his old self again. He didn't need Caitlin Saunders. After all, she was just another one of David's cast-offs.

Chapter Thirty-Six

Marc visited Caitlin every day in the hospital, but no matter how hard he tried, he was unable to get more than polite conversation and distant smiles from her. It was as though she was on the outside looking in through a window at her own life. Derrick had pulled the rug out from under her, and, wobbly as she was, Caitlin was apparently unwilling to reach out for help, not knowing who would be there or who would pull it out once again.

Caitlin had been home from the hospital for almost two weeks when Marc decided it was time for her to get out, to begin getting involved in life again. He showed up on her doorstep late one morning. She was still in her chenille robe, un-showered, drinking coffee. "It's beautiful out, Cate. A perfect September morning. Get dressed and we'll take a ride to the Bond. And then maybe out for a small bite. You'll be surprise how much has been done since you've been there," Marc said.

"I can't."

"Sure you can. Just throw on a pair of jeans. Or take an hour and make yourself ravishing. Whatever makes you feel good. I'll wait."

"Being left alone is what makes me feel good," Caitlin said, walking back into the kitchen to refill her coffee cup.

Marc followed right behind, ignoring her attempt to ignore him. "Cate, don't do this to yourself."

"Do what?"

"Walk away from life. From me. I...love you. I didn't plan to tell you like this. I thought maybe we'd be better dressed for the occasion." Marc tugged at the ties of her robe, hoping to get a smile out of her.

"Don't. I'm not interested," Caitlin said, turning away from him.

Marc gently took hold of Caitlin's shoulders and turned her around, tucking his fingers under her chin so her eyes met his. "I know this is soon in terms of what happened with Derrick and all, but we've known each other for a year now. We've worked with each other, shared sorrows, become good friends. I love you and I want us to have a life together."

"I can't. Just leave me alone." Tears stung her eyes. "I rushed into marriage with Derrick because I was afraid to be alone. I don't want the same thing to happen again."

"Do you honestly think it would, with me?"

"I don't know."

"Caitlin, you rushed into marriage with Derrick because he manipulated you. He played mind games at a time when you were most vulnerable. That has nothing to do with you and me, with how we feel about each other."

"It has everything to do with me," Caitlin said. "I let him do it. What does that say about me? I have to take responsibility for it. There's too much going on inside of me, too many questions I still need answers to. I can't work on me if I'm spending my energy loving you."

"Does that mean you do love me or that you could love me?" Marc asked.

"I'm not sure what it means. I just know that I need time. I'm going to stay away from the Bond for a while. You'll all manage fine without me, I'm sure. And I don't want you calling me. Or coming by. I mean it. I need to be alone-- really alone. It's the only way I'll be able to figure out my life."

"Cate —"

"I mean it, Marc. If I mean anything to you at all, I'm begging you... just leave me alone."

"Derrick...he ruined it all, didn't he? We belong together, you know that. But I'm going to do what you ask. Because I do I love you. Maybe someday you'll see that. I just hope it's not too late."

Chapter Thirty-Seven

Sara Livingston opened the door to her small, tidy home, inviting Caitlin and Josephine inside. "How was the ride down?" she asked. "Did your ribs survive?"

Caitlin and Josie had left Connecticut early in the morning, making the ride to Cape Cod for another reading. This time it wouldn't be Tarot cards, Sara had said. They would use another method to explore how Caitlin's past lives were influencing her present one.

She led Caitlin to a wooden straight-back chair and immediately poured freshly-made lemonade into tall flowered glasses. Everything about Sara seemed to be flowers—her long skirt, the chintz-covered sofa, the matching curtains, even the scent of her perfume. It was an odd contrast to her dark looks and abrupt manner.

"We're fine," Caitlin assured her.

"Speak for yourself," Josie laughed. "My bladder, or ribs for that matter, will never be the same. The long drive to the Cape is nothing, but the road into this place—it's brutal. We hit every bump and pothole imaginable."

"I know," Sara said. "But it does cut down on traffic. I like my privacy. Now, sit. Relax. Use the bathroom if you need to. We start only when you're ready."

Once they were all settled and comfortable, Caitlin turned to Sara, leaning forward slightly in her chair. "I need to know what's been going on. My dreams. Derrick. Why I said the word again like I did—I asked Josie to tell you all about it—it's been plaguing me. It's as though everything was repeating itself from some other time."

"Life. Life repeats itself." Sara nodded her head knowingly. "Sometimes our past comes crashing into the present, like a head-on collision. We have all this wisdom. We don't use it. So life hits us in the head. To make us understand things we should already know." She laughed merrily. "And you got hit!"

"And hard!" Josie said.

"I guess." Caitlin smiled weakly.

"Your gut." Sara pounded her stomach. "You didn't listen to your gut! Not to worry." She walked over to Caitlin and patted her hand kindly, reassuringly.

"Tell me exactly what we're going to do," Caitlin said. "I'm a little nervous."

"Nervous!" Sara laughed and winked at Josie. "Looking for the truth makes our friend nervous. Not to worry. Truth is freeing. You will feel better with the truth."

"But what exactly are you going to do?"

"It's not what I'm going to do. It's what you're going to do. Your soul's memory has been stirred. I'm here to guide you, to help you find out why."

"I don't know...I don't understand all of this..." Caitlin hated cryptic non-answers.

Josie was quick to answer for Sara. "Remember when I explained karma and everything to you way back? Well, sometimes we choose to have a lifetime that's dedicated primarily to resolving old karma. And when that happens, we find ourselves faced with problems very similar to those in a past life-- and with the same people, or souls, if you will. In this case, it will be very interesting to see how many times in the past you knew Derrick and just what your relationship was to him each time."

"Oh, God. I'm scared," Caitlin said, rubbing the palms of her hands across her lap.

"Catie, you don't have to do this. We can just pretend we drove to the Cape for lunch," Josie said.

"Oh, yes, I do. I've come this far. I'm not turning back. Just tell me exactly what you're going to do, Sara, and then let's get started."

"I'm going to hypnotize you. You'll continue to be aware of everything that's going on, and when you come out of it, you'll remember everything that happened. I'm going to ask you to go back, before your birth, to those lives that are having a vital impact on this lifetime. You'll use your inner eye, your mind's eye, to view past life scenes. Because you see a veiled curtain in all your dreams, we'll use that imagery in taking you back."

Caitlin took a deep breath. "Okay, I'm ready."

Sara began, her voice becoming soft and soothing, losing all hint of harshness. "First we'll call for spiritual protection. Imagine a pure white light, Caitlin, entering the top of your head and filling your entire body, surrounding each and every muscle. We ask that this white light protect you, and that only good can flow from you and only good can flow toward you. We ask this in the name of the Lord. Now, Caitlin, relax. Take a deep breath. Exhale. Feel the beat of your heart and be aware of its regularity. Be aware of the rhythm of your breathing. Feel the air as it enters your body, as it fills your lungs, and then as it leaves your body. Take a deep breath and exhale completely. You are becoming more and more relaxed as you set aside your conscious mind and allow your inner eye to work for you. When you awaken, you will be relaxed and alert and filled with a renewed sense of purpose. You will remember everything that has happened. Take a deep breath and exhale completely. Every muscle in your body is now relaxed. You are completely comfortable."

As Caitlin began to sink into a state of total relaxation, she felt a heaviness in her arms and legs, a sense of not wanting to move. Sara's voice seemed to come from some place completely removed and far away.

"Caitlin," Sara continued, "you are now completely at ease and unafraid, for there is nothing to fear. You are at that final curtain, the one from your dreams. I want you to pull back that curtain and walk through the corridor of bright light until you get to the other side. That's right, pull it back and walk through. See how calm everything is. When you get to the end, there will be more curtains, this time all set in front of you, in a long horizontal line. Each curtain is pulled across a stage, a stage that represents a past life or a significant past life experience. Walk back and forth in front of the stages, touch each curtain, see how it feels and smells, and then pull back the one that you seem most drawn to, the one, perhaps, that will show a strong correlation to your present life. Take a look, Caitlin, pull back one of the curtains. Tell me what you see."

"A town. Horses. It's a Western town."

"Do you see any people?"

"A woman. She's walking to the sheriff's office. She has something in her hands. It looks like a plate, covered with a napkin. It looks like dinner. She's bringing dinner to the sheriff."

"Who is she? What is her name?"

"Molly. Molly Walker."

"What does she look like? Describe her to me, Caitlin."

"She has long, light brown hair. It looks thick, naturally wavy. It's pulled back from her face, but she wears it long. Not like the other women in town. Most of them wear their hair up. She's tossing her head, like she enjoys being different. Her face is round and she has ruby red lips."

"What is she wearing?"

"A dress. Long. High-necked. It's checkered."

"Take a close look at Molly, Caitlin. Who is she? Do you recognize her."

"It's me."

"What year is it?"

"1880."

"How old are you?"

"Eighteen."

"Tell me what's happening. Why are you bringing dinner to the sheriff?"

"I always do. It makes him happy. We're going to be married soon."

"Look at the man. Do you recognize him as somebody in your present lifetime?"

"Yes."

"Who is it, Caitlin?"

"It's Derrick. Only his name is Austin. He loves me. We're going to be married."

"Do you love him?"

"I don't know. I must."

"All right, Caitlin. Move ahead, a few days, a few weeks, to any significant events that might affect this relationship. Go past the ordinary events, until you come to something special."

"He's so handsome."

"Who is?"

"The man, getting off the train. He's so handsome. My heart can't keep still, just at the sight of him. I want him to notice me. And he does. He tips his hat and says hello."

"Take a close look, Caitlin. Who is this man?"

Caitlin took a good look at the man, at the small, deep scar on his left cheek. He had a moustache, sable-brown eyes, and a way of smiling that said he appreciated the sight of a good looking woman. "Oh my God! It's David, and I'm hopelessly in love with him, at first sight. It's like I've known him all my life—"

"Okay, Caitlin, move ahead now. Let your mind's eye float in and out of different scenes here until you come to one that's important. Tell me what you see and hear."

"Austin is crying. He's begging me to stay with him. He's calling Grant—that's David's name this time—he's calling Grant all sorts of names. Grant is a Pinkerton Agent and Austin says he's just using me. That he has women all over the place. But Grant loves me, I know he does. We're going to be married. I don't love Austin."

"What happens next?"

"I'm with Grant in a beautiful green meadow. It's filled with wildflowers. We've been here all afternoon. Grant is giving me a present. A cameo." Caitlin involuntarily reached toward her neckline. It was the same cameo sitting at home in her jewelry box. "I'm putting it on. It's so lovely. We kiss. I love him so much. We're going to be so happy together. It's getting dark. We lost complete track of the time. Grant wants to head back; we're such a long way out and it wasn't a very good road. We start riding home in our buggy. It's such a beautiful night, so clear. I can see every star in the sky. Oh my God, NO! Grant, do something. Grant!" Caitlin began to sob. "Grant, please Grant, don't be dead. Oh my God, I can't move, my legs, I can't move them!"

"Caitlin, move ahead in time. Go beyond the pain and sadness. You can't feel it now. Tell me what happened."

"Grant's dead," Caitlin said almost inaudibly.

"How did he die?"

"It was Austin's fault. He was spying on us. He wanted to stop us, to scare Grant away. He was going to run him out of town. He cut in front of us, right in front of our horse. It was only a small buggy, with one horse. The poor thing was so scared. He bolted and we went like mad. The path was so bad, so filled with rocks. We kept going, faster and faster. We hit a boulder and tipped over. Grant was thrown against a tree. He died immediately. Everybody said it was an accident. Nobody blamed Austin. After all, he was the sheriff."

"Go forward a couple of years. Where are you?"

"In my house. Sweeping. But it's hard. I have to walk with a cane. My leg always hurts. It was crushed in the accident. I have a terrible limp now."

"Are you happy?"

"Not really."

"Are you married?"

"Yes. To Austin."

"I thought you didn't love him."

"I try. He's a good man. He loves me."

"Why did you marry him?"

"Because he loves me. I didn't want to at first. I felt he killed Grant, but he convinced me it was all an accident. He told me nobody else would want me because of my leg. He wanted me to be happy. He would take care of me. I believed him."

"Okay, Caitlin. Close the curtain. You're going to leave this stage. Take a deep breath. Now exhale. Feel the air fill your body. You're very relaxed. You feel no pain, no sadness. We know Derrick and David have been a part of your present life. Take a look at all the other curtains, in front of all the other stages. Walk back and forth and touch them again. Is there any other life you'd like to examine, perhaps another one in which one or both of them have played a significant role?"

Caitlin didn't hesitate. She knew exactly which curtain she wanted to pull back, which life she wanted to examine next. She smiled broadly at the scene now in front of her.

"I'm so pretty," Caitlin said. "I love my hair. It's the color of copper. I just had it bobbed. It's the latest thing."

"What year is it?"

"1921."

"What are you doing?"

"I'm having dinner with my brother. We're in this grand dining room. I'm bored at the moment. He's lecturing me again on finding a suitable mate. We're quite rich. There's a fur coat draped over my chair. Anyway, I'm not interested in what he has to say. I've found a suitable mate."

"What's your brother's name?"

"Charles. Charles Griswold. And I'm Rebecca Griswold. Everybody calls me Becky."

"What does Charles look like?" Sara asked.

"He's quite handsome, in a skinny kind of way. At least all the girls think he's handsome; they're always swooning over him. His chin is too pointed, but he has wonderfully fair skin and deep brown eyes."

"Now, go beyond the looks, Caitlin. Take a deeper look at Charles," Sara said. "Is he someone you know in this lifetime?"

"Yes. He's Derrick."

"How does he treat you?"

"He's a very good brother, but sometimes he's too possessive. He's always trying to manipulate me, to make me do things his way. But it's just because he loves me. It's especially been that way since Daddy got sick and can't run the family business. Charles thinks he's boss."

"You said you've found a suitable mate. Who is he? Is he there with you?"

"Todd," Caitlin smiled. "His name is Todd. He's not here tonight. Charles wanted to be alone with me. Todd and I...we're going to be secretly married. Charles doesn't think Todd is good enough for me, but what can he do once we're married? He'll have to accept him."

"Okay. Let's move ahead, say three months. Where are you now?"

"The same place. It's New Year's Eve. We're having a wonderful party. Daddy's feeling much better. He threw this party for all our friends."

"Look around, Caitlin, can you see the name of the place."

"Yes. It's on a matchbook. Oh my God, it's the Bond Hotel."

"Where are Charles and Todd?"

"Oh, they're around. Todd and I are going to announce our engagement at midnight. I decided to have a big wedding after all. Charles got wind of it and he's fuming. But he'll settle down. He just doesn't like Todd because he's an artist. But he's going to be a famous artist. I just know it."

"It's almost midnight, Caitlin. What happens now?"

"I'm looking all over for Todd. I can't find him. It's not like him to abandon me. He's always so attentive. There he is, on the staircase, talking with Charles."

"Where are you?"

"I'm just standing there, at the bottom watching them. Finally, Todd sees me. He turns and smiles. But he doesn't look happy. Something's wrong."

"Describe Todd to me, Caitlin."

"He's tall, almost lanky. Very artistic looking. He has dark brown hair that's always falling down on his forehead, and long wonderful fingers. His eyes are deep blue."

"Do you know him, Caitlin? Is he with you in this lifetime?"

"Yes."

"Who is he?"

"Marc. Marc Gallagher."

"Okay, you're all on the stairs. It's nearly midnight. What happens next?"

Patricia Sheehy

"They're arguing. Charles hands something to Todd. He takes it and heads down the stairs toward me. His face is so...so...tortured. I'm scared. I can feel that something is very wrong. He just looks at me. There are tears in his eyes. I'm sorry, Becky. That's all he says. I'm sorry, Becky. And then he leaves. He's leaving me! I'm running after him. It's so cold outside. It's beginning to snow. My dress is so thin. Todd, Todd! I keep shouting his name, but he's gone. I can't see him anywhere. Charles comes out and puts his arm around me. It's midnight. I can hear the clock chiming, and everybody inside is shouting and laughing. I let Charles hold me, even though I hate him. I know he chased Todd away."

"Move ahead, Caitlin. Do you ever find out what happened?"

"Yes." Tears slid down Caitlin's cheek. "Yes."

"Can you tell me?"

"Charles bribed Todd. With a trip to Europe. He always wanted to go to Europe, to see all the great paintings. It was his one big dream. All expenses paid for a year. The train for New York left that night. Charles promised Todd he could marry me when he got back. That he wouldn't stand in our way. Todd believed him. He wrote and told me everything. He asked me to forgive him."

"Did you?"

"Mostly. I was still hurt. But I loved him."

"So what happened. Did Todd come back?"

"I don't know?"

"What happened, Caitlin?"

"I couldn't bear the shame."

"What shame?"

"Todd never knew."

"Never knew what?"

"About the baby. I was pregnant. Only a month when he left. At first I thought it would be okay. I would have the baby and Todd would marry me when he got back. Finally I wrote and told him, thinking he'd come right back."

"And he didn't?"

"No."

"Are you sure he got the letter."

"He must have. Charles promised me he would mail it by special delivery."

"So what happened?"

"Nothing. I waited and waited. Every day, I expected to see Todd on the doorstep, begging to marry me. Finally I lost my courage. I'd have to tell Daddy soon. I couldn't bear to shame the family. Charles took care of everything for me. He arranged it all."

"Arranged what?"

"The abortion." Caitlin's face twisted in pain. "The doctor came to the house. Mommy and Daddy were away for the weekend. It was all very civilized. Very neat and tidy. Except the sheets keep turning red. The blood. There's so much blood. Charles is holding my hand now, trying to keep the pain away. But it hurts so much. I'm so weak." Caitlin held onto her stomach as tears poured down her cheeks.

"Okay, Caitlin. Relax. Take a deep breath. Inhale. Exhale. There's no more pain. No more sadness. Move to the next day. Tell me about it."

"There is no more pain. Everything is beautiful. The light—it's so bright and so warm. I'm heading toward it, but I can still look down and see myself. I'm so pale. Poor Rebecca. She lost so much blood. She couldn't hang on. Charles is crying. He's so sad."

"Where are you now, Caitlin. Where's Rebecca?"

"Rebecca is in the bed. Her body will have to be buried. But I'm home now. It's so peaceful here."

"Caitlin, on the count of ten, you will reach an active state of awareness. You will remember everything, but it will not burden you. You will feel refreshed. You will take what you need to learn from this without experiencing any of the guilt. One, two, three..."

Chapter Thirty-Eight

The seasons changed and Caitlin changed with them. For the first time since David's death, she allowed herself to feel the emptiness. She no longer hid from loneliness behind false relationships or frenzied activities. With November came the long, dark evenings, and Caitlin pulled into herself, like a bear hibernating to gather strength for the spring. She read constantly. Anything and everything, from contemporary novels to philosophy to the latest self-help books. She was on a quest. She needed to try and understand herself and maybe a little of the human condition. How did it all fit together? What was her role in life? Her purpose?

Throughout it all, Josie remained her one touchstone. "Let go of it," she told Caitlin one snowy December afternoon as they drank cocoa, curled up in Caitlin's family room. "You're doing exactly what Sara told you not to do. You're letting the whole thing burden you, drag you down."

"I know. I'm becoming neurotic over the whole thing. I just can't seem to help it. The one good thing is that the dreams have stopped. Except I almost miss them. It was my one way of still having David."

"His job here was done. He's let go. Now it's your turn."

"I know. But you know, Josie, with all the reading and thinking I've been doing, and all that exploration into karma and past lives, I still can't figure out why David died. That's the hardest part for me, not having an answer."

"Maybe, you never will," Josie said. "Maybe your purpose here is simply to begin the quest for answers. Maybe he died to put you on that path. Or maybe David died because you both agreed at the beginning—before you were even born—that he would help you, once and for all, resolve your karmic cycle with Austin-Charles-Derrick. And his dying was the way to do it—recreate the emotional situation from the 1880s and hope that you could reject his manipulation this time around. And maybe, Catie dear, his death was just an accident, plain and simple, with no hidden messages."

"You don't believe that."

"You're right, I don't."

"You know what I miss most, even after all this time?"

"What?"

"His hugs. When you live alone, there are no more hugs."

"Would a hug from a friend help?" Josie asked, halfway out of her chair.

"No. Thanks, Josie. You're sweet, you really are. I miss David's hugs. They were always so...so what? Sturdy. Maybe strong is a better word. They made me feel safe."

They both sat, listening to the wind whip around corners of the house, feeling the deep winter chill as it tried to find its way inside. The sun fell from the sky quickly, leaving them in a room embraced by the hushed winter twilight. Caitlin got up and turned on a few lights. Josie went into the kitchen to rummage through Caitlin's refrigerator. She came back with a plate of cheese and crackers, two glasses, and a bottle of uncorked wine. "Is it any good?"

"I don't know. I can't remember when I opened it."

"Oh well," Josie said, pouring the wine as she talked. "A little vinegar won't hurt us." She eyed Caitlin as she handed her a glass. "By the way, are you finished being angry at Marc?"

"You didn't tell him anything, did you...about Sara...what we learned?"

Josie ran her fingers across her lips. "Zipped tight, my dear. This is not my life story to tell. But, Catie, he's miserable. He really misses you."

"I miss him too, when I focus on the present. But then I think about this past life thing. I mean, if it's true that I had an abortion because of him...Josie, he abandoned me and I died. How can you expect me to get beyond all that?"

"Because it's just that, a past life. Not a present one. Obviously, a little knowledge is a dangerous thing. You don't know the whole truth. You only know your version of the truth, and just a slice of it at that. Who knows what Charles said to Todd that night. All right, let's say he was weak and took the pay-off for a chance at Europe. But maybe he really was going to return. Maybe he never got your letter. Maybe Charles never mailed it. And, just maybe, Catie dear, he would never have gone if you'd been honest and told him you were pregnant."

Caitlin laughed out loud. "Sounds like a soap opera. Maybe we should write one, call it Days of Our Past Lives!"

"Listen, you crawl back into that hole of yours, Catie, lick your wounds, do whatever you need to do, but eventually you have to come out and live. Otherwise, think of this—you'll have to come back and do it all over again."

"God forbid." Caitlin laughed, but she knew Josie was serious.

During the week of Christmas, a huge white poinsettia arrived. The note card wasn't signed, but Caitlin recognized the large scrawl: Hope this puts a smile on your holiday. She didn't call Marc to thank him, but she did tuck a solitary ornament into the branches: the same perfectly shaped scallop shell she'd used to adorn last year's plant.

Caitlin would never confess it to Josie, but sometimes she drove by the Bond hoping she could tell from the outside how the renovations were going. One time she saw Marc come out the front door, his arm protectively around Beth's shoulder as they headed into the brisk winter wind. She quickly turned down a side street before Marc spotted her car. She almost didn't recognize Lauren. She'd lost a lot of weight and her hair was cut chin-length. Almost like mine, Caitlin observed. They looked so easy and comfortable together. A quick, sudden ache stabbed at Caitlin's heart. She couldn't expect him to wait forever; maybe she would lose him after all. Maybe she'd already lost him.

It was the loneliest Christmas of Caitlin's life. She spent some of it with Adam and Josie, but they only served to contrast her single and very separate status, so that it was almost easier to be alone. And she couldn't bring herself to accept Liz's invitation to Christmas dinner, although part of her wanted to, just to be with Jessica and Jason again. Liz came by a few days before Christmas to invite Caitlin personally, explaining that Steve was willing to forget everything—Caitlin would be allowed back in their life "just as if nothing had ever happened, as long as she behaved herself."

"You mean like on a limited trial basis?" Caitlin countered.

Liz looked sad, almost shriveled. "Catie, don't make this so hard. Let's just go back to the way things were."

"I don't think we can."

"We can if we want to. If you want to." Liz twirled a strand of blonde hair around her index finger. "All you have to do is be your old self again."

"I don't think I can do that, Liz. I know I can't do that. And you can't accept me the way I am now."

"Oh, Catie..."

"I'm sorry, Liz. I'm really so sorry."

"I have a Christmas present for you." Liz dug into her large tote-style purse. "Don't get offended or anything, it's just something I thought you should have. I brought it with me in case...I guess I had a feeling...I knew you wouldn't come to dinner." Liz put on her mink coat and edged her way toward the door. "Here," she said, shoving the gift into Caitlin's hands and running out toward the security of her gray and white colonial across the street.

Caitlin closed the door behind Liz, feeling weighted down and free all at once. But mostly, she felt alone. She held the gift in her hand a long time before finally tearing away the green tissue paper. *The Way*. Liz had given her a hardcover copy of *The Way*, an illustrated edition of *The Living Bible*. Caitlin smiled as she put the book on the shelf next to the copy she'd bought for herself months ago. She would miss Liz. She would miss her a lot.

Chapter Thirty-Nine

By March, Caitlin was tired of introspection. Life was what it was, and it was for the living. David had been gone twenty months now—almost two years—and she'd finally mourned him. With each piece of clothing she packed away for the homeless, with each trinket she stored in a box (perhaps someday to give to Maryanne), she said goodbye to her husband. Once again, spring was around the corner. Life would be renewing itself, and it was time she did some renewing of her own. And by now she was certain that if she didn't get it right this time, she'd only have to come back and do it all over again.

But first, Caitlin, had to face one final goodbye.

Getting out of the car, she wrapped her jacket tighter around her body to ward off the chill in the air. There were still patches of frozen white under trees and around rocks, but the worst of winter was now over. Caitlin brushed aside a few dead leaves and sat down on the damp grass in front of David's grave.

Tucking her legs under her long skirt, Caitlin leaned forward to touch the cool marble marker, tracing her husband's name etched in the gray stone. David Andrew Saunders. How impersonal it all seemed. What trappings we give death, she thought. Her David wasn't here in this cemetery, lying in a cold box covered with tons of dirt. No, her David was off somewhere. Up there, maybe? She looked up toward the sky. Looking down on her? Protecting her?

"We never said goodbye. If you had to go, I just wish it didn't have to be so sudden. I wish we could have said goodbye." Caitlin felt the dampness of the grass seeping through her skirt, stinging her skin. She focused on the sensation, on the prickling and stinging, on the cold, wet ground. If she focused hard enough, she wouldn't feel the heaviness in her heart.

"You know, we didn't talk enough," she said out loud, absently playing with the dirt around the base of David's marker, poking away at the grass, feeling the coolness of living things between her fingers. "Oh, we talked. But I mean really talk. I should have told you how much I wanted a child, instead of crying in the bathroom where you wouldn't see me. That was wrong. I should have told you."

She could smell the dampness of the rich earth. It reminded her of their last Memorial Day when they'd spent the entire weekend planting flowers and bulbs, creating a perennial garden. They'd had so many good, special moments. But a child would have made it perfect. "It's funny, you do the most personal things with another person—you touch each other's bodies in really private ways, you see each other naked, you make love...and yet you don't give away your feelings. I always thought giving your body was the deepest commitment you could make. Now I realize it's peeling away the fear and sharing your feelings. We never totally did that, David. And I'm really sorry about that. Really sorry."

She continued digging at the dirt. "I don't know quite what's going to happen, David. Where my life's going to take me...but it's time to say goodbye. I have to leave you. And you have to let me." She began clawing hard with her bare fingers at the cold, hard dirt until she had a small, deep hole beside a bed of daffodils that would soon bloom. She slipped off her wedding ring, put it to her lips for one final kiss, and then buried it in the small hole at the foot of her husband's grave.

As Caitlin stood to go, a gust of wind encircled her body; yet nothing in the cemetery seemed to move. Not a tree. Not a branch. Not a leaf. Only she was enveloped in the gush of air, oddly warm and extremely forceful, moving in closer around her body, pressing against her chest and shoulders, pressing harder and tighter until she felt nearly smothered by this unseen force. Just as quickly as it came, the wind subsided, leaving Caitlin feeling strangely comforted, reminding her of the hugs she used to know, the hugs she still missed. "Goodbye, David," she said quietly. "See you in another lifetime."

Chapter Forty

All the next day, as Caitlin gathered the things she would
need, her stomach clenched at her boldness. She could
barely keep down a cup of coffee, and her hands actually shook as she
packed the two large totes. She didn't tell anybody—not even
Josephine—what she was about to do. There were too many ways for it
to backfire. Too many ways for her to feel like a fool. She didn't need
an audience or even a silent peanut gallery.

Finally, it was time.

Around three in the afternoon, she drove to the Bond Hotel, parking
her car on a side street that kept her out of sight, yet provided her with
a fairly clear view of the front entrance. She wasn't exactly sure what
she was waiting for, or even what her next move would be. Everything
depended upon what happened next, what she observed and,
ultimately, what felt right. If schedules were still going according to
original plan, Marc would come out soon, give the itinerant workers a
ride back to their local shelter, and then return to finish up for the day.

She watched and waited, checking the clock on her dash about
every three minutes. What was taking so long? What hadn't anybody
come out yet? Caitlin fingered the handle of the blue canvas tote resting
on the seat next to her. Maybe this was a bad idea. Maybe she should
just go home and pretend today never existed, start her life over again

in some other way. She turned on the ignition.

And then she turned it off again.

There was Marc, pushing through the front door of the Bond, looking breezy and handsome as he talked to two older men Caitlin didn't recognize. "They must be new," she said out loud, hoping they were indeed workers that Marc was driving home. Otherwise, who knew where he was going, or when he'd return? He could be leaving for the day. How long would she wait?

Marc looked her way, and he seemed to look for so long that Caitlin was certain she'd been spotted. She slinked down behind the steering wheel, sweating in her turtleneck and jacket, despite the March chill in the air. Finally, Marc and the two men crossed the street and headed toward his car in the parking lot. Caitlin sat crouched in the front seat until she saw the old beat-up station wagon disappear from sight.

As soon as she was certain she was safe, she gathered up her things and walked across the street to the hotel. The door was unlocked, which meant someone was still there. Once inside, she couldn't believe her eyes. It was almost finished. So much had been done in the short time she'd stayed away. The lobby had been transformed into a graceful living area, but it was still a grand room with intricate ceiling trim and a single crystal chandelier--Marc's one, very deliberate, testimony to the Bond's transcendent splendor. The staircase was just as Caitlin remembered. Transfixed, she walked over and stroked the gleaming wood banister.

"Caitlin, hi!" Jake said, coming into the room. He threw his arms around her. "You look great, really great. A sight for sore eyes. But you just missed Marc. He should be back in about an hour."

"Good. I wanted to miss him," Caitlin said.

"Oh," Jake said. "I just figured, when I saw you that...well, you know. Marc hasn't been the same since you left. He's just as committed, but the enthusiasm—" He rocked his hand back and forth.

"Listen, Jake, I know this is a huge request, but can you get everyone out of here? I have a plan, and I need to be alone. You're sure he's coming back?"

"Positive. He took a couple of the guys home, then he's stopping by the hardware store. But yeah, I'm sure, I'll get everyone out, whatever you want, Catie. But, do I get to know what's going on here?"

"Tomorrow, Jake. I promise."

Caitlin headed for the dining room. There were no more wood shavings on the floor and all the woodwork and intricate trim had just received a fresh coat of ivory paint. The hardwood floor and the oak wainscoting along the bottom half of the walls had been restored to their original brilliance. Caitlin's eyes searched the room until she found what she was looking for. Folded and stacked against the back wall was the aluminum table she needed. Caitlin opened up the table, moved it to the center of the room and began her preparations.

"Where is everybody?" Marc called out when he came in about an hour later. "Hey, you bums, where are you?"

"They're all gone," Caitlin said, standing in the threshold between the dining room and the lobby. "Sent them home myself. With a little help from Jake. Come on in."

Marc looked stunned at the sight of her and the best he could do was mutter her name. Caitlin held out her hand, beckoning him to follow. Once inside the dining room, he inhaled quickly and looked at her questioningly.

"Exhale," Caitlin laughed, "or you'll die here on the spot."

Across the aluminum table Caitlin had laid her grandmother's lace tablecloth, and in the middle she had placed an antique crystal vase, just like one they would have used at the Bond in the 1920s--the very one Marc had given her last August. She had filled it with two dozen velvety, deep purple Irises. On both sides of the vase were crystal candlesticks, the candles lit and burning brightly in the paneled room.

Marc looked from Caitlin to the table and back to Caitlin again. She pressed the button on a small cassette player and sounds from the Lettermen filled the air. *It seems we stood like this before...We looked at each other in the same way then, but I can't remember where or when...*She held out her hand and Marc came into her arms. Slowly, very slowly, they danced to the strains of the music. Candlelight flickered with their every movement.

As he held her, Marc's eyes explored Caitlin's face, looking at her as though he'd never seen her before, as though he'd never held something this wonderful in his arms before. With every beat of the music, he pulled her closer to him until their breathing came in the same rapid pattern and it seemed they could hear the beating of each other's heart. Marc tipped Caitlin's face up toward his and began to kiss her, gingerly at first, exploring her taste and the heat of her skin, and then hungrily, with the desire of a man who'd waited all his life to hold the woman he loved. Caitlin kissed him back, pulling him into her with the passion of a woman who has found her destiny.

The music stopped and the tape recorder clicked off, the single sound echoing in the room, jolting them back to reality. Caitlin pulled away, but only so she could lead Marc back to the table. "Before we continue this," she said, "I have something for you. The last time we were in this room, you gave me a present--a wedding present, to be exact. Now I have one for you." She was being deliberately cryptic, enjoying the puzzled look on his face. She reached under the table and handed him a large, heavy box, wrapped in gold paper and tied up with a red ribbon and huge bow.

"What is it?" Marc asked.

"Opening it is a good way to find out."

He removed the ribbon and started to tear at the paper.

"Wait!" Caitlin ordered. "I almost forgot. Here. You have to do this." She had been chilling a bottle of Dom Perignon and she now handed it to Marc. "I can never pop these things."

The cork flew across the room, hitting the wall and bouncing onto the floor. Marc poured champagne into the two crystal glasses she had set on the table. He began to raise his glass in a toast.

"No, not yet," Caitlin said. "First, open your gift."

"You certainly have a lot of rules," Marc laughed. "Are you always this demanding?"

"Guess you'll have to find out. Now open."

Marc tore at the paper and discovered a large maple box with a brass lock. He looked at Caitlin, a mixture of pleasure and confusion on his face. "Cate..." For a moment it was as if he was afraid; then he clicked open the lock and looked inside. Oil paints. Every possible tube of color...and brushes...beautiful sable brushes. He looked at her as if to ask why.

"I figure it this way," Caitlin said, "come next September, I'm starting college, and you'll need something to keep you busy and out of trouble while your wife is studying."

"My what?"

"Your wife," Caitlin said. "That is, if you still want me."

Marc didn't say anything and for one brief, anxious moment, Caitlin worried that he'd changed his mind.

His answer came in the form of a kiss, long, slow and passionate. Holding one another in a room they'd known long ago, in the very room where they'd once planned to announce their engagement, Caitlin knew only too well the long road they'd both traveled to get to this point. This was their time.

At last...

Caitlin broke away from Marc's embrace, but not before kissing him playfully on the cheek. "Now we can have our champagne," she said.

They raised their glasses to one another.

"To a lifetime of happiness," Marc said.
"To lifetimes of happiness," Caitlin smiled.

Epilogue: One Year Later

Caitlin sat up against newly fluffed pillows looking out at the world through the small hospital window. The sky seemed to be a softer blue than she'd ever remembered, serving as a backdrop for brilliantly green trees. Everything was fresh and full of color. Even the antiseptic smell of her room couldn't dampen her spirits. Instead, it actually lifted them, reminding her of exactly why she was there.

On the window sill of the small room was a vase of long-stemmed purple irises—from Marc, naturally—and next to them was an arrangement of roses and baby's breath from her mother. Josie and Adam sent a huge stuffed bear, "to protect the little one." But what gave Caitlin the most joy was the bouquet of pink balloons tied to her bed. They were from Maryanne.

Over the last few months, Caitlin and Maryanne had begun spending time together; they were cautious and hesitant with one another, but it was enough to make Caitlin hopeful that they could find a new way to share in each other's lives. And now the balloons. Definitely a good sign. Caitlin looked at the them and smiled. And then, for about the hundredth time, she took the mirror from the bedside stand so she could see how her new necklace shimmered against her skin.

"It's the only gem that does justice to your eyes," Marc said when he gave her the single, deep-colored emerald framed by diamonds and set in a pattern of gold. He'd presented it to her in the early hours of the morning. "Just a little reward for a job well done."

He breezed in now looking remarkably rested for someone who'd been gone only long enough for a shower and short nap. He'd been with her until after dawn. Finally she'd sent him home, but here he was, back again.

"Caught you," he said as she quickly put down the mirror.

"It's just so stunning. I can't get over it."

"And so are you, Mrs. Gallagher. How are you feeling this morning? I guess it's afternoon, isn't it?" he said sheepishly, looking at his watch. He leaned over and kissed her.

"Just barely afternoon. You should have rested longer."

"I couldn't stay away."

"I'm glad," Caitlin said. "Marc, I'm happier than I ever thought possible."

He took Caitlin's hand and played with her fingers. "I know. Me too. They're bringing her down now. I just passed the nursery. I think I'm going to be a very possessive father."

"She could do worse," Caitlin laughed.

Just then the door opened and a nurse wheeled in their new daughter. She had a tuft of blonde hair and the promise of beautiful eyes. The nurse picked up the baby and placed her in Caitlin's arms.

"That was a long delivery you had, Mrs. Gallagher. How are you doing?"

"Fine. Sore, but fine. Isn't she beautiful?"

"She sure is," the nurse smiled, stroking the baby's cheek. "And don't worry about that. Ninety percent of them go away before the child starts school."

"Oh, I'm not worried," Caitlin said, looking at the strawberry birthmark on her daughter's cheek. It was almost in the shape of a heart. "It's a kiss from God."

About the Author

Patricia Herchuk Sheehy is an award-winning writer with a passion for exploring the connection between mind, body, and spirit.

Her articles and essays have appeared in local and national publications. In addition, she writes marketing and advertising copy for a wide range of businesses and organizations. She is currently working on her next novel, which explores the interplay between free will and destiny through one woman's struggle for love, acceptance, and forgiveness. A Connecticut native, Patricia holds a master's degree from Wesleyan University. She and her husband live in the historic town of Wethersfield, CT.

She invites readers to write to her at patriciasheehy@aol.com or visit her website: www.psheehy.com

Printed in the United States
19346LVS00002B/67-408